String of Fate

King's Throne

BIANCA D'ARC

This book is a work of fiction. The names, characters, places, and incidents are products of the writer's imagination or have been used fictitiously and are not to be construed as real. Any resemblance to persons, living or dead, actual events, locale or organizations is entirely coincidental.

Copyright © 2014 Bianca D'Arc
Cover Art by Valerie Tibbs

All Rights Are Reserved. No part of this book may be used or reproduced in any manner whatsoever without written permission, except in the case of brief quotations embodied in critical articles and reviews.

Copyright © 2014 Bianca D'Arc

All rights reserved.

ISBN: 1496148487
ISBN-13: 978-1496148483

DEDICATION

Many thanks to my friend, Peggy McChesney for being such a great sounding board all these years and particularly as relates to this book. Thanks also to the totally awesome Anna-Marie Chaconas Buchner. You're both terrific!

This book, as all my work, is dedicated to my family. They have always supported my crazy ideas and stood by me through all my little experiments in living. Thanks especially to Dad for giving me the courage to try new things with my writing and my career, and always encouraging me to "reach for a star."

CHAPTER ONE

"Mom, I'm coming home."

"What's wrong, Gina?" The worried voice on the other end of the cell phone call came through loud and clear.

They both knew it was a big deal for Gina to leave her apartment in the city and head, quite literally, for the hills. Her parents lived upstate in the mountains. It had been a struggle to leave home when she was younger. Her father was overprotective in the extreme and it had taken a lot to overcome his objections. Her place in the city was more than just an apartment. It was a way for her to make a stand and declare her independence.

She loved her parents. She really did. But she wanted to be on her own for a bit. She wanted to be out from the shadow of her folks and make her own way in life—just like her best friend, Ellie. They'd left together to seek their fortunes in the big city and hadn't gone back, except for the occasional visit. And now their freedom had been compromised and the only thing Gina could do was head home, tail between her legs, and ask for her parents' help.

"Ellie knows about us, Mom. She knows about shapeshifters. A panther-shifter soldier followed her home and then his partner was injured."

Ellie was a registered nurse and Gina a medical doctor. It

went, almost without saying, that they'd offered their help to the injured man. Gina knew her mother would connect the dots. Her mom had also been a nurse. She understood.

"How badly was he hurt?"

Yeah, her mother definitely got it.

"Really bad, Mom. In fact, I've got him in the car with me. He was doing a little better when we left the city, but he's having some kind of relapse."

"What happened to him?" Her mother was all business now.

Gina looked at the giant of a man passed out in the passenger seat. Between her and her mother, they ought to be able to do something for the ailing shifter.

"He was poisoned. I gave him blood and all the royal nectar I had on hand to revive him. It seemed to help for a while, but now he's unconscious again and his temperature is spiking."

"You can't give him any more of the nectar. It's too dangerous," her mother cautioned. The purple substance known as royal nectar was something used only in emergencies, and then only sparingly. It was one of the secrets of the tiger Clan, produced by a very special branch of a pharmaceutical company they owned. And it was still experimental. "For all we know, the nectar could have reacted with the poison and made it worse."

"Sweet Mother of All," Gina almost sobbed. "I could've killed him."

"What are his vitals?" her mother snapped, her professional tone calm. Unfortunately, Gina couldn't do the same. For some unknown reason, her objectivity was shot where this particular patient was concerned. From the moment she had first laid eyes on him, something about him had sparked a reaction inside her unlike anything she had ever felt before. She still wasn't sure what it all meant, but she didn't have time to stop and think about it. Time was running short.

"I can't stop to get any readings right now. We're on the

run."

"From what? Gina, do you want me to get your father on the line?"

She thought about it and arrived at the conclusion that, unfortunately, this was serious enough to involve her dad.

"Yeah." She sighed heavily, not looking forward to explaining herself. "You'd better get him. He needs to hear this too."

Gina waited, listening while her mother found her dad and they both came on the line together.

"Kitten, what's wrong?"

Just hearing her father's deep voice reassured her. He was so strong, so steadfast. Nothing could harm her with her father around. At least, that's the way he'd always made her feel.

"Hi, Daddy." Her voice almost broke, but she held it together. She had to tell her dad everything that had been happening. He needed to know.

"Your mother said you're bringing an injured man here." His tone said he was both surprised by her breach of their tight security and curious.

"Not just a man. A *tigre d'or* Royal Guard." Shocked silence met her statement. "His name is Mitch. His partner, Cade, is still with Ellie."

Ellie had been Gina's best friend since they were kids attending the same rural grammar school. Ellie was completely human and hadn't known about shifters until meeting a panther shifter named Cade. When he had asked for her help with his unconscious partner, Ellie hadn't refused. She'd put the injured man in the small guest room in her apartment and called Gina.

Mitch had gone into convulsions in Ellie's guest room and started to shapeshift. His hands and feet had become paws and there had been no way to hide the truth from Ellie any longer. Gina only hoped that after this was all over, Ellie would forgive her for keeping so many secrets for so very long.

The truth was, Gina and her parents were tiger shifters. In fact, they were the rarest of the rare—the royal *tigre blanche*, or white tigers, who were blessed by the Goddess in order to rule over all tiger shifters. Or so the story went. Gina's dad though, had stepped down from his throne so long ago that Gina barely remembered the ice palace and the traditional seat of power. Her parents lived in seclusion. Exile. All due to the political machinations of her uncle.

Gina had grown up on the isolated acreage her parents owned in the mountains of the northeastern United States. Her father and a few of his most trusted Royal Guards and their families had chosen to settle there after fleeing their homeland. The place was a fortress and larger than any of the surrounding homesteads. The terrain was rugged, rocky and not really suited to farming. Her dad had been able to buy up most of a mountaintop and installed his Guard in snug homes all around the perimeter.

When it came time for Gina to go to school, the Guards' children had gone with her and they'd all made friends among the human population of their small town. The best way to protect themselves, her father always said, was to fit in. He and her mother still spoke English with a charming accent, but Gina had done all her schooling in the States and she looked and sounded like an American.

She'd gone to college nearer to the city and then on to medical school, with her parents' blessing—and a few of the Guards' kids who were around her age. They were her own little Royal Guard, though such a thing was never spoken aloud. But Gina knew her father worried for her safety and had been training the other kids to fill their parents' roles as protectors for his daughter.

Part of that training had been in hand-to-hand combat. To keep their skills sharp while in the city, most of the shifter youngsters had taken classes at a very elite, human, martial arts dojo run by a trusted human man who had been mated to a shifter. He knew all about the shifter world and still mourned the loss of his wife. His name was Harris and he'd been one of their most trusted human contacts, but as it turned out, even he wasn't safe from their enemies.

"Sensei Harris's dojo was attacked and burned to the ground," Gina continued her explanation. "That's when Mitch was hurt. He and Cade were there for some kind of big meeting between the *pantera* Nyx and Harris."

Gina didn't need to explain that the Nyx was the queen of the *pantera noir*, the black panther shifters. If things had been different, Gina's mom would still be the Tig'Ren and her dad would still reign as Tig'Ra, king and queen of the *tigre d'or*, the golden-tiger shifters.

"So Ellie brought the Nyx's Guards to you?" her mother asked, sounding surprised even though Ellie lived one floor below Gina in the same apartment building.

"Not at first. She called me when Mitch started convulsing and asked me to come down to her apartment and take a look." Gina had enjoyed living just upstairs from her best friend. She doubted they'd ever be able to go back to their carefree lives now. Too much had happened. Too many secrets had been revealed.

"She didn't warn you they were shifters?" her father wanted to know.

"She didn't know. Not until I was already there. The men sniffed me out right away, of course. As soon as I walked into the apartment and I scented them, I knew my cover was blown, but I couldn't let Mitch suffer. He was in really bad shape, so I gave him my blood and he rallied, but it caused some partial shifting while his body fought the poison."

Gina was one of the rarest—a truly universal shifter blood type—which meant more among shifters than it did among humans. Her blood could actually heal others—shifters and humans alike. Giving Mitch a few milliliters of her blood had been a last-ditch effort to save his life and totally unorthodox as far as human medicine went. Ellie was a nurse and Gina a doctor. Only their lifelong friendship had gained Ellie's cooperation when Gina had performed the radical procedure.

"Ellie saw?" That was her mother's worried voice and

Gina could almost see the anxious expression on her mom's face.

"Yeah. That's when I had to tell her. Mom, you should have seen her. Once she accepted the idea, she was fierce when the *pantera* Alpha tried to dominate the situation. I don't think he realized what he was in for. Ellie hasn't got a submissive bone in her body."

Her father chuckled, setting her at ease though she knew she was bringing trouble to her parents' doorstep.

"Cade and Mitch are both Royal Guards. Cade is keeping an eye on Ellie. They stayed in the city to deal with the ongoing problems there. I promised to take Mitch to safety and look after him. We decided to split up so I could have a shot at keeping my secret from the rest of their shifter friends who've been called in for backup. Cade and Mitch know, but Cade promised to keep quiet for now. Mitch is with me, so he's not about to tell anyone. Especially not in the state he's in. I couldn't hide my true nature from them…or from Ellie." Her voice was subdued as she remembered those tumultuous moments.

Keeping secrets from Ellie had been one of the hardest things Gina had ever done. Telling her best friend she'd been lying by omission all these years had been even harder, but it was good to finally clear the air between them. Gina just hoped Ellie could forgive her when this was all over.

"You think any of them will give us away?" Her father's voice was gruff.

"Not Ellie. I trust her with my life. Cade tried to convince me that we were needed in the Clan, but I think he understood that was a decision for us to make—not for him to force us to make. I don't think he'll tell anyone anytime soon. He was focused on his Nyx. Someone is after her in a big way."

"They you're better off out of the city."

"I thought so too. Cade arranged for an escort to meet us at the city limits. Since the Nyx is in transit too, they're stretched pretty thin. There was only one car with one *pantera noir* Guard in it as escort and we had to split up at the last rest stop on the interstate. He suspected we might have a tail and he thought the only chance we had of making it through to the house in secret was if he peeled off and took the tail with him." She tried not to let her anxiety about the entire situation come through in her tone. "He called a little bit ago to tell me the tail had taken the bait and he was leading him well away from us. He was really sorry there wasn't anybody else available to escort us, but he thought we would be okay."

"Did this escort know who you are?" her father demanded.

"No. Cade kept his word and kept me out of it. All the escort knew was that I was a shifter doctor transporting their injured Royal Guard."

Her father grunted. "Then I might forgive them for deserting you, but if anything happens—"

She cut into his angry words, wanting to calm him. "We're almost home and there's nobody on this road for miles. I don't think we're being followed, but Mitch's condition worries me. I'm sorry for bringing this problem to you, but the only place I could think of where he could heal in safety is at home. He's way too vulnerable right now."

"He can't come to the house," her father was quick to say, crushing her hopes. "Take him to the old line cabin off Miller Road. I'll call the Millers and tell them you're coming. They'll help you get to the cabin. It's stocked and defensible. Nobody can get to you there except on foot. We'll come to you when you get there."

Relief surged through her at his ready offer of help. "Thanks, Dad."

"Drive safely, kitten."

Gina was bone weary when she finally pulled into the dusty drive near Miller Road, named for the *tigre d'or* family who lived there and had built the road. They were loyal to her father. Mr. and Mrs. Miller were both former Royal Guards who understood better than most why her father had chosen exile over the danger of ruling the Clan that was his by right.

Gina's car would be left behind at the Miller homestead, hidden in one of their barns. Mr. Miller greeted her as she drove up beside the house and she saw he'd gotten two big snowmobiles ready. At this time of year, they would be the easiest way of getting out to the old cabin that straddled the edge of her parents' land and the Miller's homestead.

"I laid in some perishables at the cabin," Mr. Miller let her know. "Your father said you had a wounded man with you." He looked toward the passenger side of the car, where Mitch was slouched, unconscious.

"I'm going to need a little help getting him out of the car. He's a big Alpha."

They walked together around the car.

"Royal Guard, your father said. Do you think it's wise to bring him here?"

"It's the only place I could think of where we'd be safe. When we left the city there was a concentrated effort to kill the *pantera* Nyx. This Guard's partner thought it would be safer for me to get out of Dodge, just in case, and I agreed."

"He knew about you?" Mr. Miller frowned in concern.

"There was no way to hide it."

She opened the passenger-side door and they spent the next few minutes wrestling with Mitch's unconscious form. Mr. Miller maneuvered one of the snowmobiles over and they got Mitch onto it. Gina would have to ride behind him to keep him on the machine. They would have to go slow, but it would work.

"Joan will stash your car while we go to the cabin. She's on surveillance right now. Or she'd have come out to greet you." Gina knew the Millers had cameras and sensors hidden all over their property—just like her father had—and a bank of screens in a hidden room, which could show live feeds from every inch of their land. "You need anything else?"

"Just the bags in the back seat. Can you take those with you?"

"Sure thing." Mr. Miller got the bags that contained a few

changes of clothing and some other supplies, and hopped on to his own snowmobile. With a roar of engines, they prowled away over the snow into the darkening night.

They arrived at the cabin as the sun was setting. Mr. Miller helped her get Mitch inside and onto the bed and then hightailed it back so he could get home before full dark. She knew the Miller family would be on high alert and would be the first line of defense if anyone with bad intentions had followed Gina's circuitous route from the city. After Mr. Miller left, silence descended. She was alone with Mitch.

She looked around the cabin, locating a few things she'd need and then turned to contemplate the unconscious tiger shifter. Another infusion of her blood might be just the thing to bring him around.

Universal shifter blood was a rare and magical thing. Gina could donate blood to any other shifter or *were* species with no fear of incompatibility. Just a few drops of her blood could purify any poison or contagion in another person's system—shifter or human. In fact, her mother had covertly used Gina's blood to save a number of students in her grammar school when they'd all been exposed to viral meningitis.

It only took a minute or two to take a few milliliters of blood from her own arm and inject it into Mitch. She'd done the same when he'd gone into convulsions back in Ellie's apartment and it had saved his life. So far. But then she'd given him the nectar. She was kicking herself over that misstep.

She might've killed him with the nectar. She felt horrible about giving it to him, but Cade had been so adamant about rousing Mitch so he could answer questions. She never should have done it. The nectar had to have caused this relapse. Her blood had been working to heal him. She knew it had.

Five milliliters of her blood was more than enough to restore good health to anyone. The human kids in her grade-school class had only needed a few drops each to rid themselves of the deadly disease.

Even this huge Alpha should have been fine with the small amount he'd been given back at the apartment, but he'd relapsed. He had rallied for a little while and then collapsed again while they were in the car. With any luck, this second treatment would do the trick and put him back on the road to recovery.

"Come on, big guy." She did her best to settle him more comfortably on the bed.

He wore a giant sweatshirt she'd bought for him on the way out of town. She'd had to make a quick stop at a large chain store to get Mitch some clothing. The shirt and pants he'd been wearing when he was attacked were ruined and it wasn't worth the risk to get his own clothing. So now the tough Alpha sported a shirt that loudly proclaimed he really *loved* New York.

It was the only thing she could find that was big enough for his extra-large frame and warm enough for where they were headed. Winter had already hit up in the mountains. His pants were likewise sweats with a drawstring waist. There was another set in her bag along with some of her own clothes. It wasn't much, but it would have to be enough for now.

They had to lay low until things settled down.

Mitch's golden eyes opened.

"Where am I?" The words rasped out of a throat raw from what he'd been through, yet his tone was still compelling. If Gina had been made of more timid stuff, she might have cowed before the Alpha. As it was, she met his unvoiced challenge on even footing. Actually, she held all the power in this situation, but she was a little too nice to point it out to the injured warrior.

"Safe. In the mountains, at a remote cabin well-guarded by others of our kind."

"Your kind or my kind, milady?" One golden eyebrow rose in an almost teasing question.

"So you remember that?" She sat back on her haunches next to him on the wide bed. She'd climbed up beside him to administer the blood and hadn't left his side as she'd willed him to wake. She'd been that worried about him.

He still wasn't out of the woods. She would have to keep close watch over him until he showed marked signs of improvement and could stay awake without yet another infusion of her blood. He was perilously close to succumbing to the poison and would have been dead already if not for the magical properties of her blood.

"That and more. I may have looked unconscious, but this particular poison seems to leave me aware but unable to respond, not even to open my eyes."

"You've been awake this whole time?"

"No. Not completely. But I was aware for some time after that first dose. I heard what Cade said and your plans to take me out of the city. I faded as he put me in the car."

"Good. So I don't have to go over too much old ground. Your partner is with my friend Ellie in the city. You're out of the action for now, I'm afraid. In fact, I'm surprised you haven't responded better to my treatment. One dose should have been enough."

"Whatever they got me with is more potent than anything I've ever experienced." He grimaced as he tried to move. "The tingling is starting again. If I go out, remember I can hear you." His voice began to slur a tiny bit. "Talk to me, milady. Keep me company." His hand gripped hers as a frisson of fear entered his eyes. "Stay with me."

She covered his big hand with hers, pressing gently. "I will. I promise. We're safe for now. My father will come tomorrow and the Millers have guard duty tonight. This cabin is on the edge of their land where it meets my parents' retreat. They're a good and loyal *tigre d'or* family. Mr. Miller and his wife were Royal Guard, like you. When my father went into exile, they went with him, as did a handful of others. Your recovery will be guarded by those like you, Mitch. Trust their skill to keep you safe as they have kept my family safe all these years. I bet they've forgotten more things about stealth and secrecy than you've even heard of."

His grip relaxed as his muscles went slack and only a small grunt followed. The poison must be doing its work on him again. Dammit.

She was really worried. She leaned over him, peering into his golden eyes.

"Are you still with me, Mitch?"

One hand rose to cup her waist loosely, surprising her. He wasn't completely under, though his motions were sluggish and his eyes half-lidded. The heat of his hand on her body sent little shivers of awareness through her that were totally unacceptable. He was her patient. She shouldn't feel anything but doctorly compassion for the big brute, no matter that he was the most attractive tiger shifter she'd ever seen.

Not that she'd seen a whole slew of her own kind up close. No, she'd been raised away from the Clan, but her father had a few loyal families living up here in the middle of nowhere with them. She'd had *tigre* playmates and friends all her life. And humans too, though they lived down the mountain in the nearby town. She'd gone to the human school in the valley with both human and *tigre* kids. That's how she'd met Ellie and they'd been best friends ever since—even though there was one really big secret between them. Until just recently, Ellie hadn't had a clue about shifters.

But the shifter Guards and their children were always watching out for Gina. Even when she'd ventured out on her own. Her father wouldn't have let her go off to the city without some protection, especially at first.

By the time she'd graduated, at least one part of her protection detail had already mated and had cubs of their own. They lived nearby and she saw them often, but they weren't really guarding her anymore. After years living among humans with no problem, even her father had been willing to allow her to roam alone. After all, cats needed their space. He understood that better than most.

"I'm here, blue eyes." His words were slurred even more and his gaze spoke of the same attraction she was feeling—and fighting. Only he didn't seem to be fighting it right now.

"You're lovely, Gina."

Now that was a little more intimate than she was comfortable with. Especially coupled with the way he drew her closer, tugging at her hip as he slid his hand over her waist to urge her forward.

Her balance was precarious as she leaned over him on the soft bed and she found herself unable to resist the pull. Before she knew it, she was within range of those firm lips and he was kissing her.

It wasn't a light buss, but it also wasn't the tempestuous claiming she'd feared. It was a sweet kiss, full of promise and wonder. Something she wouldn't have expected from the tough Alpha, even in his weakened condition, and it completely seduced her.

She gave back all that he asked and more. Her hands went to his wide shoulders for balance, though the simple act of touching him turned easily into a caress. He was bigger and more muscular than any man she'd ever kissed before and she liked the sensation of his muscles moving under her fingertips. Such a feeling could easily become addictive.

When he ended the kiss, it was a gentle parting, like something out of a fairytale. Gina was stunned momentarily while his eyes searched hers.

"Tell me true, milady. What are my chances?"

His words hit her like a bucket of cold water and her heart wrenched to think this man—this gentle man who had kissed her with such beauty—might still die. Her hands tightened on his shoulders and though she tried, he refused to let her move away. The hands that secured her waist made certain of it.

"I don't know," she whispered.

"My arms and legs tingle like they don't want to work. I can also feel myself slipping back into that nightmare of being aware but unable to move." A little of the horror he must've felt came through in his voice, though she knew he tried to put on a brave face.

"No matter what happens, I'll be with you, Mitch. Now that I know you're aware at least some of the time, I'll keep you company. Nobody can get to us without considerable trouble here, and my father will be by in the morning. He may not have the title any longer, but he certainly still knows how to organize and protect things. This area is part of his fortress of solitude. It's well hidden and protected by more than you can imagine. He'll keep us safe while you heal, and my mother is a registered nurse. She'll help too, if we need her. You'll have the best care any shifter could hope for."

"You have my thanks, milady. And if the worst should happen, I have no family to return my bones to. Just tell Cade. He'll know what to do with my few possessions."

"Don't talk like that, Mitch. So far, my blood is keeping you alive and awake for longer periods of time. It might just take more of it than usual. That's okay. I'm willing donate whatever you need."

"You're not only a princess, but an angel as well." He still had strength enough to tease her and his face brightened in a weak but devastating smile.

She wasn't unaffected. Mitch had more than his share of charm.

"Not a princess or an angel. Just a doctor. With a family and loyal friends that will keep you safe while you heal." She knew the predator in him paced at the idea of being unable to protect himself from others who would prey on any weakness.

She kept reinforcing the idea that he would be safe, knowing it would reassure the beast side of his nature. Even Alphas needed to take time to heal once in a while. As long as she could placate the beast inside him, his rest would be peaceful and healing.

"I'm not used to trusting anyone but my partner or other Royal Guards," he admitted. Some of his natural protections had dissolved along with his grasp on reality. He seemed to be floating in a half-awake sort of state, though she knew it was the poison affecting him. He was aware, even if the poison took him under again and he appeared to be unresponsive.

"What about the Nyx? Would you trust the *pantera* queen to see to your safety?"

"Ria? I protect her. Not the other way around."

His dedication to his duty was impressive, but not unexpected. Each of the big-cat shifter monarchs had a group of loyal Royal Guards to see to their safety. That was the way their society had been designed back during the European Renaissance. The Renaissance had influenced the names they called their monarchs as well. There had been a decided classical and Egyptian influence.

The queen of the *pantera noir* was called the Nyx as a nod to Greek antiquity. Black panthers saw the humor in naming their ruler after the goddess of the night. Just like the golden tigers, or *tigre d'or*, named their leader after the Egyptian sun god, Ra. The Tig'Ra was the king of all tigers and he was always a rare white tiger. The tiger queen was known as the Tig'Ren. The last royal couple to reign in the ancestral stronghold had been Gina's parents, but they'd had to leave it all behind due to murder and treachery.

"Okay then." She refocused on their conversation. "What about the Tig'Ra?" Whatever it cost, she had to get him to feel safe so that he could heal. "My father may not rule the Clan anymore, but he does rule over these lands. You're in his realm now. Nobody gets through the perimeter unless he lets them through. He has a small Pride of loyal tigers. They're stationed all around. I bet even Dad is prowling around out there tonight. He loves padding through the snow fog. It's his best camouflage."

"I've never seen the white tiger," Mitch mused sleepily. "I would like to see him before I die."

She squeezed his shoulder, regaining his attention. "You will *not* die, Mitch. I won't allow it. And you will meet my father tomorrow. He's demanded it. You can't let him down. Very few golden tigers are granted an audience with him these days. In fact, none in the past decade that I can recall. You need to honor that meeting."

"I will," he said sleepily as the poison overtook him again.

"Just don't leave me, Gina. I'll stay as long as you do."

"You have my word."

He was gone again. Under the spell of the poison.

Gina was physically exhausted by all the excitement, the drive and the trek to the cabin, but she stayed by his side, talking long into the night. Even though he looked unconscious, he'd told her the poison left him unable to respond but aware. She took that to heart, talking to him, telling him about her childhood escapades here at the cabin, where her family sometimes camped when teaching her survival skills. Many romps in the wilderness had ended with a toasty fire in this cabin and burnt marshmallows on sticks.

Her parents had doted on her but had not skimped when it came to her education—both in her tiger form and in her human shape. They taught her how to live as a tiger, how to hunt and how to survive. They taught her the same things in human form too, along with other skills like self-defense and evasion. All this, before she'd even become a teenager. It had been fun to learn those things at first—when she hadn't realized the deadly game had very real consequences.

But after an attempt on her father's life while they were on one of their rare trips abroad, where friends had died in the course of saving her family's lives, she'd learned the truth. She'd learned the true nature of the world and how her family was hunted simply because of what they were. Hunted by humans. Hunted by their own kind who wanted her father's power.

After that, she'd become more serious about learning how to defend and even attack should it become necessary, in both her forms. Her father had been her teacher. He was a skilled fighter who kept in shape, training with his friends, the loyal Royal Guards who had come with him into exile.

There hadn't been an attempt on his life in many years. Of course, that was probably because they were so well hidden, none of their enemies could find them way up here.

After a couple of hours keeping up her one-sided dialog, Gina found it impossible to stay awake. The cabin was warm and Mitch was in the only real bed. It was big enough that she could lie down next to him and not touch. She doubted he'd wake easily from his unconscious state, but she wanted to be nearby just in case. It wasn't entirely professional, of course. She'd never even entertained the idea of sleeping in the same bed with any of her other patients. Still, the extreme situation called for extreme measures.

She lay down beside Mitch and closed her eyes. She was asleep before she took another breath, so great was her exhaustion.

Sometime later, in the middle of the night, she woke to a great shaking. Fighting through her sleep fog, she realized quickly that Mitch was in distress. His whole body was shaking as he fought through another round of convulsions.

"Dammit," she cursed, sitting up on the bed, reaching over Mitch's straining body to the night stand where she'd put the medical supplies. She had to get more of her blood into him to counteract the tenacious residual poison.

She swung her leg over him and sat on his thighs, trying to hold him in place so he wouldn't hurt himself. Gina checked to make sure his airway was clear and placed a small stack of wooden tongue depressors between his pearly white teeth to give him something to bite down on.

"Hold on, Mitch," she spoke to him while she prepared to take the blood from her arm. "I'm going to give you a bigger dose this time," she thought aloud as she stuck herself. "I've never given even half this much to anyone before, but you're big enough to handle it, I think. I've never had to dose anyone more than once before either, but with you I'm hoping the third time will be the charm."

She filled the syringe with as much blood as it would hold while his body shook under her. It was an all-or-nothing strategy and it had to work this time. It just had to.

She lay across him to keep his arm still while she administered the injection. His convulsions were a little less violent than the last time, when they'd still been in the city, in the apartment. That gave her hope. Perhaps his body was fighting back a bit more now, though whatever he'd been poisoned with had to be something fierce. She'd never had to give anyone this much of her blood. Never.

She shot the dose home, into his arm, using all her weight to keep him still enough for the procedure. His muscles clenched, making her job a bit more difficult, but she found a way to get the life-saving substance into him. It was either that or watch him die—and she absolutely refused to do that under any circumstances.

Within moments, the convulsions subsided, though his hands began to shift shape and his skin sprouted fur. Mottled orange, black...and white?

No way.

Gina looked more closely. No doubt about it. A small portion of his fur was white. Not the normal tawny tones of a *tigre d'or*. Now wasn't that interesting?

"It's probably a side effect of the large amount of my blood in you right now. Maybe it'll go away once you recover." She shrugged, holding his arm down as the partial shift stopped and he returned to a fully human form once more.

He didn't shift again, which was a good sign, and his body stopped convulsing and dropped into an exhausted sleep. On closer examination, this sleep seemed more normal than the state he'd been in before. His breathing was easier and at a more natural rhythm and pace. His pulse was healthy and strong. His pupils responded and he even batted one hand at her forearm as she shone her small penlight into his eye. He hadn't been able to do that before.

He seemed utterly exhausted but definitely in better shape than he had been in before this episode. She only prayed the improvement would last this time and continue until he was well again.

As the adrenaline rush left her, she felt the weariness sweep back into every bone in her body. She put the supplies back on the table, including her little penlight, and flopped back down beside Mitch. It might not be proper to sleep with him, but she was glad she had. If not, she might not have realized he'd been in crisis, for he hadn't made a single sound through the entire ordeal. Only his uncontrolled shaking had woken her and she wouldn't have noticed it had she slept on the couch across the room.

All in all, it was better she stay next to him. At least until he was out of the woods for certain.

CHAPTER TWO

Mitch woke to warmth and a luscious female form pressed against him. He didn't immediately recall much about where he was or who he was with, but he knew he wanted the woman pressed against his side. She smelled of tall grass and moonflowers. She smelled…right. Perfect, in fact.

He was only half awake, but his body knew what it wanted. Her. Always. Forever. In every way.

Mitch reached out, absently noting the soreness of his muscles. Straining his muscles was nothing new to a man who spent a lot of time pushing himself to his physical limits in an effort to be the best he could be. He dismissed the tight sensations across his shoulders in favor of the soft fabric and even softer skin of the woman under his fingertips.

He rolled slightly, aligning his body with hers. She was a perfect fit. But she wore too many clothes.

He buried his nose in the curve of her neck as he dragged at the soft jersey knit of her top, pulling it upward to bare her midriff. He touched her bare skin and paused, learning the feel of her as his nose drew in the scent of her flesh. He licked her, tasting the salt of her skin as his body absorbed the shiver that went through her.

He liked the way she responded to him. Already, he could tell this was going to be a fuck to remember.

"Mitch?" Her groggy voice reached his ear and he liked the way it slid over his senses. She had a voice edged with sin that made him draw her closer.

But she slipped one small hand between them and it felt like she was pushing against his chest. Pushing him away.

The beast inside him growled. It didn't like that. Neither did the man.

But her strength was nearly a match for his. That was new. Few women—even shifter women—could make an impression on him with their physical strength. She wasn't large. She fit into the planes of his body with feminine petiteness, but there was a core of steel in her that made him pause.

Oh, he could have overpowered her easily enough. He was an Alpha in his prime, after all, but that wouldn't be right. He was a Royal Guard and he lived by a code of chivalry handed down over the centuries through the ranks of Royal Guards. He would not stain his honor by forcing a woman. Not ever.

Slowly, the fog began to lift as his brain started to function.

"Where am I?" His voice was rougher than he expected. And his throat was raw with strain. What had he been doing to make his whole body hurt this much both inside and out?

The pain of his condition began to penetrate the sensual fog that had held him in thrall. As he drew back, he began to feel the aches in every muscle and the pain of healing wounds. He'd been in a fight. No doubt about it. He remembered very well what the day after a bust-up felt like.

Memories began to return. He'd been ambushed by a werewolf in half-shifted form outside Harris's dojo. They'd fought, but the werewolf had had friends. Someone had come from behind and jabbed Mitch with a needle. He'd fought for a few minutes more, but then the lights had gone out. He'd only surfaced for short periods since then. It was all really foggy after the needle jabbed him.

"You're in my family's cabin. You're safe." Her voice comforted him and he began to recognize it.

"Gina?"

"Yes, Mitch. I'm here." She pressed her palm more gently against his chest, but she was still trying to put more space between them. He took the hint and released her a little more but didn't let her go completely. He wanted her inside the circle of his arms.

"How are you feeling?"

"Like I got run over by a herd of elephants."

The quality of her touch changed from pushing away to assessing. Her hands went to his shoulders, rubbing the tight knots of his aching muscles.

"What do you remember?"

"Guarding with Cade. Then the ambush. Getting slashed and stuck with a needle. Then…not much. Until you. And Cade and another woman in an unfamiliar apartment. Then a car ride. Then…you again, princess. How am I doing?"

"You've got most of what you were awake for at least. That's a good thing."

"So what did I miss?" He liked the feel of her hands on his body. She had a gentle, healing touch.

"Let's see. Two rounds of convulsions and three jabs with a needle packed with universal shifter blood."

"Your blood," he confirmed. "I remember that part." He raised one hand to take hers and squeezed gently. "Thank you for that, milady. If I didn't say it before, let me say it now."

"You're welcome." Her gaze held his for a long moment and he was about to say to hell with protocol and tradition. He was angling in for a kiss when there was a pounding on the door of the cabin.

Mitch instantly released her, climbing to his feet, hoping to defend her from any possible threat no matter how bad a shape he was in. His legs trembled under his own weight but he refused to acknowledge the weakness.

Gina came out from behind him and he growled low in his throat in warning. She only sent him a somewhat worried smile.

"It's my dad. I'd know his idea of a gentle knock

anywhere."

Mitch tried to move but couldn't seem to walk. He growled again in frustration and watched helplessly as she went toward the door.

"Be certain it's him before you open up." It was the only thing he could do to keep her safe, and it wasn't much. He was in bad physical shape and he plopped down on the side of the bed as his wobbly legs gave way. One hand propped him up as he leaned heavily on his uninjured side, glaring at the door and the woman heading toward it.

"Dad, is that you?"

"Who else?" came the roar of a full-grown tiger from the other side of the heavy wooden door.

A tiger in human form, of course. The Tig'Ra. That much Mitch remembered. Gina's dad was the rarest of the rare, the magic-touched, born-to-rule, *tigre* of all *tigres*. The white tiger. The Sun King. The one blessed by the Goddess and meant to govern all of his kind.

Mitch tried hard to stand up straight but he couldn't even manage that as Gina opened the door and launched herself into the arms of the older man at the threshold. He hugged his daughter, but his sharp blue eyes sought and measured Mitch even as he greeted his daughter.

"How's my girl?" The king lifted Gina off her feet for a quick moment as he stepped into the cabin. He let her go and shut the door behind him, securing it before he turned his full attention to Mitch.

Mitch felt every inch of the once-over he received. It was hard not to feel intimidated, even though Mitch was secure in his own skin. Or at least he had been—before meeting the Goddess-touched tiger king.

"And you must be Mitch."

He tried to drop to one knee, but it was more like a fall rather than the graceful gesture he'd intended. Gina and her father each reached out and took one of his arms, steadying him, much to his chagrin.

"Whoa there, son. No need for that," Gina's father's voice

came to Mitch as if from a distance and he knew he was in danger of passing out again. "Give us some room, Gina," the older man ordered gently.

And then the room spun as the king himself reached out again, shooed his daughter away and lifted Mitch up, one strong hand under each arm. He placed Mitch in a sitting position on the edge of the bed. The older man offered support while the room steadied and then stilled. Thank goodness, the spinning had stopped, but Mitch didn't make any sudden moves, just in case the room decided to start dancing around again.

"My apologies, sire," he mumbled, embarrassed by his weakness and humbled before the greatest and most blessed of all tiger shifters. "I'm not as strong as I should be."

"No, you're not. And I'm here to find out why." The king pulled up one of the sturdy wooden chairs and sat at Mitch's side. Gina perched on his other side and together they told the story of how Mitch had come to be under her care.

"My partner and I have been guarding the *pantera noir* Nyx for several years," Mitch answered, when the king asked how Mitch had come to be in the city. "She had to move and we had what we thought was a solid contact in a human named Harris who owns the Silent Tiger dojo. Unfortunately, Harris was betrayed and the dojo was attacked while the Nyx was inside. Another team of Royal Guards got her out. I'm ashamed to admit I walked into an ambush."

"They were waiting for you with a needle?" Gina asked, her voice indicating her horror at the thought.

"Near as I can figure. All I remember is fighting a wolf in battle form. He scratched the hell out of me." Mitch raised the hem of his T-shirt to expose a few of the red lines that had mostly healed. Gina's magical blood and his own shifter constitution had done the work of healing his physical wounds, but whatever poison was still in his system, making him weak as a kitten, was something altogether different. "While I was distracted by the wolf, someone jabbed me with a needle from behind."

The king bent closer to inspect the wounds and Mitch heard the angry growl in the back of his throat. Thankfully, his displeasure wasn't aimed at Mitch, but rather at the coward who would betray his own kind so that another could poison him.

"Whoever did this wants us warring among ourselves," Gina's father said in a low, angry voice. "If you had died of the poison, not many of us would look beyond the claw marks for a reason for your departure from this realm. We would have blamed another shifter."

"I believe so, sire," Mitch agreed, thankful that he was feeling well enough to converse with the Goddess-blessed leader of his people, even if this king didn't want the job anymore. "I also believe that whatever was in the syringe was meant to kill me. Only your daughter's blood saved me and allows me to continue." Mitch turned to Gina, daring to reach out for her hand. "I want you to know, while I am still clear-headed enough to tell you...I won't blame you if I don't survive this. It won't be your fault. You've done more than anyone could have done for me. For that I thank you. Allowing me the time to help our people—to let them know it wasn't a shifter that killed me—is a true gift. Whatever happens, I want you to know that. Thank you, princess."

Mitch cursed inwardly. The woman had tears in her eyes. If not for her father sitting next to him—glowering at him now—Mitch would have taken her into his arms and kissed those tears away. As it was, all he could do was squeeze her hand and hold her watery gaze, hoping she could read the truth of his words in his eyes.

"I promise to do my best for you," Gina whispered.

Anything more she would have said was cut off by her father. "Can you save him, kitten?"

She lifted her gaze to her father and nodded, her lips pressed tightly together as if to hold in her emotions. "I think so," she finally answered. "He stays lucid for longer each time and the convulsions weren't as severe last night as they were the first time. Each subsequent treatment seems to negate a bit more of whatever it was they injected him with. Giving him the nectar was a mistake. It made things worse and it's taken a lot of my blood to bring him back from it." She bit her lip before continuing in a more timid manner. "There's just one thing that worries me. When he convulses, parts of him shift. His hands and feet. And the last time…there was white fur amid the gold."

Mitch was shocked. He'd always been a golden tiger.

"Is it some kind of side effect from the blood you've given me?" he asked, truly puzzled and feeling more than a little spooked.

White fur was the province of the king and his family alone. Mitch was *tigre d'or*—a golden tiger—as were all other tiger shifters in the world. Only a rare few were *tigre blanche*—the sacred white tigers.

"Are you certain, kitten? You saw white fur?" Gina's father asked in grave tones.

Gina nodded. "I've dosed people with my blood before—including other goldens—but I've never seen this kind of response. Of course, I've never given anyone as much as I've given Mitch. I've shot him up three times, each time with a higher dose."

"Well, it could be a side effect of your treatment, but then again…" Gina's father stood abruptly. "I have to think about this. I also have to check the perimeter and talk with the Guard. No one will trespass to interfere with your recovery, Mitch." The exiled king nodded at him and Mitch felt the impact of that decisive gesture. "Heal him as best you can, kitten," the elder said to his daughter. "He might be more important than you know."

And with those disturbing words and a final hug for his daughter, the powerful man left the cabin in a whirl of snow as he opened the heavy door. Apparently, sometime during their talk, a storm had rolled in, blanketing what Mitch could see of the sky in a dark, uniform gray.

"Looks like we'll be snowed in here for a bit," Gina said, barring the door behind her father. "How are you feeling?"

She leaned back against the wooden door, her gaze roving over him with a critical eye.

It was the look of a doctor evaluating her patient, but there was an added component…a component of attraction of female to male—and vice versa. Mitch had been attracted to the beautiful doctor from almost the first moment he'd laid eyes on her. Certainly from the first moment he'd laid *coherent* eyes on her. Gina was a beauty with Goddess-given regal lines and a reticence that seemed at odds with her competent manner.

"I've felt better," Mitch admitted, running a hand through his hair.

He was certain he looked a fright, but until now, such things hadn't bothered him. Only with Gina—and especially in front of her father—he wanted to make the best possible impression. Instead, he'd nearly fainted at the king's feet and he probably stank too. He'd been through hell since the last time he'd taken a shower. Was it only a day before? Or had it been two days since the attack on the dojo? He'd lost track of time somewhere along the way.

"Are you going to keel over on me again?" She smiled as she pushed off the door and walked a few steps toward him.

"I certainly hope not." He tried to laugh it off, but he really did feel lousy. "But I won't be running any races for a while."

She walked right up to him and touched his shoulder. It wasn't exactly an impersonal touch, but it wasn't the full-body contact he longed for. How he could think of the tiger princess that way was beyond him—especially after the audience he'd just been granted with the most elusive of tigers, the Goddess-blessed king of them all. But Mitch couldn't control the attraction he felt for Gina.

And what was worse—he didn't want to control it. Maybe it was the poison affecting his judgment or the knowledge that he could easily die of it, but he wanted her touch. He wanted to feel her kiss again. He wanted it almost more than he wanted his next breath. But she was back to business as she felt his forehead with the back of her hand and then checked his pulse.

"Any more dizziness?" she asked, all business.

"Not now, but you saw what happened when I tried to kneel," he admitted grudgingly.

"Dad doesn't go in for all that rigmarole anyway," she said as she examined his eyes, shining her small penlight at his pupils one at a time. "He's a fairly simple man."

"Honey, I hate to break it to you, but he's the Tig'Ra. There's nothing simple about him and there never will be. Nothing simple about you either, princess." His voice dipped to intimate tones on that last part and she met his gaze with a tinge of fear and determination in her own.

"Maybe not, but it's what he's chosen. What he was destined to do."

"Destined?" That was news to Mitch.

He'd never really thought about why the king had gone into exile. Nobody knew the reason, other than the violence that had hounded him and his family. Mitch had never quite believed that the king of all tigers would run from danger, but he hadn't known the details behind his departure.

"Dad doesn't talk about it much, but he once told me he'd been directed to do what he did. He answers to a higher power, you know. Being the Tig'Ra is more of a spiritual position than most believe. I believe he's had direct contact with the Mother of All, and I know for sure he believes She guides our actions."

"Have you ever had *direct contact*, as you put it, with the Lady Goddess?" Mitch dared to ask. He wasn't a particularly religious man, but he had great respect for the actions of the Goddess in all their lives. He'd seen evidence of Her divine intervention too many times to discount it.

Gina's head tilted to the side. "I'm not entirely sure, but I think at times I have felt Her influence. Look at how you came into my care. I think it was fate or destiny, or whatever you want to call it, that brought us all into the same place at the right time."

"Without you, I would already be dead, milady," he agreed. "So maybe the Goddess did send you. And if so, I sincerely thank Her for Her intervention."

Gina smiled and it was as if the sun had come out on a cloudy day. For a split second, Mitch thought he saw the sparkle of magic in the air and heard the divine notes of the Lady's chimes in the distance, but it couldn't be. Mitch was only a poor servant. He would never be so blessed. He wasn't nearly devout enough for such fancifulness.

It was probably the poison still coursing through his system.

"You should lie down," Gina instructed. "Dad will take care of security for now. I know it goes against your Alpha nature, but for the time being, you have to trust in him and his loyal helpers to see to your safety." She smiled to soften her words and he gave in and scooted back on the bed as best he could while she adjusted the pillows and covers, tucking him in.

"I know when I'm beat. Right now, I'm about as weak as I've ever been," he admitted. "I meant what I said before. If this kills me, I want you to feel no responsibility. You've done your best for me at every turn. Thank you, princess." He caught her hand and pressed the back of it to his lips for a tender kiss. She stilled, looking down at him with a startled yet pleased expression on her lovely face.

He tugged on her hand and pulled her closer, but she halted just out of reach of his lips. How he wanted to kiss her, but his energy was beginning to fail. It didn't feel quite as scary as before, so maybe he wasn't going to die just yet, but if he did, he was at peace. He had met the white tiger and had known the gentle, healing touch of the princess. He could die a happy man.

The only thing that could make him even happier would be if Gina closed the distance between them and laid her soft lips against his. He wanted her touch, her kiss, her skin against his. He knew he wasn't good enough for her, but that didn't seem to matter to his inner cat, who wanted the tigress in her to submit to his dominance. Ill as he was, Mitch knew he wasn't very dominant at the moment.

Gina stayed with him. She nursed him back to health as best she could. She gave of her own magical blood to heal his injured body. Surely she had the biggest heart of any being he had ever met. She was selfless in her care for him—a relative stranger.

She knew *what* he was. A Royal Guard. A golden tiger. An Alpha sworn to protect the shifter royalty. But she had yet to learn the deeper facets of his personality. She didn't know *who* he was. She didn't know *him*. The real him. Not really. But if he survived this ordeal, Mitch vowed to find some way that he could stay near her for the rest of his days.

He didn't delude himself that he might be considered good enough by her kin to mate her, but even without that ultimate bond, Mitch felt drawn to her. Now that he knew of her existence, he would never leave her in this life. He would do his duty as a Royal Guard and protect the tiger princess with every breath left in his body. He would quit the Nyx's employ and move to be near Gina, wherever she chose to go from here. From this day forward, she would never be unguarded again. It was his duty. His honor. He *needed* to keep her safe from all who might harm her.

He had never felt such a compelling desire to guard the Nyx, though being a Royal Guard was something he'd trained for almost his entire life. He would die for the Nyx. It was his duty. But the need to take care of Gina was even stronger.

Acknowledging that soul-deep truth, Mitch allowed himself to relax and close his eyes. Sleep claimed him, but not before he felt the touch of Gina's lips on his forehead. A gentle benediction to help him sleep. He had never known before that such a small, gentle touch could mean so much.

CHAPTER THREE

The next time Mitch woke, he was much more clear-headed. He looked around for clues about how long he had been asleep but found it hard to feel the passage of time. He knew he had been out of it for a long time though, by the stiffness of his muscles. Or maybe it was the poison that made him so achy? He wasn't really sure.

There were a few small windows in the cabin and all had curtains drawn over them. No light leaked around the fabric, so Mitch assumed it was dark out. Night time.

He raised his head and looked all around the cabin, but Gina was nowhere to be found. That worried him into sitting up. Where could she be? He didn't think she would have left him alone, unconscious and unprotected.

Then he heard the unmistakable sound of claws against the door handle as it turned from the outside. The door opened just enough to admit a sparkling white tiger. A female.

Gina.

Mitch's breath caught at her beauty. She was gorgeous in feline form, and her striped white fur crackled with magical energy in the dark. A few flakes of snow followed her inside, swirling around her sleek, powerful body as she padded in on silent paws and then turned to secure the door before moving farther into the room.

Mitch felt the chill of the outdoors, but only in a peripheral way. All his attention was on Gina and the amazing picture she presented. She was ethereal. Her glowing coat spoke of the magic of other realms. Goddess-touched.

Mitch felt like dropping to one knee in deference, but he was still prone and the aches in his body told him he wouldn't be able to move without considerable pain and possible further embarrassment. He'd tried to kneel to Gina's dad and had failed miserably in the attempt. He didn't want to make a fool of himself a second time. Still, Gina inspired worship without even trying.

She nodded her regal head at him when she turned around and realized he was awake and then loped off behind a curtain that partitioned one side of the room. He heard the rustling of fabric and a moment later, Gina stepped out from behind the curtain in human form, dressed in a dark T-shirt and jeans. She was just as beautiful in her human guise as in her fur.

"Have you been awake long?" she asked, coming closer.

"Just a few minutes. What time is it?"

"After midnight. I'm sorry I had to go out. Dad wouldn't take no for an answer. He knew how badly I needed a run and he had the Millers guarding you for the short while I was away. I knew you were out of the woods and sleeping normally. You've been asleep all day."

"Sorry. I feel more alert now, but I ache all over." He didn't like admitting to his own weakness, but she was his doctor as well as the tiger princess. He had to give her the truth at all times. "Do you know where my phone is?"

"I think Cade might have it. I know there was some worry over the fact that it had been lost during the fight. If it's okay with my dad, I can get you a spare. Dad keeps pre-paid burn phones available for emergencies up at the house, even though I'm usually on communications lockdown when I'm here. He won't even let me call Ellie most of the time. He's pretty obsessive about maintaining security here."

She shrugged and sat at his side, perching on the bed while she ran the back of her hand over his brow to test his temperature. She then felt for the pulse at his wrist and looked into his eyes. The doctor was checking on her patient first and foremost, and Mitch enjoyed her gentle fussing.

"I guess it's too late to call anyone right now. And I'm not sure what good it would do anyway."

"And there's the tricky question of saying where you are exactly. We can't compromise my parents' location. I hope you understand."

"Honey, I'm a Royal Guard." He saw the disappointment in her gaze and was quick to reassure her. "That means I guard our monarchs, no matter what. Your dad is still the Tig'Ra, no matter how much your uncle claims to rule in his place. And you're the tiger princess. I could no more put you in danger than the Nyx. If your dad wants to stay hidden—if you want to stay hidden—then who am I to question the will of the Goddess-blessed white tiger?"

A smile bloomed over her face and he was glad he had put it there. And then she blushed a bit, charming him even more. "You know, I wasn't raised with all that. I'm just Gina. I'm not a princess, no matter how many times you call me that."

Mitch bowed his head slightly in acknowledgment. He'd humor her wishes, but she would always be royalty to him—and to every other *tigre d'or*—no matter if she acknowledged it or not.

"I bow to your will, milady," he murmured with a grin, knowing she'd take his words as teasing, even though he truly meant them. He would follow her direction for the rest of his life, if she let him. And that brought up another thought...

"Gina," he began hesitantly. When she looked at him expectantly, he found the courage to continue. Never had he felt so timid before, but his future was riding on the next few moments. "I intend to resign from the Nyx's service. If she still lives." He looked away, ashamed of his weakness. He hadn't succeeded in his job and he would live with the stain on his honor for the rest of his life.

"Why?" Gina interrupted his depressing thoughts. "You're a Royal Guard. What else would you do?"

"I'm not sure," he stalled, needing to find the right way to put forward his deepest desire. "But I know I've failed the Nyx and I will bear the shame of that failure. Her enemies know who I am now. Or, at least, they know my face. I cannot go back to her service, or those enemies might trace her through me. I'm a liability." He acknowledged the grim truth at last. The life and job he had known were both over.

"They probably think you're dead. Even an Alpha as strong as you are couldn't have lived through that poison."

"Not without divine intervention," he agreed. "And it's probably for the best if I stay dead to the Nyx's enemies."

"Then what will you do? Is there family you can return to?" She cringed. "I'm sorry. I remember you saying there was no one," she apologized softly, seeming sad for reminding him of his lone state.

Tigers prowled alone sometimes, but family was everything. For Mitch, the Clan had been his family after his parents died, but he'd found friends and family of a sort among the panthers. Cade was like a brother to him, but he wasn't a tiger, and sometimes their differences stood between them.

"I may be no good to the Nyx, but I still have my uses. I intend to offer my services to your family—to you in particular, princess—if you will have me."

There it was. He'd laid his soul on the line. If she rejected him, he truly didn't know what he would do.

And maybe she saw some of that desperation in his gaze, because she didn't laugh at his offer or turn him down out of hand. She stood and paced, her expression tight with worry and...fear? His little princess was afraid and Mitch couldn't imagine of what. Not of him, surely?

Perhaps it was the fear of facing who—and what—she truly was? That made sense to him, though it was painful to watch. For the few days he'd known Gina, she'd been confident, funny, strong and gentle. All qualities he associated with the strength of character he expected of a royal bloodline. Ria, the Nyx, was very much the same, if a bit younger than Gina.

Mitch truly liked Ria and had enjoyed serving her and keeping her safe. She was a good leader to her people and a benevolent ruler who kept her people's welfare above her own. He would miss her.

But to see such worry and uncertainty on a royal face was something Mitch wasn't used to. He had trained among other shifter royalty and each had carried themselves with surety and strength, even in private. None had doubted themselves as Gina seemed to—or feared their true selves.

King Frederick had done his daughter no favors by raising her in isolation. If she accepted Mitch as part of her Guard, he would do his utmost to help her realize her own strengths and become the princess she truly was. Subtly, of course. Mitch wouldn't chastise her. He would guide and help. He would be her right-hand man, if she let him. He would be there for her when she needed him.

It was all he could do. Guard her and keep her safe. She was precious to him.

If things had been different and she wasn't the tiger princess, he would have done his best to make her his own. Mate with her for life. Protect her and love her and sire cubs with her.

But that wasn't meant to be. She wasn't for him. She was above him in all ways, and Mitch, an orphan golden tiger—albeit an Alpha Royal Guard—knew his place.

Finally, she stopped pacing and turned her worried gaze to him. "Is that what you really want?"

Mitch sighed. When had a royal ever asked him what he wanted? Not often, that was for sure. Gina was only reinforcing Mitch's high opinion of her. If she would return to the Clan and take her rightful place, all tigers would be blessed by her wisdom.

Again, he bowed his head to her. She was more like the

monarch she had been born to be every time he looked at her.

"I miss the company of other tigers," he answered evasively, but truthfully.

"It must be hard on you, serving among *pantera*," she commiserated.

Surprise made him look up at her. "Not that hard, milady." He had to smile, thinking about the life he had led up to now. "Cade is my best friend. He might be a panther, but he's one of the most steadfast men and talented warriors I know. I will miss him, but he is sworn to his Nyx and I am useless to her now. The *pantera* are good people of strong convictions. They welcomed me as one of their own, even though we wear different fur."

"My father tells me it is a rare thing for the secretive *pantera noir* to accept any outsider into their ranks, much less allowing one to guard their monarch. Dad was impressed." Gina smiled and walked a step closer, her expression softening.

"Cade and I met when we were both in training. We were well-matched and usually ended up sparring together. We became friends, and when he realized I had no close family, he sort of adopted me." Mitch shrugged.

The way he had been welcomed by Cade and his family still made Mitch feel sentimental, but he strove not to let it show too much. Cade was his brother in every way but blood, and always would be. Some bonds could never be broken.

"I'm glad. And not just for you. I think your friend Cade may have designs on *my* best friend, Ellie." Gina smiled as she sat on the chair by his bedside. "Please tell me he's not a tomcat chasing everything in a skirt."

"Cade?" Mitch had to laugh at the description. Sure, Cade didn't lack for female companionship, but he'd never shown an interest in a human to Mitch's knowledge. If he was showing signs of courting Ellie, it had to be serious. "Are you sure?"

"Oh, yeah. A woman knows the signs. And I've never

seen Ellie so worked up over a guy. If they don't get together, I'll be truly amazed."

Mitch was floored by the idea of Cade hooking up with a human. "I hope your friend is strong enough for him. Cade is more Alpha than most."

Gina laughed. "If I were you, I'd be more worried about Cade. Ellie may be human, but she's as fierce as any tigress. Even my parents love her. She'd have been adopted into our familial Pride long ago if things were different."

"If she weren't human, you mean?" Mitch asked, tilting his head.

"No. Dad's never had a problem recruiting allies even among humans," Gina answered in a more subdued tone. "I meant, if dad wasn't in hiding, he'd have granted her official status in the Pride when we were kids. For my sake, if for no other reason. But Ellie has proved herself over and over. She would have—should have—been let in on the secret a long time ago, except for dad's need for secrecy." Gina frowned. "I haven't liked lying to her all these years. And I really don't know if she's ever going to forgive me."

Mitch reached out and took Gina's hand. He couldn't help himself. Gina looked so forlorn.

"She'll understand. How could she not forgive you if you're as close as you say?" He tried to coax a smile out of her, but Gina wouldn't be swayed out of her concern. "If anyone can make her understand about shifters and our need to keep our secrets, it's Cade. He's *pantera noir*, after all. Ninja of the shifter world. They don't come more secretive than the *noir*."

Gina sighed. "I guess you're right. I mean, I *hope* you're right. I just worry. She's like my little misguided, innocent sister. There's so much she doesn't know about."

"Cade will teach her. And he'll look out for her. There's nobody better at what he does than Cade." He stroked the back of her hand with his thumb. It was a small gesture, but she seemed to take comfort from it, so he continued. "But you're avoiding my question. Will you let me stay and be your

Guard?"

Gina met his gaze, the worry creeping back into her eyes. "If you ask my dad, he'll say yes. He's been after me to accept more protection for years." She squeezed his hand and then pulled her fingers free of his. "Let me think about it, Mitch. After all that's happened, I'd like to see how things settle out with the Nyx before I make any decisions. As of right now, I don't even know if I'm going back to the city after this is all over. I might be stuck here for a while. Maybe even permanently if Dad has his way." She rolled her eyes a bit in frustration as she shook her head slightly. Living in secret her whole life couldn't have been easy for such an outgoing spirit.

"No matter where you go, I'll follow and protect, Gina. If you let me." His voice dipped low. "Please let me."

Their eyes met and held, the silence between them charged.

But she was saved from answering by the loud knock on the cabin door. They had a visitor, and visitors this late at night couldn't mean anything good. Mitch jerked upright, willing the room not to spin. He was still too damned weak, but at least he was feeling stronger than he had before, even if his head spun.

"That's not your dad," Mitch whispered, pretty sure the soft knock wasn't the Alpha of all Alphas.

Gina shook her head and tried to go to the door, but Mitch stopped her, rising to his feet. He couldn't help swaying a bit, but he'd be damned if he was going to let her answer the door alone at this hour of the night.

"Is there any way to see who it is remotely?" he whispered.

Her eyes widened for a moment before she grinned. It looked like she'd remembered something. Reaching into the bedside table's top drawer, she pulled out a small tablet. She pushed a button and the screen flared to life.

Camera feeds. Nice.

"It's Mr. Miller. Looks like he brought us some supplies."

"At this hour?" Mitch questioned even as Gina visibly relaxed. She put the tablet on the nightstand and moved toward the door.

"Relax. I've known him all my life. He helped me get you here."

Mitch wanted to stop her but he was still too wobbly on his feet, much to his chagrin. He could only hope Miller was the friend Gina believed him to be and that he didn't come bearing bad news.

Gina opened the door and Mitch held his breath.

"I hope I'm not bothering you, but I saw the light and thought I'd check in with some supplies."

"Light?" Gina looked concerned, and Mitch realized that the windows weren't just curtained, they were light-proofed. Nice.

"Up top," Mr. Miller pointed above his head where a vent allowed air to flow into the cabin. There was a small flap of dark fabric pushed to one side near it that was obviously intended to cover even that tiny source of potential light at night.

Gina blushed and bit her lip. "Darn it."

"It's all right, sweetheart," Mr. Miller reached out to pat Gina's arm in a fatherly way. "Just be glad it was me who saw it and not the big guy. He'd chew your head off for forgetting even something as small as that."

Gina tugged on a string that had been tucked next to the doorframe and the little flap came down over the vent. With that done, she stepped back to invite the man inside. He accepted her invitation, shaking snow off his boots on the doormat before entering, his arms laden with a basket that looked more suited to a picnic than camping. He handed it over as soon as the door was closed behind him.

"Joan sent some fresh bread and a few other things," he said in a pleasant voice. "I see your patient is awake." Mr. Miller focused on Mitch and he felt the piercing gaze of another Alpha.

Mitch was at a decided disadvantage, but he stood his ground. He recognized the look of the man. He was Alpha. Gina had said Miller had been a Royal Guard in his time.

Mitch decided to go on the offensive—in what small way he could, weak as he was.

"I'm Mitch Thorburn." He held out his hand and Miller grasped it for a firm shake, informing Mitch that his first name was Tom. "Thanks for helping get me here. Gina told me about the snowmobile ride." Mitch smiled slightly, showing his teeth. He liked what he saw of the older man and knew this Alpha had been quite a tiger in his day. He was older now, but he didn't seem to have lost any of his strength.

"Gina tells me you're Royal Guard," the man said with a measuring look in his eyes.

"I am," Mitch confirmed but didn't go into detail. The less people who knew about the Nyx being in the area, the better.

"Me too," Miller confirmed, stepping back, giving Mitch space. "So is my wife. Our children guarded Gina when she was young."

"Quite a family," Mitch complimented the older man with a nod.

Being a Royal Guard was a very special thing. It required not only Alpha traits but a particular temperament that wasn't common. It required selflessness and the instinct to protect others that not all Alphas could claim.

"The big guy said you work for panthers." Again, Miller treated Mitch to a statement that sounded more like a question.

"I've decided to resign my post. I'm a liability now that I've been seen, though the attackers probably think I'm dead. I'd be more effective elsewhere for now." Mitch looked at Gina, but her expression was unreadable.

"That's more or less what Gina's dad said as well," Miller agreed. "But you have time to heal here, and after you're back on your feet, we'll discuss a great many things."

Now that sounded promising. Mitch was taken by surprise by the new, welcoming tone in Miller's voice.

"I'll look forward to it."

Miller backed away, turning to Gina for a few quiet words about the supplies while Mitch pondered the undercurrents in the man's words. It sounded like Gina's dad was already thinking along the same lines as Mitch. If the tiger king was interested in secrecy, what better way to make sure Mitch didn't give away his location than by taking him into his employ?

Miller stayed for a few minutes more, chatting with Gina in low tones. Mitch could hear them talk, but it was mostly about Miller's children and how they were doing. He left a short while later without much further ado, shaking Mitch's hand before taking his leave. All the same, Mitch was glad to see him go.

Mitch's strength was failing again and the moment he was certain the door was secure, he sank back on the bed, grateful for its support. Gina came over to check on him, but he couldn't rouse the energy to even open his eyelids.

The next thing Mitch knew, he woke up what felt like it had to be hours later. Time was a fluid thing when you were on the mend, Mitch knew. And with the blackout curtains blocking all light, it was even harder to tell what time it was inside the cabin.

Mitch had lost track of how many days it had been since the attack. Had it only been two? Three? Four or more? He wasn't really sure.

But what did it matter really? He was out of the action for now. Well out of it. Contacting his teammates would only serve to possibly put Gina and her family in danger. There was nothing Mitch could do from here to help the Nyx. Cade, no doubt, had the situation well in hand. There wasn't a more capable Royal Guard than his soon-to-be *former* partner.

Mitch was better off laying low for now, healing and doing the best he could to protect Gina and her family from discovery. That was about all he was capable of at the moment. Which made him wonder where Gina was.

Mitch sat up in bed. It was a lot easier this morning and the room didn't tilt. In fact, his head was clearer than it had been since he'd been attacked. Moving carefully, he swung his legs over the side of the bed and sat for a moment.

Still good. He might just be healed.

Mitch looked around the small cabin and spotted Gina curled up on the couch across the room in front of the fireplace. She was sound asleep, but she opened her eyes the moment Mitch stood.

And then the world spun.

So maybe he wasn't completely healed yet. But he was a lot better than the last time he'd woken up. He'd take that and run with it. Well…not exactly run. He'd have to keep it to a careful trot for the time being.

"Good morning." Gina stretched as she woke up, looking soft as a kitten and just as adorable.

Mitch wanted nothing more than to go over and cuddle with her on that couch, but he couldn't. Not only was he not up to it physically, but he had to carefully control all the carnal thoughts he'd had about Gina over the past days. Now that he was more clear-headed, he realized he'd let his fantasies go a little too far. Sure, Gina was the most intoxicating woman he'd ever met, but she was also the tiger princess.

Too good for the likes of him. Way too far above his station in life.

He'd be a fool to fall for her. A fool who would live the rest of his life alone because he couldn't have the woman of his dreams.

"Good morning, milady. Please tell me you didn't sleep on the couch all night."

"I didn't sleep on the couch all night?" She said it like a question as she rose to a sitting position and began to tidy the blanket and pillow she'd used.

And that's when he knew he'd stolen her bed. He'd thought nothing of the sleeping arrangements in such a small cabin until just that moment. He could only blame it on his fuzzy head and whatever poison he'd been dosed with.

"Damn. I'm sorry. You get the bed tonight. If I'm still here tonight."

"What does that mean?" She paused, stilling her motions as she looked at him with a concerned expression. "You feel better, right? Your vitals were strong all night. I checked your temperature and pulse every hour and you were okay."

"I feel a lot better physically, but I'm feeling like a royal heel knowing you've been reduced to sleeping on the couch and watching over me all night." He filed away the realization that he hadn't woken up when she'd checked him every hour. Normally, Mitch had much sharper reflexes. The slightest noise out on the street would wake him instantly. He was always on alert. And yet, somehow, Gina had touched him and he hadn't woken up once.

"I've slept in a lot of worse places than this comfy couch," she assured him, standing and continuing to fold the blanket. "And taking care of people is my job."

He had to give her that point, but he didn't have to like it. It rankled that he'd been so inconsiderate of her comfort, but he'd make it up to her. He promised himself he would. Somehow.

"Regardless, tonight we switch places." He rubbed a hand over his hair and realized how grungy he felt. He probably smelled pretty bad too. "I need a shower." He'd used the bathroom a few times, so he knew there was a fully equipped, if small, shower.

"I'm way ahead of you. Dad stopped by earlier this morning and dropped off some clean clothes for you."

Damn. Not only had he not woken when she'd checked on him *every hour* last night, but he'd slept through the king's visit to the cabin entirely. He was really slipping.

"What time is it? I'm all turned around."

"It's almost noon."

Mitch was a little shocked. "I lost more than a few hours in there somewhere."

"Yeah, I know you were sleeping really deeply, but it appeared to be a normal sleep and you were doing a lot better than you have been previously, so I concluded that your body was working through the remnants of the poison. If I'm right, you're out of the woods. I'm still ordering bed rest with maybe a little gentle exercise later today if you're still feeling good."

"I'd love to go for a prowl." He knew running was beyond him at this point.

"It's just possible that could be arranged, but only if you're still in good shape later. For now, I think the shower is a good idea, as long as you're steady enough on your feet. Can you stand on your own?" She had walked toward him until she stood in front of where he still sat, his hands grasping the edges of the mattress.

He'd be damned if he was going to continue to coddle his weakness. Mitch gathered himself and pushed to his feet. Only a moment of disorientation hit him, but it wasn't as bad as it could have been. Still, Gina reached out and placed one soft hand on his chest and one around his shoulder.

He loved her nearness but not the reason for it. He had to be stronger than this. But having a gorgeous woman's hands on his body wasn't something he'd pass up lightly. He allowed her to help him regain his balance and then walk with him toward the small bathroom.

"Don't lock it," she cautioned, nodding toward the bathroom door as he reached out to grab the doorframe and she let go. "Just in case."

He wouldn't let himself pass out, but he understood her advice. It was only wise to take precautions.

"I won't. But I'll be okay." He didn't like the worried look on her face, so he decided to tease her a bit. "Of course, if you want to come in and scrub my back, I wouldn't say no." He let his voice drop into suggestive tones and shot her a wink for good measure. It was way over the top and he knew it. He wasn't surprised when she laughed. In fact, it was precisely the reaction he'd wanted.

"Nice try, Casanova, but I'll take a rain check." She was still smiling when he closed the door between them.

CHAPTER FOUR

Gina did end up opening the door to the bathroom before Mitch was done with his shower, but it wasn't for any sort of exciting reason. He heard her come in and turned toward her, but the frosted glass showed only the vague outline of his magnificent body.

"Just dropping off these clean clothes. Some big guy distracted me before." She joked with him, trying to forestall the unreasonable attraction she felt for Mitch. "How are you doing in there?"

"Why don't you come in and check for yourself?"

If he only knew how much she wanted to. But she feared his teasing was just that. Teasing.

He knew who she was. Her secret was out—at least to him. She couldn't be sure he was flirting with her for the person she was or for the princess she had never really had a chance to be. Anything that happened between them—romantic or otherwise—would be colored by that annoying little fact of her birth. She was royalty. And he was a Royal Guard. Alpha. Strong enough to guard, but not elite enough to mate.

No matter how much her inner tigress urged her to open that shower door and jump his bones. Tigers liked the water, and her cat wanted desperately to come out and play, but

Gina didn't dare. She didn't allow the tigress to rule her. She never had. She'd made a deal with her wild half long ago.

She let the cat run, but she didn't allow her to dictate Gina's actions in the human world. There was an uneasy peace between her two halves, but she made it work for the most part.

Until now. Until Mitch had crashed into her life, changing everything. She wasn't even sure she'd be able to go back to her life in the city. Or her job.

"If you're strong enough to flirt, you're strong enough to finish your shower and dress yourself," she quipped. "I'll be outside if you need anything. We'll eat and then we'll see about that little walk outside."

She left the steamy bathroom and shut the door behind her. The scent of soap and clean man was kind of intoxicating, and the tigress was scratching at her insides to get out, but Gina kept hold of her control. Just barely. She made it out of the room with her pride intact and then leaned against the closed door, trying to catch her breath.

She spent a few minutes putting a meal together, figuring she could gauge Mitch's physical status best by watching him rather than asking questions. A tough guy like him would probably answer every one of her questions with the standard *I'm fine*. Well, that wasn't going to be of any help. She had to gauge for herself whether or not he was up to shapeshifting and taking a prowl around the property.

Mitch came out of the bathroom dressed in some of her dad's sweats. They were about the same size. Powerful Alphas in their prime.

He was using a towel to rub his wet hair. He wore it short. Clean cut. No nonsense. Masculine. And all too attractive.

Down, girl.

He walked over to her on only slightly shaky bare feet to claim the place at the small table that she had set with a plate and silverware. His scent had changed. Up to now, he'd emitted a thick chemical smell that she could only assume was from the poison with which he'd been injected. As the days wore on, the scent of his illness had grown strong, though she had done her best to keep him clean while he'd been out of it.

But now he was completely clean for the first time since she'd met him. His natural scent was almost clear of the chemical taint. Her sensitive nose told her that the poison was well on its way to leaving his system altogether.

If he was strong enough after lunch, she would not only permit, but encourage, him to shift form into his tiger. The magic of the shift would, in all likelihood, remove the final bit of the toxin. If they were very unlucky, it would trigger something worse. But she really didn't think it would. She wouldn't risk his wellbeing if she thought shifting would harm him more. All the same, she'd be watching carefully to make sure all went well and be prepared in case something went wrong.

"I'm feeling a lot better since that shower," Mitch said in between bites of the thick, roast-beef sandwich she'd prepared for him. "Will it be a problem to prowl a bit in the immediate area?"

"Dad owns all the land around here and the perimeter has state-of-the-art detection equipment. If a chipmunk enters the area, Dad's security knows about it right away. So the short answer is, yes. Plus, I think a shift will help clear out the rest of the toxin. I would've recommended it right away except for the convulsions. I've never really seen a shifter have them before, and knowing this poison was probably designed for our kind, it's just possible that doing a shift while the chemical was still at full strength would've killed you for sure. But at this low concentration, I think your normal shifter magic will clear up the rest of it. Just don't overdo it. A quick shift. A gentle walk. No running. No battle form. Taking it easy is the order of the day."

Mitch smiled as he wiped his mouth with a paper napkin. "All right, Doc. I hear and obey."

"I'll hold you to that." She motioned him to sit while she collected the few dishes they'd used and put them in the sink.

She'd deal with the rest of the cleanup later. For now, he was looking refreshed after eating his first really good meal in days. Now was the time to try the shift.

"There's a special feature of this cabin that I think you'll like." She led the way over to a hidden door concealed in the rough wood timbers of the cabin. "There's a passageway between this wall and the outer wall of the cabin. It forms an L-shape around this side of the building and the door on the other end leads directly into the forest. Dad designed it. We can leave our clothes in the passageway. There are hooks for that purpose."

Mitch peered into the passageway after she opened the hidden latch and looked around. "Ingenious," he murmured, inspecting everything he could see in minute detail. She liked the way he took in his surroundings. Cats were naturally curious and he seemed even more curious than most. "I never would have suspected this was here and I've been trained to look for hidden passageways."

He stepped into the passage and started to strip off his borrowed clothes by the light coming in through the open door. Getting naked in order to shift was something Gina knew about, and she was a doctor, after all. She'd seen and handled naked men in her time. But she'd never seen Mitch entirely in the buff. And definitely not when he was conscious and moving around under his own steam.

She'd noticed his muscles and the broad planes of his chest with interest even when he'd been close to being comatose. It wasn't professional, but then nothing about this situation with him was normal. He was outside her experience entirely.

It seemed he thought nothing of stripping off in front of her and she supposed if she'd been raised among a normal group of tigers, she would think nothing of it—though how any red-blooded female could take Mitch's nudity casually, she'd never know. The man was stunning. Every inch a male animal of superior strength and breeding. His body showed the obvious physical training he did, but far from being a muscle-bound Neanderthal, he was sleek like the cat that shared his soul. There wasn't a spare ounce on him—especially since he'd been so ill of late. His muscles were hard and long, powerful and lithe.

He was a work of art. And she was duly impressed. A little too impressed, if truth be told. She felt her body responding, the tigress inside clawing to get out. Gina was almost afraid what would happen when she let her cat out to play. Would she pounce all over the big male or play coy? Gina hoped like hell she was able to exert some control over her animal half. The last thing she needed was for the tigress to play games with Mitch.

Without asking for advice or permission, Mitch began his shift almost the moment he was completely nude. The shift was slow, cautious, which she approved, but when his fur began to sprout, he turned his half-human face toward her and his eyes held confusion.

"Something's different," he growled in a voice that wasn't quite human. He passed quickly through the battle form and into his full tiger in the shadows of the passageway, but she could see enough to...

"Sweet Mother of All," Gina exclaimed when she got her first good look at the tiger Mitch had become.

His eyes were troubled and she thought she sensed worry. She could understand that. Mitch had shifted into—

She didn't dare put a name to what she was seeing.

"Come inside," she counseled, wanting to take the worry out of his golden eyes. "You're okay, but..." She trailed off, leading the way toward the small bathroom at the other side of the cabin. She threw open the door and he padded in behind her, stopping short as she flipped the switch to flood the room with light.

And there in the mirror was Mitch. A newly minted white tiger.

Mitch couldn't quite believe what he thought he was seeing. He looked okay in the bathroom mirror. He'd put the pads of his front paws on the vanity so he could reach upward to look at his face and as much of his body as he could in the mirror that started about waist-high on a human.

From the tip of his nose to the end of his tail, he had lost his golden color. He couldn't see all of his mid-section, but judging by the way Gina was staring, he thought he was probably bleached out there too. He was still striped. Only the black and gray stripes were on a field of pure white instead of his usual orangey-gold color.

Holy shit.

He looked at Gina and a sound of distress came out of his mouth. Even his tiger half was confused. He'd known it when he first started to shift. It felt different. Not bad, but somehow easier. More natural. Not at all painful and very, very magical. Mitch had always been a strong Alpha, but now he felt like he could take on the world. It felt like the shifter magic was shooting through his paws and down deep into the earth.

And he was…aware of things…on a whole new level. He felt the pulse of the earth coming up through his claws and into his body, aiding his shift. As if the magic that made him what he was came from the Earth Mother Herself. Gaia. The Goddess. The Mother of All.

Mitch couldn't get over it. He was *tigre blanche*, and he thought he finally understood what it was about these rarest of tigers that gave them domain over all others. Magic. Incredible magic.

Would it last? Was it some temporary gift of the blood Gina had given to heal him? And most of all…what did it mean?

One thing was for sure, the tiger was mostly in control at the moment and would not allow him to shift back to his human form. Now that was odd. Mitch hadn't had to fight his tiger for supremacy since he was just a youngster learning how to shift. He and his animal side had a nice partnership going on and they had nurtured each other through many escapades and deadly situations over the years.

But something was different now. The tiger was stretching. Becoming.

The tiger wanted to go out into the snow and practice blending. Stealth. He wanted to try out his new stripes and see what they could do in this best of environments for a white animal. Snow. The only thing better would be ice fog. For now though, the cat wanted to play in the snowpack and frolic in the flurries.

And he wanted Gina's cat prowling alongside him. Forever.

What was he thinking? Thoughts like that were all too tempting—and forbidden. Gina was a princess. Royalty.

He nosed past her, prowling with determination toward the secret passage. The door was still open. He'd figure out how to get out on the other end. It couldn't be too hard, right? It was designed for people with paws, after all.

Something was calling him. Making him go outside. To be in the snow. In the ice. In touch with the earth.

Here in the mountains, the early season snow was thick on the ground. It hadn't yet snowed in the city at its lower elevation. The concrete jungle had almost completely stifled Mother Nature with its steel and asphalt. Only in small green places did She show Her face.

Not like here. High in the mountains, well north of the city that never slept, there was only one road and a few gravel lanes leading to the dwellings that were built of wood and natural stone, part of the earth and its creatures. Part of the heartbeat he could feel under his paws. The slow, steady, strong beat of Mother Earth.

She was fire and She was ice. She had hidden depths where lava flowed and sparks danced with untold energy. Up here on the surface, She was sometimes tranquil, as now, and sometimes the tempest itself.

He could feel all of that through the pads of his paws. He felt it in his newly awakened heart. In the beast-half that had always been closer to nature than his human form. He felt it in his soul.

As anticipated, the latch to get out of the secret passageway wasn't hard to operate with paws. There was also a tiger-height display that let him see what was waiting on the other side of the door from four different camera angles. He checked it before he opened the door, noting the squirrel gathering nuts in the upper right quadrant of the screen and the birds pecking at some kind of hardy berry in an evergreen bush on the lower left. The small animals weren't disturbed by anything and he couldn't see any obvious threats, so he proceeded to open the door and step out into the sun.

Mitch had only walked a few feet into the forest before the white tigress joined him. Gina. She was so beautiful he had to blink a few times to clear his vision. She sparkled in the sun, the crisp winter light reflecting off her white fur and dark stripes as it reflected off the snow and ice melting and dripping all around them.

The trees sparkled too. The earth was alive with the dance of sunlight on frozen water, melting, changing, ever transforming. The Goddess in her guise as the Crone. The not-so-barren Lady Winter. The Snow Queen.

And Gina was the princess.

Mitch felt the tug of magic leading him on. He moved off into the woods, following a trail that existed only in the magical energy swirling around and through him. An energy he'd only felt fleeting bits of before now.

He followed where it led, trusting his instincts and the call of the Goddess. He could hear her rhythms in the earth under his paws, in the rivulets of water melting off the trees, the ice chiming as wind blew frozen branches into one another. It was a symphony of light and sound of the most magical variety. A blessing from the Earth Mother. A call to Her service.

Mitch could no more deny Her than he could deny his true nature. The nature that had led him into service to the Royals rather than to found his own Pride. He was Alpha enough that he could have easily done so, but he'd felt the need to serve and protect even stronger. It was who he was.

Who he was born to be.

He felt Gina pacing along beside him as he followed his senses through the unfamiliar woods. He'd never prowled here before, but something about this place spoke to him. It was completely foreign, yet at the same time welcoming and familiar. He liked the pines and the bare trees that had lost their coat of leaves for winter. He enjoyed the scent of damp earth under the melting snow and the crisp bite of the cool air ruffling his fur like a caress.

He didn't know how he knew where to go, but when he arrived at his destination, it was completely obvious. He broke through the dense forest into…a sacred circle of standing stones.

Of course. He should have known.

There was a joyous hum in the air as he stepped into the circle of stones on the top of a small hill. The cabin was far behind and below him and he had the sense of the surrounding area. He somehow knew there was a bigger house on the other side of the hill they were on. The main house where the Tig'Ra and his queen lived.

Gina's parents. Gina herself stepped into the circle behind him and came to sit on her haunches at his side. For a moment, they just sat there, facing the direction of the main house until finally, he realized why he'd been drawn here.

Two people stepped into the circle. A man and a woman, both in their human forms, but Mitch knew who they were. Their magic spoke for itself. As did their commanding presence. These were Gina's parents.

He'd met her dad before, of course, but he'd never even seen her mother. Gina had her mother's kind eyes and gentle smile, but she'd inherited her father's stubborn chin and determined jaw, it seemed.

The tiger king looked Mitch over and sighed heavily as Mitch bowed his head. Mitch kept his eyes raised to the king in a show of respect. It was their way to not dismiss a warrior's power. Averting the eyes meant disrespect in the shifter world.

"I should have known this would happen when Gina talked about your fur sprouting white. In fact, I've been waiting for this day for a long time but was almost afraid to hope it was near. Be welcome to the *tigre blanche*, Mitch Thorburn, formerly of the *tigre d'or*."

As the words were spoken, a shaft of bright sun broke through a momentary cloud, illuminating the circle and all within. For a moment, the light almost blinded Mitch, making him wince, but then something happened. The sun felt like it was focusing on him, bathing him in its warmth.

And then he realized it wasn't really sun. It was magic. A sparkling, magical beam carried on the sunlight, sent by the Goddess.

In that moment, his heart opened and his soul became one with the cat whose nature had changed, just a little. The change had been enough to make him feel odd when he first shifted, but now, with the Lady's intervention, the oddness had gone. It was replaced by a surety that he had never experienced. Mitch finally knew his purpose in this world—to serve and protect as before—but his duties had been expanded to include not just the royalty, but every tiger everywhere.

Starting here and now. Mitch basked in the magical beam of sunlight a moment more, and then it was gone, dissipating in a shower of rainbow-colored motes of light. Dazzling and enchanting. By far the most magical thing Mitch had ever experienced. He was left standing in front of the Tig'Ra and his lady, who were both still in human form, and Gina wearing her fur at his side.

"Go back to the cabin for now," the king of all tigers said in a kind, yet gruff voice. "You're still on the mend and we have a lot to discuss. I'll be down shortly."

Mitch bowed his head in respect and then, conscious of the fatigue now weighing him down, he made his way out of the stone circle with Gina still at his side. She had stuck by him through all of it, a silent witness to the life-changing events of the past few minutes. He wondered if she'd sensed what had happened, or was it something only Mitch had have been aware of? He wasn't entirely sure.

They loped down the small hill and made their way through the icy trees and snow cover to the backdoor that led to the secret passageway that wrapped around one corner of the cabin. He allowed Gina to work the hidden mechanism with her dainty white paws and followed her inside.

She shifted and went straight into the cabin, opening the door so he had some light. Not that he really needed it. He had excellent night vision. Still, it was a considerate gesture.

He allowed the change to take him while she watched over him from just outside the passageway. It was easier this time. Felt less odd. More natural.

He picked up the clothes he'd discarded before and put them back on, enjoying the stretch of his muscles. He'd had too many days of inactivity. He'd need to really get some exercise tomorrow or the next day. As soon as Gina gave him the go-ahead. She was still his doctor, after all. And his princess. He'd do whatever it took to make her happy.

Ducking his head to fit through the small door, he reentered the cabin and shut the passageway's secret entrance behind him. Gina had moved into the room to sit at the table. They'd left coffee on the warmer and she'd already poured herself a cup. He went and did the same. He could use the caffeine at the moment to give him a little boost of energy. He didn't want to admit how much that small journey had taken out of him. He was still weak but getting better all the time. He had to be happy with that.

A few days ago, he'd thought he would die for sure. Now, he had a new lease on life, and it was all thanks to the delicate woman sitting here with both of her hands wrapped around a steaming stoneware mug. She looked worried.

Mitch got his own coffee and sat down across from her at the table. She looked up, meeting his eyes with a troubled gaze.

"What just happened?" she whispered.

Something wondrous. Something magical. Something

almost inexplicable. But he had to try.

"I...changed." It was the best he could come up with.

"I don't think that was temporary. Dad said it might be, when I told him about how some of your fur sprouted white when you were convulsing and your hands shifted. But it was only a little. You were still golden too. But now..." Her voice trailed off as her hand shook, but she took a deep breath and regrouped. "I felt something in the circle. The presence of the Goddess. I've felt it before a few times, when Dad's been doing something up there. But this was you, Mitch. She came for you this time."

"You really think so?" He was still flabbergasted by the idea. "I mean, I thought I felt what you're describing, but it seems so unreal."

Her gaze met his and held, but they didn't say anything more, the enormity of what had just happened lying between them...until the exiled king's pounding sounded on the heavy wooden door.

Gina rose to let her father in. The big man swept into the cabin, his coat dusted with fine specks of snow that soon melted. It was flurrying again outside.

Mitch rose as the tiger king came over to the table, shrugged out of his coat and put a leather pouch that looked very old on the table. Gina took the coat and spread it out to dry before rejoining them at the table. They sat in silence, the weight of the day's events laying heavily on them all, it seemed.

Finally, King Frederick reached forward and opened the leather pouch to pull out an antique-looking leather-bound book from within. He passed it to Mitch with great ceremony.

The language was arcane, but even as he looked at it, the ancient characters resolved into something he could read. More magic.

"*The Rule of Fire and Ice,*" Mitch read the golden title inscribed in the worn leather of the book. His gaze rose to meet the other man's.

"Well, that answers that question. If you were not meant to be *tigre blanche*, you could not read the ancient script. Only those of our line, or those blessed to become part of our number have the magic to read the ancient words of the Lady, handed down through fire and ice." King Frederick replied.

Mitch was across the small table from the king, Gina at the side, between them. She watched them both with equal parts worry and confusion on her beautiful face. Mitch wished he could reach out to her and tell her everything was going to be all right, but he just didn't know if this bizarre situation would turn out good or bad. The only thing he knew for a certainty was that from now on, things would be…different. Very different, indeed.

"You must study the Rule, Mitch. Learn the words, passed down from the Lady Herself. Only after you have mastered the Rule, will you be knowledgeable enough to challenge my brother, Gisli."

"Challenge?" Gina's voice rose in alarm, but her father sat back, seeming utterly weary.

"It is the only way I see this situation resolving. Mitch's change was blessed by the Mother of All. You witnessed what happened in Her sacred circle. You cannot deny he is Goddess-touched. I can only believe that the stalemate we have lived with for so many painful years is at last to be challenged."

"I always heard that you chose exile, your majesty," Mitch said respectfully. There was more going on here than he knew and it seemed imperative that he understood all facets of what might be asked of him now that the Lady had taken a startlingly personal interest in his existence.

The Tig'Ra sighed heavily. "It was the only choice that made any sense at the time. It was the only way I could safeguard my family while avoiding killing my own brother." He seemed so defeated, Gina worried for her dad. "To understand, you must know how this all started. I was born to a family of golden tigers. When I got old enough to shift for the first time, everything changed. I was *blanche*. Immediately, my family went from being merely related to the royal line to having the heir apparent. The old king's family had all been killed in human wars and shifter conflicts and he was despondent until I came along. We moved to the stronghold and he took me under his wing. He was my father's uncle and I'd known him growing up, but after I shifted white, he took an even stronger interest in my life, teaching me about the Rule and all that a good king should know. Eventually though, he passed on to the next realm and I took the throne. My parents were still young enough to have cubs and the Goddess blessed them with my baby brother, Gisli."

Silence reigned while the king contemplated his next words. Finally, he continued. "I don't know when it started to go wrong for Gisli. Maybe it was the mages we had to bring into the stronghold to magically hide it from human discovery. Gisli was always so fascinated by the magic users. He befriended them and learned from them. He learned things our parents would not have taught him. He learned how to lie and how to steal. Or maybe some children are just born selfish. I really don't know, and I've had a lot of time to ponder it over the years. So much happened so fast and only in hindsight do I really understand how those events unfolded so long ago. Gisli came of age and he was as golden as our parents. He was so upset about it. He'd thought for certain he would be like me and his first shift would prove him to be royalty. When it didn't happen, his bitterness began to overcome his goodness. Over the years that followed, he changed. I didn't see it. Not for many years. During that time I married and had children. Gina and her older brother, Fridrik junior."

Her father looked so upset by the retelling of the tale that Gina reached out to put one hand on his arm, offering what comfort she could. He covered her hand with one of his, meeting her gaze for a short moment before going on with his story.

"Little *accidents* started happening. As a toddler, Gina fell down a flight of stairs. She was okay, but I think Gisli or one of his cronies pushed my little girl with the intent to harm her. My wife's car had its brake lines cut and she wrecked it on the road. She was injured but made a full recovery. Then they killed Fridrik." His voice broke and Gina clutched his hand, gripping tight. Tears were in her eyes as she remembered.

"Fridrik and I were both white when we first shifted. He was a few years older than me and we both trained with the Guard to hone our skills. One day when we were out with our teachers practicing stealth in the snow, we were attacked by a group of human hunters. They weren't just any hunters though. They had a mage with them and it was pretty clear they were there to kill us all. Fridrik died protecting my trail." A tear rolled down her cheek and she paused to wipe it away. "They all died. All except me—the smallest. I was hurt, but I ran as fast as I could back to the stronghold and right into my father's arms."

"I sent out help right away, but it was already too late. The Guards found the scene and it was a bloodbath. All the tigers were killed, but they'd taken out a good number of the hunters as well. All human. All with the stink of magic about them. At least one survived and stole a piece of my son's pelt. I shudder to think what the murderous bastard has done with it all these years." Her father growled, and Gina wiped away the tears, allowing anger to stiffen her spine.

"When it was clear magic was involved, I began to suspect Gisli, even if the rest of the Clan thought he was a great guy. He had them all fooled back then, but I knew how much he always liked mages. I would've torn his heart out, but the Rule does not allow for brother to kill brother, and I had no evidence to punish him or strip him of his rank. I prayed. I went up to the sacred mountain and sought the Lady's counsel. The vision I received in answer told me what to do." He paused a moment as if remembering that desperate time.

"I made preparations to leave for America. Gisli's allies

tried to stop us, and several of my loyal Guards were killed in the process, but we got out of there and took the most loyal Guards with us, as the Lady had counseled. I wish I could've fought Gisli and done away with the problem for good, but *blanche* cannot spill their family's blood. There are so few of us. It is one of the sacred tenets of the Rule, which you will read in the book. Bound as I am to uphold the Rule, I could not fight my brother. He knew this. He knew I would never challenge him, which is why he could do what he liked to me and mine with no fear. He would not hesitate to kill me and my wife and remaining child as well. But he knew I would never do the same. So we struck an unspoken deal. I would leave and go into exile with my immediate family. I left the Guard Captain in charge of the Clan, but when that Alpha died under mysterious circumstances, my brother took over as steward of the Clan in my stead. Somehow, in the middle of all of this, Gisli managed to finally turn white and the people accepted him as my royal steward. It was a bitter pill to swallow, but I had no choice." He sent Gina a loving, regretful smile. "I could not let him hurt you, kitten. Or your mother."

Mitch didn't speak right away, allowing the father and daughter their moment of silent communication. He mulled over the king's words and thought he finally understood the man's motivations. After such a devastating loss, if he had a mate and young, he would do all he could—including giving up everything, as the Tig'Ra had done—to protect them.

The king rubbed one hand over his brow as he sat back, remembering. "It was so long ago. But the Mother of All gave me a vision. A fleeting hope that one day, another white tiger would come. One that wasn't related to us by blood, who could fairly challenge my brother." He looked straight into Mitch's eyes. "I believe you are that tiger."

"I think you're right, sire, based on the flashes of insight I gained at the sacred circle."

"You saw something?" The king leaned forward in his chair, bracing his forearms on the table.

"A charred, black landscape where molten rocks spewed from a glowing fissure. Barren land covered in thick sheets of ice and snow. Ice fog. And two white tigers locked in mortal combat, their blood staining the snow." Mitch admitted to the strange scenes he'd glimpsed in his mind while the beam of light had hit him in the circle of stones. He hadn't understood them at the time, but clarity was dawning. "I think I'm one of those tigers, though I haven't really seen all of what I look like now. Still, the stripe pattern on one of them looked a lot like mine, only bleached out."

"A tiger does not change his stripes, even when he goes from *d'or* to *blanche*. Only the coloration and appreciation for the magic of the Lady changes," King Frederick confirmed.

"I never knew tigers could go from gold to white." This was something outside of his experience, training and education. It was part of the many mysteries surrounding the *blanche*, and they guarded their secrets well.

"There have only ever been a handful of white tigers in any generation. In order to keep the line going—and in some cases where all the *blanche* were wiped out—the Lady intervenes, taking a worthy *d'or* and turning him or her *blanche*. It doesn't happen often, but it does happen."

"My mother was born golden, Mitch," Gina said softly. "She turned white over time, after my parents were married. In fact, I still remember her being golden when I was little."

"It usually happens like that for those who marry into the line," the king added. "It's a gradual thing that affects our mates over years. But the change in you, Mitch, is much more dramatic. Only a handful of times in our recorded history has such a thing occurred, and never by this method. Usually the white shows the first time a youngster shifts, like it did with me…and Fridrik and Gina. Or, in times of trouble, the Lady sometimes appears to a worthy older candidate and turns him or her white in a blinding flash of light, then sends them on a quest or puts them directly on the throne. For you to have changed in this indirect way—through blood—is both more interesting, and somewhat confusing. If you were a consort, I would expect the change to happen in the usual, gradual way, but your sudden change—particularly while Gina and I still live—is troubling."

"What does it mean?" Mitch was still very much stunned by the turn of events.

Those flashing images he'd seen in the stone circle didn't give him a great deal of confidence. The two tigers had been evenly matched and both were bloodied. There was no reassurance to be taken from those images that Mitch would prevail if he followed through and challenged Gina's uncle.

"I can see several possibilities," the king admitted. "The most likely of which is that you are destined to be the champion who challenges Gisli. Whether or not my family and I survive to see it is what troubles me most."

"I will lay down my life to protect you and your family, sire," Mitch said immediately. He would give anything to protect Gina—even his life. She was that important to him.

"I thank you for the thought, Mitch," the king said kindly. "But as you have experienced today—often things are not in your control when you are *blanche*. Whether we live or die is up to the Lady's desire. I have done my best to serve Her, but if She wills it, I will go to the endless snowfields of eternity with the knowledge that you have been chosen by Her to set things right among our people."

It was just possible that Mitch's role was to die in the challenge, changing things enough so that Gina could claim the throne that her father had given up. Or so the king could return to his rightful place. Mitch would give his life for Gina, but he wasn't exactly *eager* to die. He wanted to know that his sacrifice would be worth something.

The alternative was equally daunting. What would happen if he actually won the challenge? To his knowledge, no Tig'Ra had ever allowed a champion to fight in his place. In most shifter traditions, the victor of the challenge fight became the Alpha—the ruler of the group. So did that mean if Mitch won, he'd become the king of all tigers?

It seemed impossible. And yet—

"What did you study in school?" the king asked abruptly, shaking Mitch from his thoughts.

"I have an MBA and my undergraduate degree was a double major in business and history." He didn't understand why the king was asking, but the older man seemed pleased by his answer.

"Excellent. I will bring another book tomorrow. A book of history. Lighter reading than the Rule, but no less important." The king stood decisively, eyeing Mitch as he also rose to his feet. One did not remain sitting while the king stood. "You will read the Rule today and be ready to discuss what you have learned tomorrow when I arrive for lunch."

"Yes, sire." There was no other answer Mitch could give to the king in exile. It was pretty clear no other answer would be acceptable.

"Then we will discuss the ice fields and the earthen fire you saw in your vision. Iceland. That's where you must prepare to go. The traditional seat of power of the *tigre blanche*." He nodded toward his daughter. "Gina was born there, though I doubt she remembers much about the Grim. But you must go there, according to your visions. I will seek answers of the Lady, but She does not always answer in ways we mortals can readily understand. And perhaps she has already given you the answer. It is clear you bear her favor. Now it's up to us to prepare you for the ordeal ahead as best we may."

The king held his gaze for a long moment before nodding once. He then gave Gina a peck on the cheek before turning to stride toward the door.

Once the door closed behind the exiled king, Mitch was able to breathe again. The man had a way of filling a room that was more than intimidating. It was just one aspect of his power, which Mitch was learning was even more immense than he'd always believed.

CHAPTER FIVE

Gina nibbled on a cuticle as she sat before the gas fire next to Mitch. He was reading the sacred book. She knew very well what it contained. She had studied it herself as a youngster, at her father's knee, to the point where she could almost quote every last word of the ancient tome.

She worried over Mitch's reaction to the sacred Rule. There was a lot in there that would probably be hard to stomach if you weren't born to the responsibilities of the white fur. Being *blanche* required more of a person's character than normal shifters. The coloration carried with it a special blessing and a heavy responsibility. Her father's predecessors had written the Rule in ancient times to guide subsequent generations of tiger rulers.

Gina didn't know how Mitch would take some of the archaic language and old-fashioned ideas of duty and the multitude of blood oaths written in the Rule. There were good things in the Rule too. Things meant to protect those who swore their allegiance to the Tig'Ra from his absolute rule. But the Rule carried a high price to those who swore to uphold it.

Every Tig'Ra and Tig'Ren had to swear the oath. Her uncle had not, which is why he'd gotten away with the power play that had forced her family into exile. But if what Mitch had seen in the circle and her father's interpretation of it meant what they thought it did, that situation would soon come to a head.

Gina chewed on her fingernails—a bad habit she'd picked up in medical school when the pressure to perform had grown too stressful—and worried about what the upcoming battle would mean for Mitch. And for her.

She didn't want him to die.

Far from it, she wanted him for herself. Her tigress had taken only a little time to convince her. The tigress knew and accepted that Mitch would be her mate, if the Goddess allowed it. Unlike other shifters, the *tigre blanche* had to consider more than just their own desires when mating. Very often, the Lady Goddess stepped in directly and blessed one union over another.

Gina sent up a silent prayer, asking the Lady to allow her time with Mitch. Time to be with him—if that's all she could have—before he had to face her uncle in mortal combat. She knew her family. She remembered her uncle. He was a savage fighter. As strong as her father, if not stronger. And he'd held his position of power through many challenges over the years, savaging all those who had tried to remove him from the sham of a *stewardship* he used to control all the tiger kingdom's resources and people.

Many knew and understood why her father had chosen to leave rather than spill his brother's blood, and many had been lost in the attempt to champion the exiled king. So many loyal Royal Guards. So many friends. So much death. All at the hands of the usurper. Her uncle, Gisli.

A hand on her knee roused her from her dark thoughts. She looked up and found Mitch watching her, concern on his handsome face. He had a little bit of beard stubble just shadowing his chin in bright gold and it was sexy as all get out.

"What puts such a worried look on your face, sweetheart?" His words were pitched low, in a sexy rumble that thawed her from the inside out, melting away her fears.

At least for the moment.

She moved closer to him and rested her head on his shoulder. "It's nothing."

"Come on, sweetheart." He turned her to face him, one hand cupping her cheek briefly. "You can tell me anything."

Caught. She wanted to burrow into his arms and seek reassurance, but she knew full well there was none to be had. His vision showed him fighting Gisli, a warrior to be reckoned with. She couldn't undermine Mitch's confidence by admitting to her fear that he would not prevail.

"Just worried you're going to balk when you read some of the stuff in the Rule. It's a little hard to stomach if you weren't raised to it, I'd imagine."

The distraction worked as he hefted the book in his other hand. He was more than halfway through it already.

"Actually, the majority of it makes a lot of sense and most of the concepts are not unfamiliar to me. The Guard has something similar, though not quite as extensive and certainly not geared toward those who would rule, since we protect them. We are *not* them. Which is why I can't figure why your dad wants me to read this. Unless it's just so I understand the weight of what lays on his shoulders."

"Mitch…" Gina didn't quite know how to say what was in her mind. Maybe flat out. That was probably best. Like ripping off a bandage. Taking a deep breath, she went for it. "If you challenge Gişli and win, according to the Rule, you can become Tig'Ra."

Mitch turned away from her and put the book down next to him, his eyes widening as he blew out a stream of air. The unconscious gesture spoke more than words about his state of mind. He was troubled—and very obviously surprised.

"I guess I haven't gotten to that part of the book yet," he finally said, not looking at her but staring into the fire. "If what I saw was me fighting a challenge, I figured I'd be acting as your father's champion. I wasn't born to rule anything, Gina. I'm a soldier. A Guard. That's my job. My calling. I'm not fit to be king. If that's what your father wants, I'm going to have to respectfully decline."

Her heart broke a little at the shock and denial in his eyes. She sought to reassure him. "Look, don't think about it right now. Neither of us knows the will of the Goddess. She gave you the white fur for a reason. Maybe it's so you can return my father to the throne. Maybe it's something else. There's no way to know until it happens. I think my dad is just preparing you. It's his way to prepare for every contingency. The more you get to know him, the more you'll realize how unbelievably *prepared* he is for everything. He could be one of those doomsday preppers if he wasn't a shifter. I think he gets most of his new ideas from those end-of-the-world websites lately." She tried to lighten the mood and it appeared to help a little. He moved his arm around her shoulders and sat back on the sofa, squeezing her close next to him as they both watched the flames dance in the fireplace.

"I can see the level of thought he put into this cabin. A gas fire that doesn't give off smoke to betray our presence. Blackout curtains over every conceivable source of light leakage. And that pantry has about a year's worth of rice and beans in it, not to mention the cistern on the roof and underground fuel tanks."

Gina was a little amazed at how much he'd observed. She hadn't seen him obviously looking around and he hadn't asked any questions, but he saw more than the regular guy, that was a fact.

"This is just a cabin. You should see the main house," she quipped, glad the mood was lighter now. "That place is a fortress. More like a bunker, actually."

"I can only imagine." Mitch stroked her shoulder in a gentle caress. It was a simple motion but it made her feel warm...and appreciated. It also made her hunger for more.

"Mitch...I..." Gina trailed off, turning toward him. Their eyes met and held and there was no need for words. He felt it too—this amazing connection, the undeniable attraction.

She closed the space between them, seeking his mouth with hers. And then her lips were on his and he was kissing her. This was no tentative exploration. No repeat of the sweet salute he'd given her before. No, this kiss started out calm but then swirled into passion like a raging torrent. Deep, drugging, intoxicating passion.

He maneuvered her into a position under him, lying flat on the couch while his starving body pressed her into the cushions. He loved the feel of her against him and wanted more. So much more. Did he dare push the limits of propriety? She was a princess and he was…nothing. Just nothing. He didn't have any right, even to this kiss, but then she pushed against his shoulders, making him draw back.

Rather than pushing him away, she was only demanding more room to move her hands. Those dangerous little fingers of hers went right under his shirt and started stroking him in ways that made him forget all his objections.

He leaned into her caressing fingers, loving the gentle way she stroked his skin. She was petting him and he felt a purr rumble up from deep within his chest. That almost stopped him cold. Purring in human form was significant, but he couldn't stop to think about it now.

He kissed her with all the pent-up longing within him, all the dreams of what could be—if he let things go too far. He didn't want to hurt her, but how could he deny the fire that flared between them? He was too weak to resist as she pushed his shirt up and out of the way. He moved back for a tempestuous moment to let her to shove the bunched fabric up, over his head and arms.

When he returned, he was bare and wanted nothing more than to feel her soft skin against his body. He let his fingers trail to her waist, seeking the hem of her stretchy top. Going slowly, seeking permission with every touch, he lifted the soft fabric upward, exposing her midriff. He paused there, stroking her skin and learning the feel of her. She felt like soft, heated velvet against his rough fingertips. So feminine. So warm and delicate.

And then he dared to push the fabric higher, up over the satin cups of her bra. He let his fingers toy with the hard-pebbled tips he felt poking up from under the fabric. She shivered and he lost a little of his control. He tore the shirt off over her head with her very willing cooperation. He reclaimed her lips almost immediately, their kisses growing deeper and more desperate with every passing moment.

The couch limited his movements. Making no conscious decision, he lifted her in his arms, mouths still clinging to each other, and walked with her to the big bed on the other side of the room. He deposited her there, taking only a moment to unhook her bra and let it fall down her arms.

Then he paused. His hands cupped her soft breasts, his mouth still devoured hers, but something inside him stilled. He knew he couldn't take this too far. He also couldn't be a cad and leave her hanging. She was panting against him, her body primed for pleasure. He'd be a total asshat if he left her wanting after taking it so far.

But he couldn't claim her. He couldn't make love to her and then pretend nothing had changed in the morning light. And he wasn't the kind to fuck a woman and then leave her head spinning as he withdrew to a safe, protected corner. No, he had to be stronger than the primitive urges driving him. He would give her pleasure tonight because he *wasn't* a cad, then he'd leave her be.

That way was safer for them both. And for the tiger Clan. He had more than just himself to worry about now. Anything he did with Gina could potentially impact many more lives. She was royalty. He was just a lowly soldier, who until a short time ago was as golden as any other tiger. A quick change in color didn't change who he was deep down inside. He had to remember that.

Decision made, Mitch lifted his mouth from hers. He couldn't keep kissing her and maintain even a sliver of control. He had to do the right thing here—even if it was one of the hardest things he'd ever tried to do.

Mitch let his mouth roam downward over her soft skin, licking, tasting and nibbling on her as he went. She tasted divine. Like the heavenly dew on a pale morning rose. Like the nectar of the moonflowers she reminded him of so much. She was like no other woman he'd ever tasted before. And Mitch feared very much that this stolen interlude would ruin him for any other.

But it was worth it. Hearing her little whimpers of pleasure as he finally took one nipple into his mouth was worth anything—everything that might come later. This one moment out of time was his for eternity and he would never regret it—or forget it.

Gina's body strained toward his and he loved the feel of her softness against his bare skin. She was quickly losing all control and he both feared and wanted it. The sooner she found her bliss, the less his control would be tested, but he also wanted to draw out this moment, to savor it and give her as much as he could in this one, stolen moment out of time.

He switched to her other breast, allowing one of his hands to reach downward, between them, seeking the warmth at the apex of her thighs. She eagerly opened for him, the cloth an annoying barrier between them. He needed to get closer, but he also didn't want to remove that last barrier that was helping him retain his very tenuous control.

Compromising, Mitch felt for her waistband and was relieved to find just enough give in the stretchy fabric to fit his hand down the front of her pants. He wouldn't have to remove them if he did this right. It just might kill him, but it would also help him stay in control.

He sucked hard on her tight bud as his fingers found the moist cleft that he sought. The little button at the top was his goal and soon after he found it, she cried out, her sleek muscles going taut under him as she reached a climax at his hands.

She was so beautiful. So responsive. He knew he could drive her even higher—if he allowed himself to touch her even more. But that would be wrong. His entire existence was in a massive state of flux at the moment. He didn't know what the future would bring. Hell, he didn't even know what the next hour would bring.

He couldn't subject her to the uncertainty that was his life right now, any more than she was already involved in it. He couldn't be the tiger she needed at her side and in her bed. She needed a prince. A future king. A consort she could be proud of for the rest of their very long lives.

The only thing he was sure of at the moment was that he could be the protector that made sure she got the chance to live out the rest of her very long life. He would defend her with his last breath. He would die for her and he would live for her. But he didn't think he could be the man at her side and in her bed for the rest of their lives. Gina was too special for the likes of him, and Mitch was too damn confused by it all to even begin to think about where he fit into the larger picture of the Clan and Gina's life.

For all he knew, he would die in the challenge against Gisli. If so, he didn't want to leave Gina brokenhearted. Better they not get any closer than they had already been. Tonight was a fluke. A lovely, amazing set of circumstances never to be repeated.

Even if it killed him.

When she tried to touch him as her small climax passed, he gently put her away from him, tucking her under the covers and wrapping her in his arms. The blankets were between them while he took the time to try to cool off. It was hard to do. Hell, he was hard as a rock and his body wanted nothing more than to claim Gina in the most basic way. But no. He wouldn't let it happen.

He held her, not giving her the chance to ask the many questions he could see in her beautiful blue eyes. He kissed her gently each time she tried to speak, shushing her in a loving way. Eventually, she gave up and gave in to his softly spoken instruction to sleep.

Her breathing evened out long before his did and she fell into a restful slumber in his arms. Mitch held her for a long, long time, enjoying the feel of her next to him. Eventually though, sleep claimed him as well.

When Gina woke the next day, Mitch was still in bed with her, but he was sitting with the ancient book in his hands. He was very close to the end, judging by the number of pages left, and his face was a study in concentration.

She didn't want to wake up and let the peaceful moment pass. Who knew how many mornings she'd have like this, waking to find him near? She would cherish every moment, fearing the worst and hoping for the best. But this moment—this moment—was to be savored.

Mitch's golden gaze caught her watching him. And then he smiled. A warm, encouraging, almost sinful smile. She wanted to remember that smile all her life.

"Sorry. Did I wake you?"

"No," she answered, her voice rusty with sleep as she stretched a little. "It's okay. I usually wake up long before this. I think I overslept. What time is it?"

"Just after eight-thirty," he replied, closing the book and putting it on the small bedside table. When he turned back, he bent down and nibbled her neck. The nibbles turned hot and then molten as he pecked at her lips, eventually taking her mouth in a kiss that was temptation itself. When he finally pulled back, he gave her one of those sinful smiles again. "I've been wanting to do that for the past hour."

"Mmm. You should've woken me up." She smiled back at him, loving the moment of communion between them. Nothing else mattered. Just this. Just them. Together.

But reality intruded as her cell phone rang. Gina reached over to the nightstand to answer it. It was an unexpected, though not unwelcome, call from Paul Miller, the eldest of the Miller's many children. He wanted to know when he should come up to the cabin with more supplies. She told him any time that morning would be fine and he agreed to stop by after breakfast.

Gina ended the call with a fond smile. Paul had already been a grad student when Gina started college and he'd helped look after her when she first ventured out into the big, bad world. He was an orthopedic surgeon and unofficial

Royal Guard, having learned everything about being one from his parents. It wasn't until she graduated that she fully realized why Paul and his siblings had been her constant companions in those years she'd been at university. They'd been protecting her.

More than that though, they'd been her friends. She'd grown up with the rambunctious family practically next door and had loved having them with her in school. They were classmates and buddies. It hadn't really dawned on her that they'd also been watching over her all those years at their parents' behest.

In fact, she doubted her father would have let her go to school at all if the Miller's brood hadn't all been around the same age and attending the same schools. Okay, maybe that was stating it a little too broadly, but sometimes she wondered.

She hung up and rolled back toward Mitch, but he'd already risen from the bed. He headed toward the kitchen area, the book tucked under his arm.

"You get the bathroom first and I'll get some breakfast going. Sound good?" he asked casually.

So much for a little more early morning snuggling. Unless… If she was just a tiny bit more secure about where she stood with him, she'd walk right up to him and jump his bones.

But she just wasn't that confident. Not after he'd called such a definite halt last night just when things were getting interesting. No, she wouldn't risk his rejection and invite her own humiliation.

She had a few days to work on him yet. She'd find a way to break through his reserve. She had time to negate the mindset that had him turning away from her when all she really wanted was to have him make love to her. And mean it. That was the big thing that held her back.

She was pretty sure she could get him to have sex with her, but she wanted something more. Even the tigress in her soul wanted more. Raw sex would be nice, but *making love* would be even better. Even if it was only for a short time, she wanted whatever time they had together to mean something.

Gina shook off her troubling thoughts, scrounged up some clean clothes and headed for the bathroom. She'd take a shower, get her head on straight and then come out to tame the tiger presently making coffee in her kitchen.

When Gina stepped out of the bathroom a short while later, the first thing she realized was that Mitch was no longer alone. Paul had shown up early—with his sister, Maribeth—and Mitch had apparently invited them to stay for breakfast.

A little gremlin of jealousy reared up in Gina's mind. Maribeth was a knockout, as well as a little indiscriminate when it came to her bed partners. Maribeth was, in short, a bit of a slut—even among shifters, who were not known for their abstinence. And the moment Gina walked out of the bathroom, she was well aware Maribeth was up to her old tricks, flirting up a storm with Mitch.

Gina had to suppress a growl. The tigress had her claws out and ready to swipe at her old friend who dared flirt with the male the tigress considered her own. Wow. Gina had never reacted that strongly to Maribeth before. Usually, Gina found her friend's outrageous flirting and loose behavior kind of amusing. But not when it came to Mitch.

Maribeth was laughing, batting her ridiculously long eyelashes at Mitch when she suddenly became aware of Gina. She turned her head and caught Gina's gaze, immediately stiffening and coming to her feet.

Hmm. Maybe Gina hadn't done such a good job hiding her annoyance. She tried to dial it back, but it was much harder than she expected. The tigress was flaring her claws inside Gina's skin, making her presence known in a way she seldom did. Gina guessed her eyes were glowing blue with the tigress's annoyance too. Damn.

"Hi, Gina," Maribeth turned her head slightly in a show of obedience though she was an Alpha in her own right. Still, she had always deferred to Gina, even when they were kids.

Such deference was one of the perks of being *blanche* that

had always annoyed Gina, setting her apart from the other kids. But today, she was glad of it. *How dare Maribeth make a play for Mitch?* the tigress demanded silently, outraged. Gina's human side felt both the tiger's anger and a very human hurt.

Somehow, Maribeth seemed to see it all. She moved closer slowly, reaching out for Gina's hand.

"It's good to see you," the other woman offered in a soft tone. "It's been too long."

"I didn't know you were here," Gina offered, still trying to rein in her spike of temper.

"I just got in this morning. Dad called us all home when you showed up with your...friend." Maribeth's gaze darted toward Mitch.

Now that was news. Gina hadn't considered that Mr. Miller would call in reinforcements and start circling the wagons when Gina brought Mitch here.

"Sorry to put you to such trouble. It's probably unnecessary."

"Maybe not," Mitch spoke finally, coming over to place a mug of coffee in Gina's hands. It was a thoughtful gesture that made her tigress back down a little bit. He'd fixed her coffee just the way she liked it and she sent him a smile of thanks as he continued to fill her in on what she'd missed while in the shower. "Paul was telling me that there were some perimeter incursions last night. He and his dad were out checking the boundaries starting at about four a.m. They found a few tripped sensors and human-shaped boot prints." Mitch frowned and Gina felt a pang of concern.

She knew her dad and the Millers had strung all sorts of motion, heat and even sound sensors all over the property. They had redundant systems and cameras everywhere. If anything bigger than a chipmunk entered their territory, they knew about it.

"It was near the entrance to our road," Paul added. "Could've been just some kids out drinking on a country lane. There were a few cans and bottles in the ditch. We collected them and sent them for testing."

Mitch nodded, apparently pleased at their uber-vigilance, though Gina thought it was overkill. Gina knew they did get kids around from time to time who were looking for an out-of-the-way place to have a kegger. There was no real reason to think last night's perimeter breaches were anything out of the ordinary.

"What did my dad say?" Gina asked, suppressing her annoyance with Maribeth's blatant come-on to Mitch in light of the new information. Even the tigress within her knew how to prioritize threats.

"Just to keep our eyes open for now. Our dad thought yours sounded as if he almost expected something like this." Paul's gaze pinned her. "What gives, Gina? What was the magic surge our mom felt yesterday?"

All eyes focused on Gina, including Mitch's. Not sure how much to reveal, she looked at him, answering the easiest question first. "There's a mage somewhere back in Mrs. Miller's family tree. She's more sensitive to magic than most shifters."

Mitch nodded, apparently satisfied with the explanation, but the Miller siblings were still giving her questioning looks.

"The magic was…" How did she say this? How *much* should she tell them? She decided to hedge. "The magic was Mitch."

Now the siblings turned their questioning glances on him. It wasn't fair of her to have deflected onto him, but really, it was his life. His decision on what these people knew about him.

"I'm a Royal Guard," he explained. "I was in service to the *pantera* Nyx, but my cover's been irrevocably blown, so I'm no good to her anymore. Gina saved my life and brought me here. Since then, I've been recovering. And yesterday, I went up to the stone circle. The magic surge your mother felt came from up there."

"It's a powerful place," Paul agreed, "but it usually doesn't have that kind of effect on people on an ordinary Tuesday." The statement was clearly an invitation to say more.

Mitch ran a hand through his hair. "You two were trained as Royal Guard by your parents, right?" At their nods, Mitch went on. "Did that include taking the oath?"

Paul stood and his expression became rock hard. "I took the oath when I was ten."

Maribeth stood and moved to her brother's side, facing Mitch and Gina. "I was fourteen when I took it. We may not live in the mainstream of tiger shifters, but we live true to the code and have taken the oath."

Despite her tendencies to sleep around, Maribeth was a wicked fighter and a very smart cookie. She had degrees in molecular biology and earth science. Sometimes, Gina thought the Miller kids had spent a lot more time in school than they otherwise would have simply to stay nearby while Gina was in college and then later, in med school. Of course, none of the Millers would ever admit it.

Mitch gave the brother and sister a hard look as if evaluating them, then he seemed to come to a decision. "We are alike, you and I. We both live by the code and have taken the oath. We know what that means. I would die to keep Gina and her family safe. I would have died trying to protect the Nyx, but for Gina's help." The Millers nodded, clearly in full agreement tinged with respect. "The thing is..." Here Mitch hesitated and a bit of troubled chagrin entered his expression. "Something changed. Yesterday when I shifted fully for the first time since coming here, I wasn't as I always have been."

Paul's eyes narrowed, intrigued concern on his face. Maribeth's expression was a little harder to read, but her flirtation had ended, for which Gina was grateful. It was all business now. Professional. Gina could handle professional—and the tigress within approved.

"What happened up at the circle?" Paul asked finally.

Mitch didn't seem to want to say it, though it was clear what he'd been leading up to. Gina took his hand in hers, looking up to meet his gaze. "Mitch's beautiful golden fur...is now white."

Stunned silence filled the room while Gina held Mitch's gaze, trying to communicate her pride and confidence in him with a single look. She'd never seen him seem so unsure, even when he'd been close to death. He'd faced his demise with a calm acceptance and bravery she admired, but this simple—earth shattering—change from golden to white had him stymied.

"For real?" Paul finally asked in an awed tone. "Can that even happen?"

"According to my dad, it's happened a few times before, in the distant past. And it had the clear blessing of the Lady. That's the power surge your mom felt from the circle. The Lady's Light engulfed him," Gina said, remembering the amazing moment the day before. "It was so beautiful. So powerful."

"What does it mean?" Maribeth whispered.

"It means—" Mitch seemed to recover from his momentary uncertainty, "—I'm probably going to be taking on Gina's uncle in a challenge fight. And to do that, I'm going to need to sharpen my skills. Are you up for a little sparring, Paul? Maybe later this afternoon?"

Paul frowned and really looked at Mitch, giving him an assessing once-over. Paul was bulkier, but Mitch was taller. Gina knew how ferociously Paul fought and thought he would be more than a challenge for Mitch—which both worried her and spurred her competitive streak. Her tigress purred inwardly, looking forward to seeing which male would prevail in the matchup.

"It would be my honor to help you prepare. We have a barn we use as a dojo down by the main house. Gina can show you where it is or I can send up one of my brothers to guide you down. Is that acceptable?"

Mitch shot her a questioning look that she answered with a nod. He then turned back to Paul. "We'll come down around three, if that's a good time for you?"

Paul agreed readily, and it was Maribeth who brought up the subject that hung in the air between them all. "Does this mean your father is going to take back his throne?" she asked Gina.

"To be honest, I'm not sure. My father is coming for lunch, so hopefully he'll make his intentions clearer then. But whatever the goal, one thing is for sure. The status quo is about to change in a big way."

CHAPTER SIX

The Miller siblings took their leave a short time later, leaving Gina and Mitch alone for a while. They finished breakfast and then Mitch settled down with the book again. He wanted to finish it before the king showed up for lunch.

Mitch had dined with royalty before. He wasn't nervous about sharing a meal with the exiled king. He was more concerned that the man was Gina's father. He wasn't sure what the exiled king thought of Mitch sharing the cabin with his daughter. Mitch's intentions were sincere, but his mind was all screwed up. Since the change from golden to white, he hadn't had much time to consider his place in the universe. What had he become? What was his role now? What was his destiny?

Or was it conceited of him to think he had such a grand thing as a *destiny*, at all? Mitch was used to thinking of himself as a soldier. An Alpha. Top of the food chain—as far as that went. But still a soldier in service to the rulers of their kind.

That he'd been serving the *pantera* Nyx and not the Tig'Ra didn't matter. He still had a definite role and a place in big-cat shifter society. But now? What was he now? Neither royal nor Guard, he didn't quite fit in either place.

When a cub was born with strong Alpha tendencies, they were usually driven to create their own familial Pride once they reached adulthood, strengthening the Clan as a whole. A precious few Alphas felt a higher calling to forsake their own power in service to a higher authority—the royal families who served the Goddess. The structure of big-cat shifter society had been set up in Europe during the time of the Renaissance. They'd taken the titles for the kings and queens of each big-cat shifter species from different traditions.

The mysterious *pantera noir* had chosen to call their queen the Nyx, after the Egyptian goddess of the night. The *tigre* Clan had chosen to be a little more straight forward since the Mother of All had given them an easy way to know who was chosen to rule over them all. They simply used the names of the colors in French. *D'or* literally meant gold in French. *Blanche* translated to white. Simple words to cover such complex differences. But they'd also gone back to antiquity to give their king the title Tig'Ra after Ra the sun god of ancient Egypt. The queen was called the Tig'Ren—in which a bit of liberty was taken with the spelling of *reine*, the French word for queen.

The white tigers, it was said, had come about after the first conclave when the tiger Clan's greatest priestesses had gathered. They'd prayed for a sign by which to know which of two great warriors should rule over the entire Clan as Tig'Ra. After a week of unrelenting prayer, the two candidates were called into the sacred circle and the Lady answered the prayers of Her servants, turning one of the mighty tigers white. He then had become the very first Tig'Ra.

That was real royalty. Every subsequent generation had been either descended from that great warrior in some way or singled out by the Mother of All in a blinding flash of light. None had ever changed the way Mitch had, and he didn't know what to think of it all.

He wondered what the *real* royalty thought of him? What did Gina's dad expect of him? And would he blow a gasket if he realized that Mitch and Gina had shared the bed last night?

He was a father. An overprotective tiger father, at that. Of course he'd be upset. And he had every right to be.

Even knowing that, Mitch wouldn't have traded last night for the world. Holding Gina in his arms—just once—was worth her father's wrath. If she was any other woman, Mitch would have claimed her already. Taken her body and made sweet, sweet love to her. Made her his in the most elemental way.

But she was the tiger princess. Off-limits.

Or was she?

There was a little devil sitting on his shoulder that kept whispering that things were different now. He was *blanche* now. Could it possibly mean that he was now good enough for Gina? Could he somehow win her heart? Or was he only dreaming?

A princess and a guy like him? Wasn't there a line from an old movie like that? He didn't remember how it had worked out for the characters in the movie, but that little imp on his shoulder kept making him hope that somehow, some way, it could work out for him and Gina.

If he didn't die in the challenge first.

He had to keep that always in the back of his mind. It wouldn't be fair to give in to his baser desires, to make love to her, only to leave her alone and unprotected should he fall in the challenge. He wouldn't do that to her. He loved her too much already to toy with her emotions in that way. Not to mention her safety. If he fell in battle, she would be even more vulnerable. He had to maintain a professional distance—as best he could.

They'd already gotten much closer than he ever would have allowed had he himself not been in dire straits when they met. His professional detachment was shot to hell. He'd been as close to death as he ever cared to be and hadn't been thinking rationally for the first few days they'd been together. He'd said things he otherwise would never have said. He'd done things he wouldn't have dared had he been in his right mind.

He'd allowed himself to feel things. Dangerous things.

He'd allowed himself to need her. Like he'd never needed another woman. Ever.

If Gina were a regular woman, he'd have staked his claim. He wanted her until his dying breath. He felt more for her than he'd ever felt for any female. He *needed* her until it physically hurt. Emotionally, the wound was raw as well. He needed for her to be safe. As safe as he could make her in this crazy world where her uncle probably wanted her dead.

Mitch knew one thing. He would give his life—if that's what was needed—to ensure her safety. He would die for her.

And that was something he had taken for granted in his line of work. He'd said the same thing about Ria, the young Nyx. But with Ria it had been a matter of duty. Of honor. When he said he would die for Gina, there was some previously unknown emotional intent behind the words. His heart—which he had thought was frozen in ice—was fully involved in the declaration. He *felt* something for Gina that he had never felt for the Nyx. It was more than duty. More than his honor. It was his heart on the line. And though he had readily put his body in front of danger for his charges in the past, never had he put his heart out there.

It was a stark realization. If he'd had time, Mitch would have shifted form and taken a good hard run to help him put it all in perspective and figure things out. But he didn't have the time. He'd finished reading the Rule a few minutes ago, though he'd pretended to still be concentrating on the last few pages as he sat there at the small table.

Gina was puttering around the kitchen area, getting things ready. Her father was expected shortly.

When the knock came at the door to the cabin, it wasn't the distinctive thundering of the tiger king. No, this was a gentler sound. Made by feminine hands. Apparently, the queen had decided to come to lunch as well.

Mitch stood, crowding Gina as he checked the small screen he'd found hidden discreetly near the door. Every entrance and exit—including the small windows—had hidden cameras trained on them. The exiled king didn't take security lightly even here, on his home territory.

Sure enough, both of Gina's parents showed on the screen as she went to open the door. It was safe.

Nevertheless, Mitch moved to stand behind her in a respectful pose. He had often adopted such a stance when guarding the Nyx. It was a position from which he could easily protect her if such a thing became necessary. It was also second nature to Mitch after so many years as a Royal Guard.

Gina greeted her parents with hugs as she ushered them into the cabin. The queen held a basket, which Mitch took from her. It was heavier than it looked and his estimation of the queen's strength rose a notch. She looked so delicate—shorter even than Gina—but perhaps this queenly tigress had more to her than met the eye.

Mitch stood and waited while the lunch was set up. Gina had prepared what they had left in the way of provisions, but the basket the queen had brought contained a great deal more food. They set it out and soon were sitting around the small table. Mitch waited until the others sat and then only joined them at the king's specific request.

The king sighed as they began to eat and turned his attention to Mitch.

"Look, Mitch," he began with seeming resignation. "Although I am glad of your manners and respect for our position, you must realize by now that things have changed drastically for you in the past days. For that matter, things changed drastically for my family when I chose exile over bloodshed. I renounced the position, and unlike you, I cannot change my stripes." A hint of humor crossed his lined face. "Your formality is appreciated but unnecessary. I am no longer king and you are no longer *d'or*. We are equals, and you must call me Fred."

Mitch was shocked by the invitation to such familiarity. Speechless actually. And it only got worse when the queen joined the discussion.

"And I am Candis," her majesty added. "When we decided on America, we changed our names. Even Gina's. She was very young at the time. Her real name is Gleda. In our old land, her name was meant to be a wish for her. Happiness. I didn't like the sound of Gladys, which would have been a closer translation, but I always thought Gina had a nice ring to it."

"You picked right, Mom," Gina smiled wryly. "I don't think I'd have enjoyed being a Gladys in grammar school." The women chuckled as Mitch tried to understand what was happening.

"Fridrik Americanized easily to Frederick," the king added. "But Snaedis had a little harder time until she decided on Candis. It's close enough in sound, though there is no comparative name that we have found in English for my snow goddess."

Mitch knew the Icelandic language. He'd been born in Iceland, though he'd left there as a child to go to his adoptive parents' home in the States. Most tiger shifters learned the language since the traditional seat of power had been in Iceland for centuries. It hadn't really occurred to him that Gina and her folks had given up their homeland in order to come the States. Not only that, but they'd had to give up their original names as well. It seemed like adding insult to injury.

"Of course, the *blanche* didn't always live in Iceland," the queen put in when the silence dragged on a bit. "If you go back a little further, our people emigrated from Europe, like most of the other big cat shifter species."

King Frederick lifted a book from the basket his wife had put on the floor next to him and placed it on the table. "The rest is in here. A history of our people. As far as it goes. There are some parts missing. Lost to the mists of time. But most of the past few centuries are in here. I thought it would be a good place for you to start. This book focuses on white tigers, but some big events among the golden are in here too. Might give you context depending on how much you remember from your history lessons when you were a cub."

"I admit I wasn't always the best student as a youngster." Mitch picked up the book and stroked one hand over the spine, admiring its age. "But I started to like history as an adult. It's a hobby of mine. I'll enjoy reading this. Thank you, sire."

"Fred, remember?"

"Sire, I—" Mitch began, but the king held up one hand to stop his words.

"I'll make it a royal decree if I have to," King Frederick warned. "You are *blanche* now. We are the same."

"With all due respect, we'll never be the same." Mitch's frustration with the mindboggling situation he found himself in shone through his words. "I wasn't born *blanche*. I am a foot soldier. A Royal Guard. Nothing more. I never have been."

"I wasn't born *blanche* either," the queen said softly. Her expression gave away nothing of her thoughts, but it made him feel calmer. She was serenity itself. The perfect queen. If she could adapt so well to her change, maybe there was hope for Mitch? It was a concept worth thinking about.

They went on to discuss the political situation among the various groups of big-cat shifters that had organized into its current state during the Renaissance in Europe. Mitch spoke what he could of the *pantera noir*, while Frederick filled him in on the other groups. It turned out that while Frederick had been in exile for decades, he still had his ears tuned to the doings in the big-cat shifter communities. He was very well informed.

"What it boils down to is that my brother doesn't want to be just the steward. He has made many attempts in the past to break through our defenses, though none in recent years. Gina was safe enough while she was still a cub. Even while she was in school. Gisli would not stoop to killing a cub, even as bad as he is." The king sighed heavily as they finished eating and sat with full mugs of steaming coffee. "But things are changing. The unrest among our enemies and the sorry state of the Clan's finances is pushing Gisli to action once again. Gina is an adult. Youth will not protect her. Especially now that she may soon mate and have young of her own."

Mitch looked sharply at Gina, but she refused to meet his eye. Was she involved with someone? It didn't seem possible. Nothing she had done to this point indicated she had a fiancé or boyfriend. Had he been wrong? Was she obligated to someone else? It didn't seem possible.

Mitch almost shook his head in denial but caught himself. He knew women and he knew how they acted when they were in a committed relationship. Gina didn't give off any of the signals. Perhaps her father was just talking generally. She was of an age to be taking a mate. It would be natural. But Mitch sincerely doubted there was a candidate waiting in the wings.

Unless the royal family indulged in such archaic practices as arranging marriages for their children. Mitch didn't think so, but who knew what these exiled royals had been driven to in their lonely existence?

Cats were loners at times, but it wasn't quite natural to be so isolated. Mitch hoped for their sake that they had a larger community of exiled tigers around them. Socializing with the Millers and their progeny was all well and good, but shifters needed more than just a few of their own. They needed the community. They needed the support and social structure to ground them and keep them human.

"The Clan is in shambles," Candis spoke unexpectedly, drawing Mitch away from his troubling thoughts and back into the conversation. "While we do not participate in the politics or activities of those we have left behind, we do hear things," she explained, her troubled gaze focused on Mitch. "For too long, we have sat by and done nothing. *Could* do nothing. It has been both frustrating and heartbreaking to see what has become of our beloved people. But I think the Lady has shown us clearly today that things are about to change. *You're* going to change them, praise the Mother of All."

"While I appreciate your confidence in me, I have to admit it all seems rather..." Mitch trailed off, unable to come up with adequate words. He sighed heavily, running one hand through his disheveled hair. "My apologies. I just don't know what to think."

The king sat back in his chair and placed his palms flat against the table, his gaze troubled but patient. "That's all right, son. A lot has happened to you in a very short time. I'd have been surprised if you didn't question all this." He pushed his chair back from the table. "Read the history. Study the Rule. Get back your strength. I'm always available to discuss anything you need. In the meantime…" He stood and everyone else followed suit. "I hear you've asked one of the Miller boys to spar." The statement came out sounding like a question.

"Paul agreed to help me get back in shape. All this lying around is getting on my nerves." Mitch grimaced and the king laughed outright, clapping him on the shoulder in a fatherly way.

"It is hard for a man of action to sit and watch from the sidelines. Believe me, I understand."

Mitch heard the regret in Frederick's voice and knew the sincerity of his words. What must it be like for this vital, intelligent man to have had to stand by and watch his brother usurp the power that rightly belonged to the king alone? Torture, Mitch decided. A very special, very painful form of torture.

The king and queen left shortly thereafter, promising to come back for lunch the next day as well. Mitch knew he had a lot of reading ahead of him, but he was looking forward to it. He'd always enjoyed studying history—especially the history of their people.

But right now, Mitch needed to stretch his muscles more than anything. He craved a hard workout. Either that or a marathon session of hot tiger sex with claws out and all that entailed. Since the latter wasn't forthcoming, he'd have to settle for the former. Of course, it was for his own good. If he had to fight a challenge in the coming weeks, he sure as hell had better prepare.

Coming as close to death as he'd been, he had a ways to work to get back both his strength and his speed. He would probably take a pounding at Paul's hands today, but Mitch looked forward to it with an animalistic glee. The tiger inside him wanted to stretch its muscles and try out its new fur—and any new abilities that might come with it. Mitch was a man of action, as the king had pointed out. Both sides of his nature had been sitting still for far too long.

Mitch helped Gina clean the kitchen area and wash the dishes and then went to change. He'd wear a T-shirt and sweat pants to spar with Paul. Loose clothes that wouldn't hinder his movements. After putting them on, Mitch moved to the center of the room and began a series of stretches. He'd have to do more before engaging in mock battle with Paul down in the barn later, but it felt so good to stretch out muscles that had been inactive far too long.

It was some time before he realized that Gina was watching him.

She sat at the kitchen table with a mug of coffee, pretending not to notice the play of sinuous muscles under stretchy T-shirt fabric. My, oh my, the man was smoking hot. Gina resisted fanning herself by wrapping her hands around the coffee mug.

"See anything you like?"

She'd been caught ogling his ass. Deciding to admit her attraction, she let her gaze roam boldly upward until it met his.

"What would you do if I said yes?" She favored him with what she hoped was a come-hither smile.

Apparently, she'd gotten it right. Mitch prowled toward her on silent feet, his gaze holding hers, his stare almost hypnotic. She rose from the chair, carefully placing her coffee cup on the table's surface, ready as the tension in the room rose with each quiet step. He advanced until he was directly in front of her and then moved closer still, lowering his head toward hers.

"I might do something like this," he whispered, his lips against hers.

And then he kissed her, taking what she offered and giving in return.

It just felt...right. Everything about Mitch felt right to her inner cat and her outer woman. Everything he did, every touch he gave her, every one of his inner thoughts he shared with her only made her more attracted to him. He was a man of honor that spoke to her own moral code, and he kissed like a dream.

Now if only he would take it beyond just kissing. She was old-fashioned enough to want him to be the aggressor, the dominant. Her inner tigress craved a man who could—and would—demand she give him everything, and give her everything of himself in return.

She sensed Mitch was just the man to do it, but so far, he hadn't stepped up to the plate. And it would sort of defeat her purpose if she had to tackle him...though she was increasingly tempted to do just that. She wanted him and she wanted him bad. But more than just the physical need, she wanted him to want her and be bold enough to take what he wanted.

As he was doing now. He'd been the one to call her out for ogling him. He'd prowled closer to steal this incredible kiss. Her toes curled at the magical sensations roiling through her bloodstream. And then she realized...it *was* magic. There was some kind of magical exchange happening between them, but it didn't drain her. In fact, she was gaining energy, not losing it. Was she draining him?

She put her palms against his shoulders and pushed, trying to break the kiss. He didn't let her go right away, but eventually her urgency seemed to get through to him and he raised his head. His pupils were dilated, as she was pretty sure hers were. Pleasure did that to a tiger.

The hunger in his dark-gold eyes almost made her forget why she'd denied herself more of the incredible pleasure of kissing him. But the dazed look to his features reminded her.

"Am I draining you?" she asked quickly, her voice breathless and her breathing rate still elevated from their kiss.

He shook his head. "What?"

"Power drain. Magic. Do you feel it?" She wasn't really able to string words together into a full sentence yet, but he seemed to understand. His golden brows drew together for a moment as he seemed to think about what she'd asked.

"No. If anything, I feel energized. I think you're giving me power. Are you okay?" His expression turned to one of concern as he focused on her, and his arms gentled, holding her close against his chest almost protectively.

"I'm fine. Great, in fact. I felt a boost in magical energy too." There. She was able to speak a complete sentence at last. She thought of it as a small victory.

"Really?" Concern turned to intrigue on his face.

She was getting better at reading his strong chin and gorgeous golden eyes. He didn't give away much, but now that she'd gotten to know him, she could figure out the subtle changes that echoed his mood.

His head dipped lower and she knew he was going to kiss her again…and then the phone rang. The loud bleat of her cell phone broke the spell they'd both been under and he released her. Gina swore silently that she was going to murder whoever it was on the other end of the call.

She stomped over to the end table where her phone lay charging and punched the button after seeing the name on the display. Paul Miller. Drat the man. He was one of her best friends, but he really needed to work on his timing.

"Hey," she answered abruptly, not wanting to take her frustration out on him, but he heard it anyway.

"Sorry. Bad time?"

Paul didn't usually tiptoe around her, but their relationship had changed a bit now that he was married and she wasn't constantly underfoot. When they'd been in school, she'd been his pesky younger sister. Now there was a distance between them that she didn't like but understood. They'd grown apart a bit. It was only natural, but she missed having him around all the time.

"Coulda been better," she groused, but her good humor

was returning. She could never stay mad at Paul for long. "What's up?"

"I just called to ask your guest a question or two. My brothers are around and I wanted to know if Mitch didn't mind having a few more bodies to pummel and be pummeled by."

It was odd phrasing but she knew what he meant. Paul had a way of overcomplicating the English language that never failed to amuse. Like her, he had been born in Iceland, but he'd been older and had had to learn English as a second language. Gina was lucky in that respect. She'd learned both languages side-by-side as she'd grown up. Paul didn't have an accent, but he did like to structure his sentences oddly from time to time.

"Hang on a minute. I'll give him the phone." Gina held out the small device to Mitch and he took it, jumping right into the conversation with Paul. Shifter hearing was sharp and he'd heard Paul's end of the conversation almost as clearly as she had.

The men arranged to meet earlier than previously agreed and then have dinner at the Miller's. Mitch ended the call, already gathering a change of clothing in the duffel she'd picked up somewhere along their journey here. She added a few things she wanted to bring with her and within a few minutes, they were ready to go.

They got outside, but there was only the one snowmobile. They had to ride double down the hill and over the fields to the Miller's barn. Mitch let her drive, which was only sensible since she'd practically grown up on one of these machines. But having his big body spooning her from behind made it the most...um...exhilarating ride she'd ever had on one of them.

She didn't feel the cold. Not with Mitch's big body giving off heat like a furnace. And his arms around her middle made her wish there wasn't a wad of bulky fabric between them. It made her want his hands to roam up, under her parka and sweater. Up, over the bare skin of her torso and into her bra.

Up, over her breasts, cupping them, caressing her nipples.

She had to clear her throat as she pulled the snowmobile up in front of the barn. Damn. He hadn't even done anything to her and she already needed a moment to calm down. A cold shower might help. Or a roll in the snow. Naked. With Mitch inside her.

Ug. She had to stop thinking about it and quit stalling. She secured the machine as Mitch hefted their two bags and waited in a ready stance. Ever the protector.

She realized once again how close he'd come to dying. And how quickly he'd bounced back. There was deep magic involved, of course, but her analytical side cautioned her to warn him.

Gina stepped close to him, taking one side of his collar in her fingers and stroking him through his jacket. The mood was intimate all of a sudden. Just them, surrounded by snow and the ticking of the engine as it cooled next to them.

"Promise me you'll be careful. I know you feel better, but it wasn't too long ago that you were not long for this world. It would…hurt me…if you died, Mitch."

"Hey." Mitch cupped her cheek in one big hand, his voice dipping into low and intimate tones. "I'm not going to die. Not today. And I have you to thank for the fact that I didn't die from the poison. You and your amazing blood." He stroked his thumb up and down over her cheekbone in the most tender of touches. And then he let her go and stepped back. She dropped her hand from his collar. "But if I'm going to stay alive through the challenge, I have to get back into fighting form."

There it was. The shadow that hung over him. Over them both. The challenge.

She was quickly coming to despise the thought that he was going to have to fight Uncle Gisli. She didn't know how it all would end, but there was every possibility that Gisli—deadly fighter that he was—would prevail. Just thinking about it broke her heart, but she couldn't do anything about the future that had yet to form. She had to deal with the here and now.

"Just try to be careful. You won't be able to do everything up to your usual standard right away. Be gentle with your healing body."

"I promise, *Doctor*." He smiled and winked at her, emphasizing her title. "I can't afford to pay you for any more in-home visits. I must owe you a small fortune by now."

"It's okay," she found the nerve to answer. "I don't want your money. You can pay me in kisses."

A spark ignited behind his golden eyes, making them flash amber at her. He liked her daring, it was plain to see.

"You don't say." He stepped closer to her, snaking one arm around her waist as he pulled her close. Her breath caught at his actions. This was the man she wanted. The one who reached out and took her—with her enthusiastic permission. "I'd better start paying down my debt right away," he whispered against her lips, their breath steaming in the cold.

And then he was kissing her again. A little whirlwind of a tempest that knocked the breath from her, showered her with a dazzling magical storm of energy and left her breathless as he let her go. She wanted to follow him and beg for more, but she became aware of just why he'd stopped.

The door to the barn had opened and Paul was standing in the open doorway, frowning at her. Damn. Caught necking in the snow by her would-be older brother.

Gina brazened it out, trying her best to ignore the hard looks that passed between Mitch and Paul. She stepped away from Mitch, internally aware that her balance was off. Mitch had literally made her head spin. But she did her best not to let it show on the outside as she smiled at Paul and walked past him through the open door and into the barn.

Inside, it was set up like a dojo with an entrance area with places to stow your stuff. The central area of the big building was filled with light that filtered in through high, discreet windows placed strategically on every side of the big building for maximum effect. The middle of the floor was covered in mats with other equipment around the circumference of the room.

Gina had spent many afternoons as a youngster learning how to fight and defend herself in human form in this makeshift dojo. Even more time had been spent in her fur, out in the woods, grappling and playing with the Miller brood. A quick look around the dojo told her that all four Miller brothers had come home at their father's call.

Gina greeted Tad, Harry and BJ with smiles and hugs as they came over to say hello. Paul and Mitch finally showed up inside and Gina introduced Mitch to the rest of the guys, silently wondering what had gone on outside after she'd left Paul and Mitch alone. She wouldn't ask, but she knew Paul. He had to have shared some choice words with Mitch after catching them in that clinch. He was too much her big brother to let something like that pass.

She wouldn't comment on it now. She was already feeling weird enough as it was. Better to pretend that everything was normal.

Mitch came over to her as she made the introductions and put an arm around her waist, shocking her. Was he staking a claim? Among shifters, this sort of action meant even more than it did in the human world. Was Mitch feeling possessive or merely protective? It could be either. Or even a little of both. One could mean something very special. The other less so, but still nice.

And what in the world had Paul said to him to make him react this way? Gina was full of curiosity but remained silent.

The Miller men were friendly enough toward Mitch, and before long they were out on the mats, trading punches. Gina was glad to see they started off slow and worked their way up to more intricate moves. She watched carefully from the sidelines as she began her own series of stretches. Mitch wasn't the only one who liked to keep in shape.

When the door to the barn opened about twenty minutes later, Gina was thrilled to see Mandy Risling, who was married to Tad, and Adele Miller, who was only a couple of years younger than Gina. They came in with the baby of the Miller horde, their little sister, Violet.

Gina ran over to them and exchanged hugs all around. It had been a while since their merry band had been all together in one place.

"Is that him?" Vi asked as the women settled in to watch the men at work.

CHAPTER SEVEN

The ladies would take their turn on the mats, Gina knew. And not alone. The women would spar with the men. It was good practice since you never knew who your opponent would be if you got into a fight in the real world. But for just a few minutes, they were observers as the Miller brothers escalated the workout, testing Mitch's reflexes and level of skill.

"Yeah," Gina answered, unable to keep her gaze from Mitch.

He was poetry in motion, and though she worried about the athletic level at which he was operating, she couldn't find any fault in his form or delivery. He was in the zone and clearly able to take on all the Miller men at once and still search for more opponents. He was an even better fighter than Gina had imagined.

"I heard he was a Royal Guard," Violet prompted, clearly wanting more information about the newcomer in their midst.

"Yeah," Gina repeated, knowing she sounded a bit dopey but unable to really concentrate on anything except the play of muscles as Mitch moved. He was a beautiful animal in his fur and in his skin.

Gina heard snickering from the older women that finally drew her gaze away from Mitch. Mandy and Adele were making faces at her and she swatted at them playfully, glad to have her childhood friends once again at her side.

"Ooh...Gina's got it bad, girls," Mandy said in a voice only the women could hear. "Looks like the hunka hunka burnin' tiger over there has caught the eye of our little snow princess."

"Is it true he turned white for you?" Violet asked, a flavor of awe in her tone.

Gina had to laugh. "I wouldn't say he didn't just for me, exactly. And I don't think he had any control over it. It just sort of happened. I gave him my blood and the next time he shifted fully, he was white. Surprised the heck out of both of us."

"You gave him blood?" Violet asked. Apparently, she hadn't heard the entire story.

"He was poisoned. Almost died a few days ago. It was touch and go for a while, but he's made what appears to be a miraculous recovery." Her gaze traveled back to him, watching his every move. "You wouldn't know it to look at him now, but he was as close to death as I've ever had one of my patients go without taking that final journey. I thought I would lose him a few times, but he has a warrior spirit and he fought through."

Silence greeted her revealing words. Then Mandy spoke again. "Tad said something special happened up at the circle. It sounded like Mitch has been Goddess-blessed." Quiet respect filled her voice.

"Yeah, I think he was. It was quite an experience—unlike anything I've ever seen or felt before up there, even with my dad. Mitch is special," Gina admitted.

"Special enough to mate with?" Adele asked the obvious question.

Gina couldn't speak the word, but she knew the answer in her heart. She nodded and felt the surprise of the women behind her. Each of them had known her almost all her life. They'd played together as children, gone to school together and learned about being tigers together. They knew her better than almost anyone and knew she'd never dared to give her heart to any man before.

Mating among shifters was something instinctive. Something special. Among shifter monarchs, it was slightly different, but Gina had always wanted a man who would be her true mate, not just a mate of convenience. She thought she'd found him in Mitch, but it would take Mitch's cooperation to take that final step and join their two souls.

If they mated, it would be for life. She wanted that with all her heart. She was beginning to crave it with every fiber of her being. But her female nature demanded more of her mate. It demanded that he claim her in the way of their ancestors. Her inner tigress deemed him worthy, but it was going to take Mitch to make that final connection. The claim. The demand for submission that her tigress was all-too-willing to give him—and only him.

The girls didn't have time to comment on her admission because the men chose that moment to pause for a water break. They were all sweaty and in various stages of undress. Most of the Millers had their shirts on, but Mitch's clothing hadn't been that good of a fit to start with. He'd shed his T-shirt already and was clothed only in the borrowed sweatpants.

Gina found it hard to look away from his gleaming skin and the muscles that played just underneath. He was a specimen of masculine perfection if she'd ever seen one.

Tad tossed him a towel and Mitch wiped his face. The Millers kept their private dojo stocked with supplies. A small refrigerator held bottles of water and sports drinks and Paul handed out bottles, tossing them across the length of the barn to each of them.

"Shall we show them how it's done, ladies?" Gina asked with a sly grin.

Mandy giggled and ran for the hidden control panel. She hit a few buttons and several items slid out from hidden cupboards in the walls, among them was a set of uneven bars, an extra-long balance beam, a pommel horse and a vaulting horse and several other items used in gymnastics. Adele and Violet moved everything into position while Mitch whistled once through his teeth.

"That's some setup," he observed, coming over to stand beside Gina. "You aiming for just a workout or something more?"

"Watch and learn," she countered, enjoying teasing him. "We're tigers. We're good at tumbling and jumping, and we use it in conjunction with more traditional martial arts."

"I'm familiar with the concept." Mitch looked down at her through slitted eyes. He seemed both skeptical and intrigued.

"You do gymnastics?" Gina wanted to know. He was big for it, but he definitely had the body. Those muscles were long and lean. She didn't doubt he could do more than just plain old fighting with them.

"I've been known to tumble a bit. It didn't come quite as naturally to me as to some of my shorter brethren."

"There are rings up in the rafters and a high bar we can put out if you like. Paul will probably get it out of storage before long. He likes going round and round." She made a silly face, used to Paul's antics. "There's plenty of space for even a guy as big as you to fly a bit." She nodded toward the rafters of the barn, high above their heads. The entire space was open and voluminous, built that way for just this reason.

Gina's attention was caught by a bead of sweat sliding its way down Mitch's throat as he raised a half-empty water bottle to his lips and proceeded to gulp the remainder down. He held it upward, his neck stretched as he emptied the clear plastic bottle. His throat worked, his Adam's apple bobbing up and down as he swallowed. Gina caught her breath. The man was so sexy, even his simplest motion made her wet.

She looked away before he finished with the drink and caught her staring. Again. She really had to stop ogling the man. Or...maybe not. He was just too handsome not to look at.

Violet jumped onto the balance beam and ran at a rapid pace, jumping and tumbling as she went on the tiny ribbon of only slightly padded wood. Mitch watched her, his eyes narrowing as if assessing her skill. He didn't seem surprised. He'd definitely seen this sort of thing before.

Adele started running and jumped into a simple vault, starting off slow as Mandy started stretching and tumbling a bit on the mats. Mitch's gaze went from one to the other, his gaze measuring.

"Is this the way regular Royal Guards train?" Gina had to ask.

"More or less. We all get tumbling and the unique fighting style that combines our more gymnastic abilities with self-defense as well as offensive fighting. Looks like our training in many respects, though I guess your version of it is truer to what it once was. I heard one of my teachers remark once that when your father went into exile, he took the best of the Guard with him."

"He didn't ask any of them to come. They all volunteered." She was quick to defend her father.

Mitch turned toward her. "I meant no disrespect. I'm sure they followed your father of their own free will. He is the king after all, no matter if he doesn't want to rule. If I'd been in the same position as the Millers, I probably would have followed him too. But it left a bit of a vacancy in the *tigre* Royal Guard ranks. Most of the best and most senior teachers went with your father. Those who were left to carry on were good but not exactly in the same league as those who departed. Which is part of the reason I went to the *pantera* to complete my training."

"I didn't realize..." Gina trailed off, thinking. "You went to the panthers and stayed. Why didn't you go back to your own kind? I know my uncle still fields a team of Royal Guard to protect him."

"It was a combination of reasons. First, Cade and I hit it off. He is my best friend as well as my—or he *was*—my partner." A look of sadness passed over his features for a split second when he mentioned the partnership that had been dissolved by Mitch's injury. "I wanted to partner with

Cade and he's dedicated to the Nyx by both desire and blood." Mitch's voice dipped into low, confidential tones so that nobody else could hear what he disclosed.

Gina realized Mitch was sharing a secret with her. His ex-partner was related by blood to the Nyx. Which meant Cade was probably in line for the panther throne if something happened to the young woman who currently ruled. If the panthers were anything like the tigers, they kept such things a closely held secret, and Gina didn't blame them. Being a royal put limitations on a person and a big fat target on your back.

"So you wanted to stay with Cade. That's understandable."

"I never really had a family," Mitch admitted, each word gritted out between his teeth as if he hated talking about it. Yet, he was. He was sharing a part of his past with her that still pained him to admit. That meant something. She treated his revelations with the respect they demanded. "Cade is my brother in all but blood. His family welcomed me and made me part of their tightknit group. I will miss them."

Gina reached out to him and put one hand on his hot skin. She didn't dare touch him anywhere but the forearm, but even that contact made a little frisson of electricity dance down her arm to her spine, sending tingles throughout her body. She ignored them. It was time to offer comfort and support, not jump his bones.

Besides, there were too many people around. And they were all watching her and Mitch out of the corners of their eyes. She'd have to join the workout sooner or later, but for this quiet, stolen moment, she and Mitch were connecting on a deep level, in spite of—or maybe because of—the setting.

"You don't have to give them up completely, do you? I can't imagine they'd forsake you, no matter what's happened."

Mitch turned toward her and she read a brief moment of vulnerability in his gaze before he shuttered it. "They wouldn't turn me away, but my duty is to protect them, not put them in danger. I can't go back to the way it was before. I've been compromised. The Nyx's enemies knew I guarded her, even if they didn't know my name. I will not compromise my friends by going back to them. Not now. Maybe not ever."

"I respect your devotion to duty, but where does that leave you? Alone?" Gina's heart went out to him.

"Not alone. The Mother of All has seen fit to point me in the direction of my own people. I haven't spent much time among tigers since going off for training among the *pantera*, but I know now it's time to return to my own kind and do my duty to *my* monarch, not the Nyx."

"You're right, Mitch." Gina squeezed his arm, facing the mats. "You're not alone anymore. You'll never be alone again if I have anything to say about it."

Dropping that bombshell for him to think about, she let go of his arm, then strode away toward the uneven bars. It was time to work off some of her sexual frustration and kick some ass—or have her ass kicked.

As it turned out, the score was about even by the end of a grueling workout with both the male and female Miller brood. They mixed and matched—Mitch and Gina going up against opponents of both sexes. One never knew who they'd be facing on the field of battle and enemies didn't always fight fair, so they tried different combinations of sparring arrangements.

At one point, Mitch took on all of the Millers plus Gina and knocked everyone on their asses by the end of the bout. He was something to watch, and hell on wheels as an opponent. Gina liked sparring with him, trying to score hits with her slightly quicker reflexes.

It wasn't so much that she was faster than him, more than that she was smaller. She was able to dart in and out, under his guard.

Until he caught her. The Millers were sprawled all around the dojo, having run afoul of Mitch's lightning-fast reflexes and unfamiliar, but incredibly effective fighting style when Gina danced a little too close to the dragon.

Mitch seized her, pulling a kick that otherwise would have

knocked her block off. Instead, she ended up encased in his arms, held tight against his sweaty body and her entire nervous system short-circuited. Well, that's what it felt like, at least.

The seconds ticked by in slow motion as she realized she was completely immobilized by his hold. He could do whatever he wanted with her and she was powerless against him—on so many levels. She wanted to surrender, to tell him to do his worst. Because she was certain his worst was better than the best she'd ever had. But they weren't alone.

Not that it mattered much among shifters, but Gina had been raised a little apart from the rest of her kind. She didn't always like the distance other shifters put between her and them when they knew who she was. And the only shifters she'd ever interacted with closely enough to want that normal shifter intimacy with were those she'd grown up with. In the city, she'd steered clear of Others of every kind and gave shifters in particular a wide berth. Until Cade and Mitch had sniffed her out, she'd never gotten close enough to another big-cat shifter to have been discovered.

Mitch held her in his arms, his hold loosening by slow degrees as if he wasn't quite sure what to do with her. It got to the point where she had a little bit of wiggle room and might've been able to counter the hold, but why would she? Her body was exactly where it craved to be—plastered against Mitch.

The only thing that would be better was if they were both naked. She looked up at him and their gazes caught and held. He dipped his head by slow degrees.

"I think you can let her go now." Her father's booming voice came from near the doorway.

Shit.

Mitch tightened his arms for a fraction of a second before he complied, releasing her. Gina cursed inwardly. He'd been about to plant one on her and she'd had just enough of his kisses to crave more. She thought maybe she was becoming an addict. Addicted to Mitch. Yeah, it was a harsh truth that she'd have to live with. Gina almost laughed aloud at her thoughts, but her father was waiting and the king wasn't known for his patience.

Mitch, to his credit, faced the tiger king after unwrapping his arms from around her, but he didn't let go of her completely. He kept hold of her hand as they faced her father's possible wrath side-by-side. Together. A united front. Only she was pretty sure Mitch would jump in front of her if her dad made even the slightest angry motion toward her.

But her dad wasn't going to get violent. He wasn't that kind of guy. He enforced his will with loud words and frowns, more than anything else. At least where she was concerned. He'd never raised a hand to her in anger and she knew he never would.

"How much did you see?" she asked her father, trying to defuse the situation.

"Enough." The king nodded, the frown on his face speaking of the intimate hold he'd broken up. But then his expression cleared and he looked intrigued. "Is this what the *tigre* Royal Guard is taught now? I have never seen anything quite like that fighting style. It's athletic but subtle. More stealthy than our usual fare."

Mitch finally let go of her hand and stepped forward, reaching for the towel he'd discarded earlier as he walked off the mats and went to talk with her father. Everyone else got up and toweled off, clustering around her dad to see what Mitch would reveal about the techniques that had put them all on their asses. It wasn't something they were used to. Each one of the Millers and their extended family were highly trained and very capable warriors.

"I wasn't trained fully by tigers. When it became apparent that I was outstripping my teachers, I was sent to the *pantera noir* for more advanced study. I was thirteen," Mitch revealed.

"I knew you were working for the panthers, but I didn't realize you'd trained with them too. How did that come about?" King Frederick asked. Everyone listened, waiting to hear what Mitch would say.

"One of my teachers had a contact among the *pantera noir* and he used it to get me into their training program."

"The only Guard I knew who had friends among the panthers was Geir Falkes. His aunt married into that secretive Clan, I believe."

Mitch shouldn't have been surprised by the exiled king's knowledge. Geir had been a young Guard when the king had left. He hadn't been part of Frederick's inner circle, though he'd been a hellacious fighter, even back then. The void left by the departure of so many of the top Royal Guards and their families had allowed Geir to move up the ranks quickly so that he'd become a teacher of other Guards at a much younger age than most of his predecessors.

Mitch had been a protégé of sorts. Almost a younger brother to the highly skilled warrior, who was still in his prime. It had been hard for Mitch to leave Geir behind when he'd finished his training, but he had known it was for the best.

"Master Geir was indeed the man who took me to the *pantera*. He looked after my training until I was old enough to be out on my own." And that had felt good to his seeking soul. Geir had taken Mitch under his wing and treated him like a younger brother. He was still one of his most favorite people in the world.

"You were young to leave your kin," Frederick observed.

"The Thorburns weren't my blood, though I can never thank them enough for adopting me. I took their name out of respect, but I was born Mitchell Gustavson. The Thorburns told me my parents died in a car accident."

The king looked at him sharply. "If your parents were Emile and Maria Gustavson, they didn't die in any accident." Frederick turned to face Mitch, his gaze troubled. "They died protecting me and my family. They were both Royal Guards and two of my dearest friends. Sweet Mother of All." Frederick's gaze turned heavenward as his face showed the pain he felt at the memory.

He took a moment, during which Mitch's mind spun. He hadn't known. Nobody had ever told him the truth about his parents, though they all must've known. But why?

"Mitch." The king looked back at him and put one hand on his shoulder. "I'm so sorry." The king hugged him then, a back-pounding hug of both comfort and sorrow shared.

Mitch didn't know what to say. He wanted to know the exact circumstances of his parents' death, and yet...he was almost afraid to ask.

When the king let him go, Gina was beside Mitch, her gaze filled with understanding and compassion. She reached for his hand and he took it like a lifeline. She was so good to him. He needed her touch to ground him, regardless of what her father might think. Mitch knew his place.

Mitch had just learned more about his true parents than he'd ever known. They'd been Royal Guards. Nobody had seen fit to inform him of that fact before, and Mitch had to wonder why.

"What's the big secret?" he asked aloud. "Why didn't anyone tell me about them before?"

The king sighed heavily. "Probably because of the way they died. You see, it was the last straw. The final battle that decided me on exile. Gisli came at us himself, along with a group of his loyal followers. We only had the Gustavsons and Petries with us. Both couples died to give us time to escape. Your mother shielded Gina, who was only a cub at the time, until Candis was clear of the fighting. She suffered grievous wounds getting Gina to her mother and collapsed at my wife's feet while your father was ripped open by Gisli, himself. The Petries held off the rest of the attackers until we could escape. Sadly, they too died in the attack. We met up with the Millers and a few others and hit the road. We left that very day. I didn't want any more of my friends and protectors to die in my service. I knew you existed, but I was assured you would be placed with a good family."

Mitch had to clear his throat before he could speak. "I was." He cleared his throat once more and tried again. "The

Thorburns were very good to me, but they had a hard time dealing with a child with Alpha tendencies and the desire to fight. They didn't really understand me, yet they indulged me. They found me teachers and put me into the training I craved. And Geir did the rest. I was well looked after and protected—perhaps too much—from the truth of what happened to my blood kin."

To say Mitch was stunned by these revelations would be understating it. A lot. But he was coming to some harsh realizations as well. Suddenly, things were coming into focus. Magnificent things of great scale and design. Destiny. Fate. The will of the Lady. Call it what you will, he realized events had led him to this place, this time, this woman and this king. He knew what he had to do.

"My existence as Mitch Thorburn is at an end," he declared. "That name is known by our enemies, and as far as I'm concerned, he died of the poison the day they burned Harris's dojo in the city. But Mitch Gustavson lives, and it's time to avenge my parents' deaths and put right something that went wrong a long time ago."

Silence greeted his softly voiced statement. He hadn't expected cheering, but he didn't know what to make of the silence until Gina squeezed his hand and drew his gaze down to meet hers.

"Whatever name you go by, you're a man of rare honor, Mitch." She reached up and planted a kiss on his cheek in front of all and sundry. It felt like a benediction. A touch of magic meant to begin healing the hurt places inside his soul.

He didn't really know what had prompted his decision or his bold words, but he knew the Thorburns would understand. They'd always been there for him, even as he'd grown into his Alpha role—something neither one of his adoptive parents were. They weren't afraid of him, but he'd become the leader of their tiny familial Pride by virtue of his cat's dominance. It was an odd arrangement, but Mitch would never take advantage of it and they knew he wouldn't. Still, it did cause some tension.

It had gotten better when he had been given the role he craved as a Royal Guard. He had taken the posting with the *pantera noir* and only went home to visit the Thorburns occasionally. They were good people, but it had become very obvious over the years that they didn't really understand Mitch's inner nature. They respected him, of course, and were proud of the man he had become, but they still didn't quite understand him.

"Gina's right," the king finally said, extending a hand for a strong shake. "It doesn't matter what name you go by, though I see your reasons for wanting to leave your old identity behind—both to safeguard your friends and former colleagues, and to honor your blood kin. It makes sense. And I give you your parents' place in my Royal Guard. It is your birthright, and now that you are here, it is yours for the taking. If you want it."

Mitch sank to one knee, beyond honored at the king's gesture.

"It is my honor to serve you," Mitch uttered the formal words, his head bowed.

"Then I charge you with my daughter's safety," the king commanded, surprising Mitch.

His first urge was to smile with satisfaction, but then he wondered, had the king meant more by his instruction? Had he just given Mitch implicit permission to date his daughter? Or was it what it sounded like on the surface? Mitch was confused.

"It is my honor to protect the tiger princess." Mitch made the formal reply and rose. Gina looked thoughtful and a little miffed as she narrowed her gaze at her father. The king had a somewhat smug smile on his face.

"Now that's settled," Frederick went on as if something monumental hadn't just occurred. "I think we need to talk about strategy. I assume from the performance I just witnessed that you're back up to full strength?" His gaze shifted to Gina and back again. She was the doctor, after all, but Mitch knew his own body well enough to realize he was almost fully recovered from the poison.

"Almost."

Paul Miller laughed out loud and drew Frederick's gaze. Pinned by the older man's stare, Paul spoke. "If that was his *almost*, then I'd truly hate to have to fight him at full strength."

CHAPTER EIGHT

Gina felt a swell of pride. She knew full well that Paul wasn't one to hand out compliments easily. The elder Millers had trained all their children and the children of the other families that had gone into exile with them to a high standard. They had been the best of the best when they'd left the tiger enclave, and they hadn't let their skills or abilities fade over time. They still trained every day, as did their children.

Almost all of the progeny of those original Royal Guards had followed their parents' inclinations. Only one or two of the younger generation didn't have enough skill or desire to become Guards themselves. Such was usually the way with tigers. Most of the time, blood ran true. And the few that didn't want to serve found other important roles in the Pride. They weren't Alpha enough to serve and protect, but they had other qualities that helped their Pride survive and thrive.

The rest of the afternoon was spent discussing strategy and technique with her father, the Miller kids and their dad. Paul had called up to the house and asked him to come down to the barn at Frederick's request. Mitch and his unique fighting style were the main topic of conversation. He was asked to demonstrate some of the holds, stances and other techniques he had been using during the earlier sparring practice.

And then, Gina watched in a little bit of awe as Mr. Miller and her father faced off against Mitch on the mats. Everyone watched in anticipation as the two best fighters of their small Pride took on the newcomer.

Things started slow and then built to a point where all three men were leaping, twisting and almost flying around the barn. It was two against one. Both older men—seasoned warriors—up against the younger. It wouldn't have been a fair matchup for anyone else, but Mitch was not only holding his own, he was prevailing at times, making the older men really work for the small hits they managed on him.

The gymnastic abilities of all three men came into play as they bounded off the mats, the apparatus that had been left around the edges of the practice area and even the walls. At one point, Mitch swung up into the high rafters of the barn itself to avoid a concentrated attack from Frederick, only to land behind Tom Miller, striking a point off the older man.

This went on for a half hour or more until the door to the barn opened discretely behind the watchers. A gust of cold air heralded the arrival of Gina's mom and Joan Miller. Both women seemed surprised by the main attraction everyone was watching with such intense concentration.

"If I'd known this was what was keeping you all, I would have brought a big bowl of popcorn with me," Joan Miller whispered to her eldest. Paul smiled and tucked his mother under one arm in a loose hug. She was shorter than every one of her sons, but still the clear Alpha female of the little familial Pride.

Gina's mom took a spot next to her on the end. "Your Mitch moves like the wind," she commented in a quiet whisper that wouldn't carry over the background noise in the room.

Gina started a bit. While she agreed he did move like the wind, the part that stopped her short was her mother calling him *her Mitch*. Did her parents see what was happening between her and Mitch? Did they approve? Or was it simply a convenient phrase that meant nothing of the sort? She didn't know, but she liked the tone of admiration in her mother's voice. Mitch really was something to look at.

"He's amazing," Gina agreed, not bothering to hide her true feelings. If her tigress had her way, Mitch would be her mate. Her mother would have to get used to that idea sooner or later—assuming Mitch cooperated.

"Have they been at this long?" Her mother hopped up to sit on the ledge behind her, getting comfortable.

"About forty minutes. Maybe a little more. But Mitch had already grounded all of them—" she pointed to the assortment of younger people seated next to her, "—and me, before Dad got here. One at a time and as a group. He's really something to behold when he gets going."

"His fighting style is like nothing I've ever seen," her mother commented, her gaze transfixed on the amazing speed and athletic motion of the three men fighting at the center of the dojo.

"He learned from the *pantera noir*. They trained him from the time he was thirteen." Once again, pride filled her voice.

Mitch was like no man she had ever known. He'd faced such adversity in his young life, yet he'd found a way to grow into a man of uncommon skill and unquestionable honor. He'd been accepted by one of the most secretive and selective shifter Clans. The *pantera noir* were notorious for not accepting just anyone among them. They were especially protective of their monarch. Mitch had to have proven himself in some way to even be allowed to train with them. To be trusted with the life of the Nyx, he must have done something even more powerful.

Just watching him face off against their best fighters—her father and Tom Miller—it was clear he was in the same class as both of them. Maybe even better. After all, he was coming off a grievous injury. He had admitted that he wasn't yet fully recovered. And still, he took on two of their best as if it were nothing. No sweat. No big deal. Just another day in the dojo.

He was beating them too. It wasn't an obvious, flat-out victory, but it was clear as the bout went on that Mitch was scoring more points on them than they were on him. Gina was impressed all over again. If he could do this now, what would he be like at full strength?

Most importantly, would he be good enough to take on Uncle Gisli and win? She sent a prayer up that it would be so. She couldn't lose him. Not now. Not ever. He was hers and she was his. It would just take a little more time to convince him of that unrelenting fact. She needed that time. Desperately. But she didn't think they were going to be allowed that luxury. Things were moving fast now and she had a premonition that events were speeding along and she had no choice but to be caught up in them. The whirlwind was coming and she could either fight it and lose, or allow it to sweep her along toward their destiny.

"You could do worse than a man like that," her mother observed, still in that low tone that wouldn't be heard beyond the two of them in such a large space. She nodded toward Mitch, now running literal circles around Tom Miller, much to the delight of his sons if their heckling hoots and hollers were anything to go by.

She turned to look at her mom, more interested suddenly in her opinion on Mitch as a mate than the mock combat taking place in the center of the room. Her mother's opinion mattered greatly to Gina.

"Would you and Dad object if it turned out Mitch was my mate?"

Her mother turned to meet her gaze. "Is he?"

The sounds of the room faded as the moment of truth hit her. Silently, she nodded, holding her mother's gaze. She wasn't sure what to expect, but the tears that came into her mother's eyes sparked an answering moisture in her own. Why were they crying? Was it bad? Or tears of joy? Or what? Gina was so confused.

And then her mother reached out and hugged her.

"Oh, baby girl, I'm so happy for you." The whispered emotion was thick and sweet. It was good. Her mother was happy with Gina's choice. "Does he realize it yet?"

"I'm not sure." Like a magnet, Mitch drew her gaze. "I think he's fighting it, though the indications are there…" She trailed off, not wanting to go into explicit detail with her mother.

"Sometimes men need a little push in the right direction," her mother surprised her by saying.

"But he's the dominant partner in our pairing. My cat knows and accepts that."

"That's good," her mother replied with a satisfied smile. "Having your tigress on board means this is a good match. But maybe you can coax her to be a little more forward in getting him to take the lead."

Gina wasn't quite sure what her mother was driving at, but she was getting some particularly naughty ideas. It was clear her mother wouldn't object to Mitch. And if Mom didn't object, Dad wouldn't either. It was clear just by watching them spar that her father already had a healthy respect for Mitch's fighting abilities. They'd also discussed the Rule and the history of the Clan and she knew the signs that told her without words that her father liked the way Mitch's mind worked. They'd talked a lot about Mitch's business background and experience, including his take on the world economic crisis and what could or should be done to fix it. The fact that he came from a family that had been close to hers in the past counted in his favor too, though he had been raised by others.

It looked like green lights on all fronts, except where it counted most. Mitch had kissed her. He'd even gone a little farther than that, but he seemed to shy away from the final step toward a deeper relationship with her. She'd have to fix that at her earliest opportunity. Maybe even tonight. If she could wangle a way.

She lapsed into silence, watching Mitch move around the dojo. He was poetry in motion, but her mind was on the possible scenarios she could engineer once she had him alone again. Night couldn't fall too soon as far as she was concerned.

Eventually the bout came to an end with no clear winner, but all three men were smiling and sweating. There was a bank of showers along one wall of the dojo and everybody was able to clean up a bit before heading back to the Millers' home. Joan had insisted everyone stay for dinner.

It turned into a raucous evening with all the Millers, including Tad and Mandy's baby, young Addie. She was adorable and was passed from adult to adult to coo over and cuddle. She was a peaceful baby whose true name was Asdis, which meant goddess in Icelandic, and Gina had always thought there was something a little fey about her.

Unlike her parents, little Addie had clear blue eyes that she had never grown out of. She wouldn't begin to shift until her teenage years, but Gina privately wondered what kind of tigress she would turn out to be. Very few golden tigers had blue eyes.

One other good thing to come out of the meal was that Maribeth had visibly backed off. She no longer flirted with Mitch, which calmed Gina's tigress. In fact, Maribeth had given Gina a little wink and thumbs-up when Mitch wasn't looking, wishing her good luck in the silly way they had as schoolgirls. Maribeth had ceded the conquest to Gina. Thank goodness. Gina hadn't wanted to fight with one of her oldest and dearest friends over him, but she would probably have been pushed in to it if Maribeth had continued her flirtatious ways.

When the meal was finally over and the night had grown dark and cold outside, they lingered for a while over coffee in the Millers' big living room. Eventually though, it was time to leave. A contingent of Millers—both old and young—formed an informal Guard troop of sorts to escort the king and queen back home. Some of the others wanted to do the same for Gina, but Mitch declined their help, saying he could protect her well enough on the short ride to the cabin.

After everything they had seen him do in the dojo that day, nobody cared to argue the point. Of them all, Mitch was the superior fighter. If he couldn't keep Gina safe, nobody could.

They set out quietly from the big house, taking a different route than the royals, moving stealthily back to the dojo to retrieve their snowmobile. Mitch checked it over before starting it up, exercising some of his ingrained Royal Guard caution. He waited only for Gina to hop on the seat before taking off toward the cabin.

When they got close, he stopped the vehicle a short distance out, going the last yards on foot. His approach was again, cautious. It was clear he wasn't taking anything for granted. They'd left the cabin secure, but they'd been gone for hours. Anyone could have infiltrated the building during that time.

Gina pulled out her smartphone and started accessing the cameras both inside and outside the cabin that she had set to broadcast to an incredibly well-hidden internet address. While she checked the small screen for any possible evidence of intruders, Mitch did a more physical inspection. Between the two of them, they soon established that nothing had been disturbed since they'd left.

Mitch parked the snowmobile on one side of the cabin where it was hidden from view and joined her inside a moment later. The place was toasty warm and closed up for the night. Gina had shut the blackout curtains before they'd left, knowing they'd be returning after dark. And this time, she hadn't forgotten to close a single one. They were as secure as they were going to get.

Which meant the moment of truth had arrived. Gina had been going over the discussion she'd had with her mother earlier that evening for the past hour or two. She was as certain as she could be that Mitch was her destiny. Her future. Her mate.

Drastic measures were called for in order to get him to admit what she knew in her heart was the truth. He was hers, just as she was his.

And there was no time like the present.

She shed her coat, walking up to Mitch as he did the same.

She didn't stop to think or give him time to move away. She simply stepped right into his arms and hugged him close.

He was so warm. So vital. So alive.

She could tell he was confused by her actions when his arms seemed to pause before slowly wrapping around her. He let her rest her head against his shoulder for a long moment before she felt him move back a bit to look down at her.

"What's this all about?" A confused smile played about his masculine lips and she read uncertainty in his golden eyes.

"Something I should have done days ago. The moment the poison was out of your system and I got a taste of your natural scent, I knew you were the one," she admitted. "I debated jumping you in the shower." She had to laugh at herself, knowing honesty was the best policy among mates. She would start as she meant to go on—laying out the truth, fully expecting he would do the same.

"Whoa, princess—"

"No." She felt him pulling away and she tightened her hold. She wasn't letting him get away with putting barriers of useless titles between them. "I'm not your princess, Mitch. I'm your mate."

There it was. The stark, undeniable truth. She saw a momentary flair of panic in his eyes. But then something settled down and he seemed to inhale very deliberately and close his eyes. When he opened them, the look in them was very different. Resigned. Concerned. And joyous.

She understood the mixed emotions very well. Mating was a big deal. He'd be cavalier if he wasn't worried. For that matter, mating *her*—in their precarious political position—was something to be very concerned about. She knew it. And she knew he knew it. They'd be fools to not consider what their mating might mean in the bigger picture.

But it was also a biological imperative. An undeniable force of nature that demanded they come together. In all the world, his was the one soul matched to hers. He was the one man she needed as no other. And she was the same for him. She knew it in her heart.

For that's what mating was among shifters. It was a Goddess-given bond between two souls, two people and their two inner beasts. It was sacred and special. And it could be very scary as well as intensely satisfying.

"You feel it too?" he finally asked in a rough voice, so deeply pitched it rumbled along her spine like the softest of caresses.

"Since the moment you came out of that shower without the chemicals clouding your scent. Although, if I'm honest, I'd say I was attracted to you well before then. When I first saw you in Ellie's guest room, I knew there was something about you." She reached up and pushed a lock of golden hair away from his face. "You're a handsome man, Mitch. You know that. But there was more. Some inner...something...that attracted me. I liked the way you fought against the poison that would have killed almost anyone else. I liked your spirit and your determination. You were brave too. So brave when it looked like you might not win the fight. My heart broke for you, and when it came back together, you were deep inside, never to be removed. And a big chunk of it became yours."

She smiled, stroking his stubbled cheek. The rasp of his short bristles against her fingers sent shivers down her spine to settle in her center. She loved touching him and reveled in the freedom to finally touch him like a lover.

"Gina..." he whispered, dipping his head to hers and joining their lips in a sweet, sweet kiss. He drew back but didn't go far, his hands framing her face. "You are the most beautiful woman in the world. Your heart, your courage, your compassion and strength humble me." He dipped closer, planting another short kiss on her parted lips. "I've tried to stay away. I know I'm no good for you. And I worry about the future. I could lose the challenge, and if that happens, I didn't want to leave you alone and hurting."

His gaze was deadly serious as he laid out the worst-case scenario in stark words. She nodded, raising her hands to hold his forearms on either side of her as he slid his hands to cup her shoulders.

"If that happens, I would be hurt regardless. Even if we never consummate this union, my heart knows its mate. And if you leave this plane of existence, I would mourn you. I might even want to follow you," she whispered, admitting her deepest fear.

"Never." His tone was adamant and he squeezed her shoulders for emphasis. "Promise me right now that you'll never give up like that."

She had to look away from the anger in his eyes. "I can't." Her voice broke as worry overtook her for a short, painful moment. "I don't think I'm strong enough to go on without you," she admitted in a small, frightened voice.

Loving brought vulnerability. She had learned that in the short time she'd known Mitch. It also brought strength and joy. They had to concentrate on that while they could. The worst would come. It always did. But for now, they could just be happy. Just for a little while. She just needed to convince him of it.

"You are the strongest woman I know," Mitch insisted, one big hand going to her nape and pulling her in to his chest once more. He snaked his other hand around her waist.

She absorbed his warmth and was comforted by it. He was such a good man. The world would be a sadder place if he was taken from it.

She couldn't let that happen. No way. No how.

"I'm glad you think so." She needed to change the subject. She hadn't meant to let this turn into something maudlin. This was supposed to be a joyous time. A time of discovery and celebration of the newness of acknowledging their bond. "I'd rather you thought I was the *sexiest* woman you know though, just for the record."

She looked up at him, smiling and hoping he'd follow her lead in lightening the mood. She knew she'd hit the jackpot when he dipped his head lower once more.

He took her mouth in a hot, wet kiss that left her in no doubt about how he felt. He devoured her this time, staking his claim and demanding her compliance. She gave it willingly. Surrender was her pleasure and her inner tigress purred at his masterful dominance. *This* was the man she'd been dreaming about. The man of action and confidence who knew what he wanted and took it.

He broke the kiss and stole her breath by scooping her up into his arms. He walked toward the fire rather than the bed and she wanted to purr. There was a sheepskin rug in front of the fireplace that she'd been dreaming about ever since they'd come to the cabin. With the gas flames licking happily upward and shedding both heat and a fanciful light over the area, it was the perfect setting for a magical seduction.

Whether she'd seduced him or he was seducing her was a moot point. They were together. Finally. And there was no turning back now.

Mitch laid her down on the fluffy sheepskin, loving the way the softness of the pelt outlined her gorgeous features. She was a dream to him. A beautiful, aching dream of what could be—what *was*—on this magical, Goddess-given night.

He didn't know how long this could last, but for whatever time they had left, they would be together. He couldn't let her go now. Not after the heartbreaking way she'd admitted to the truth he could no longer deny.

He had thought staying away from her would protect her. He'd been wrong. Denying the pure fact that they were destined mates wasn't doing either of them any good. Though uncertainty dominated their future, all he needed to worry about was the next few minutes…the next few hours…the next few days. The rest would take care of itself. Living in the moment was the best they could do for now.

Mitch gave in. He decided to take what time the Goddess would grant him with the love of his life and run with it. Whether they lasted a few days or a few decades was in the hands of the Mother of All, though Mitch vowed to do everything in his power to stay with Gina as long as he possibly could. It was added incentive—as if he needed any—

to win the challenge he knew was coming.

He'd do anything for Gina. But for a chance to spend the rest of his life with her? He'd move mountains. He'd find a way to make it happen.

Mitch rested on his forearms over her compliant body. He stared down into her eyes and knew there was no turning back. He'd been a fool to think he could ever resist her.

"You *are* the sexiest woman I've ever met." He gave her the words she'd teasingly asked for, and he meant every syllable. It was no joke to him.

Mitch had been pursued by women—human, cat shifter, even a werewolf bitch. He'd let a few of them catch him...for a time. He'd enjoyed women and liked to think he'd treated his lovers well. He'd thought he had a way with them. But nothing and no one could have prepared him for Gina. She was in a class by herself.

It wasn't just that she was royalty. That was pretty much beside the point now. He had used their differences in station to set them apart, but with his change of stripes, he just didn't know where that left him. And right now, he didn't really care.

All that mattered was Gina, and the hunger that could no longer be denied.

He lowered himself over her so that he was pressed against her from head to toe. Full body contact, though their clothing got in the way. He kept the majority of his weight off her and enjoyed the feeling of enveloping her, taking her in, covering her, protecting her. It made him feel stronger than he ever had before that this amazing woman gave him the gift of her trust.

"I'm going to make love to you," he warned. If she wanted him to stop, he had to know now.

"Thank the Goddess for that."

Her exasperated and relieved tone made him chuckle. Only Gina could do that. Only she could make him laugh, finding joy in the simplest of things. Being with her was a treat. A delight to his senses.

"I think we're both overdressed." He smiled down at her, remaining motionless. He was enjoying the moment almost too much. He didn't want to move, though he knew he had to if they were going to speed things along.

"Get up and I'll remedy that." Her expression dared him to play. And cats loved to play.

Mitch rolled to the side and lay on the soft fur while she did a slow striptease for him. Oh, yeah. If he died now, he'd be a happy man. Although he'd be even happier after he finally sank inside her body and made her his. He'd wait to die until at least after the third or fourth million time he'd had her…if he could.

He didn't want to think about their uncertain future while Gina revealed herself inch by slow, teasing inch. She was a beautiful woman with a lithe body, honed in the dojo. She'd impressed him with her tumbling skills and ability to defend herself. He was glad she had that training. Theirs was a dangerous and uncertain world.

But he pushed those thoughts aside as she bared her breasts to his gaze. Nudity among shifters wasn't a big deal, usually. Gina's nudity, however, set his body tingling and his blood to boil. She was gorgeous. Every inch of her skin was creamy and, as he already knew, delicious. He wanted to taste her again. Lick her like the cat that shared his soul. Wrap her in his arms and never let go.

When she was bare, she moved toward him like the cat she was, prowling over his body. She kissed him, one knee on either side of his hips, her hands on the floor on either side of his head. She leaned down and took his mouth with a fierce femininity that took his breath away. The daring in her smile as she lifted her mouth from his for a moment made him smile in return.

His little she-cat wanted to play. She dove back in, nipping his lower lip between her teeth. It didn't hurt, but it spiked his desire higher.

He raised his hands as he took control of the kiss, cupping her breasts and squeezing the hard peaks as she whimpered, telling him of her excitement. She moved into his touch, silently asking for more.

He wanted to touch every inch of her, learning her peaks and valleys. Mapping out the terrain of her desire, understanding what made her squeak and what made her moan. It would be his life's study. Learning how to please her was something he looked forward to with every fiber of his being.

He moved his hands lower as he sent his tongue into her mouth. She responded, undulating her hips, arching her back, allowing him easy access to the secret treasure revealed between her luscious thighs. Her knees were already apart, one on either side of him, so it was a simple matter to let his hand roam into the hot moisture that gathered at their apex.

One hand in front, one cupping her amazing ass, he alternately squeezed and stroked, learning her contours and what made her wiggle against him for more. He dipped one finger into her channel, loving the tightness, the way her body welcomed him and tried to hold him within. He went back with two fingers, stretching her a little, wanting there to be no discomfort when he finally put his cock inside her tight opening.

She moved on his hand, pumping up and down as if to drive him deeper. She fucked his fingers and moaned into his mouth as he deepened both the kiss and the penetration. He added another finger for good measure, stretching her even more.

Gina went wild in his arms, squirming closer and increasing her movements until she shattered. Her climax hit and she lifted her head. He let her go, watching her ride his hand and wanting to be inside her the next time she came.

He flipped her over, reversing their positions so that she lay under him as he stripped off his shirt and then lowered his pants. He sprang free, ready and eager to claim her. When she looked up at him with that dreamy expression in her lovely blue eyes, he couldn't stop himself.

Mitch lowered himself over her, glad when she eagerly

spread her legs and wrapped them around his hips. She seemed as eager as he was, despite her recent climax. He couldn't wait. He needed to be inside her. Now.

Holding her gaze, he slid into position and then took possession, watching her for any sign of discomfort. But he saw only welcome and a deep satisfaction in her eyes when he finally joined them in one long, sliding glide. They fit together like two halves of a whole. As if she'd been made for him alone and he for her.

Mitch could've sworn he heard soft notes of the Goddess's chimes as he finally claimed his mate. His mate. The concept floored him. That this special, incredible woman could be his.

"Gina," he whispered, nearly overcome with emotion. The enormity of what he was feeling expanded his heart to envelop her, taking her within forevermore.

She gasped as he began to move, slowly rocking within her, testing the motion that would not be denied. He wanted this moment to last forever, but he couldn't hold it. Urgency rode him. The driving need to come. To make her come. To give and receive pleasure. He wasn't entirely sure he'd survive it, but it didn't matter. All that mattered was Gina. Amazing Gina. And the love in his newly awakened heart for her.

CHAPTER NINE

Gina gasped as Mitch began to move. He was big. Bigger than the few men she'd dated in medical school. They'd been purely human and totally unaware of her true nature. They'd scratched an itch and stroked the tigress into satisfaction. For a while. But nothing and no one could have prepared her for the overwhelming force of nature that was Mitch.

He began to pump his hips, his long, thick cock touching her inside in ways that made her squirm to get closer. It mad her yearn for more. She wanted everything he would give her and more. She wanted him. Forever.

"Mitch," she breathed his name as he moved closer, his mouth nipping at her neck, his lower body moving faster as he picked up the pace. Her insides were quivering, waiting for the explosion she craved.

"You're mine, little tigress. Now and forever, you're mine," he whispered near her ear, driving her wild. "Say it," he demanded.

"I'm yours," she agreed readily on a gasp as he changed his pace again. Oh, yeah. But she wanted more. "You're mine too," she insisted, her voice breathy as he drove her wild with his new rhythm.

Her words made him growl and she knew he liked her possessiveness. The tigress in her stretched, reaching for her mate.

"I'm yours, my princess. My mate," he agreed, his raw, sexy voice setting little fires in her bloodstream.

His mouth claimed hers again in a tempestuous kiss as his lower body began an even more urgent movement. It wouldn't be long now. Thank the Mother of All.

And then he ended this kiss, lowering his mouth to her neck and the soft spot where it met her shoulder. He nipped her skin until he found the perfect spot. And then he bit down hard as her world exploded. She raised her head off the floor, seeking blindly for him.

She found the sweet spot and unleashed her beast, biting in return as he groaned deep in his chest, his hips stopping while he was deep inside her, every muscle in his body tensing for a long, glorious moment as they both came. Together.

Gina was blown away by the experience she'd just shared with Mitch. She hadn't known sex could be so primal, so breathtakingly raw and urgent. He'd wowed her on every level, and she was very much afraid her senses were singed by the experience and would never recover.

She lazed on the sheepskin rug in front of the fireplace, snuggled up against Mitch as his breathing slowed. He kept one arm around her, seeming to enjoy her closeness. She'd never cuddled after sex before. The humans she'd been with hadn't wanted it and she hadn't really cared enough to bother.

But with Mitch, everything was different. She wanted to touch him, to stroke his skin, to be stroked in return. She wanted it all with him. All of it. Forever.

"We didn't use anything," Mitch commented in a quiet, deliberate voice once his breathing had slowed enough to speak normally. He stroked one finger in slow lines up and down her arm, as if he too craved the touch of her skin. "Condoms, I mean," he clarified, turning his head to meet her gaze.

Truthfully, she hadn't thought beyond the moment, but

his reaction to the idea made her pause. He didn't look panicked. He almost looked...hopeful? Would he be happy if a child resulted from what they'd just done? She searched her heart and knew she would.

Realizing that, her response to his statement was simple. She put one hand over his heart, feeling it beat against her palm through his hot skin.

"I want your babies, Mitch. A whole little tribe of tiger cubs to romp and play in our house and brighten our lives." She traced circles on his chest as his heart sped up in what she hoped was pleased excitement.

She felt that he was watching her, so she raised her gaze to meet his again and found a sadness there that she had been expecting. Sadness and regret. She felt it too. They both knew this was a moment of peace in a turbulent time that could go either way for them.

"It's a dream I will savor," he said with a seriousness that she understood.

"It's a dream I want to see come true," she countered. "If I get pregnant, the Mother of All wills it. I'd like to have your cub, Mitch, regardless of how things go with the challenge."

"I wouldn't want to leave a cub fatherless, or leave you alone to raise him or her." His gaze narrowed as the troubled thoughts crossed his mind.

"All the more incentive to survive," she whispered. He looked shocked and angered, but she calmed him. "I don't mean it the way you're thinking. Our baby would never be a pawn to me. I would love and protect our child as I love you, Mitch."

He seemed to deflate as a cautious joy entered his eyes. "You love me?" he whispered, as if he didn't believe her.

On firmer ground now, she sat up a little so she could rest her chin on his chest and gaze deep into his eyes. She smiled at him, loving the feel of his skin under her hands.

"Of course I love you," she confirmed, watching his reaction. He was getting easier and easier for her to read as time went on. He wasn't an overly demonstrative man, but there were little signals that heralded his moods if you knew how to read them.

Right now, he looked like he'd had the breath knocked from him. A second later, she felt the same way as he reversed their positions and kissed her deeply while her head sank into the cushioning sheepskin covering the floor.

"I love you too, Gina," he whispered against her lips, taking them again and again. "I love you with everything that's in me. With all my heart." He punctuated each statement with kisses so sweet they made her want to cry.

Her heart was so full. All because of this incredible man.

They moved to the bed eventually and made love off and on throughout the long winter's night. Gina never wanted it to end. She almost feared the dawn and the responsibilities it would bring. For now, she was content in their little love nest. Just the two of them. Together on a voyage of discovery as they each learned what pleased the other and drove each other to ever-increasing heights of passion and pleasure.

But dawn did come, and with it, a new day in which to prepare for what they both knew was coming. They ate breakfast together and then Mitch spent some time studying the history of their people while Gina took care of some light chores around the cabin. Her parents joined them for lunch again and even though a few pointed and very speculative glances were sent their way, they had decided to keep their growing relationship to themselves for now. After lunch they all went down to the Miller's dojo for a long afternoon of training and dinner with the other family.

They returned to their cabin to make love long into the night and recover from the rigors of the day. This pattern repeated itself for about a week. After the first day or two, Mitch began a regimen of outdoor exercise in the mornings to retrain his body. He would run in his fur, going farther each day and doing the heavy chores around the cabin.

Gina went out with him for part of each morning. They would climb trees, run and scout the area. He spent a lot of time honing his skills. He taught Gina things he knew that she had never thought of, while she helped him work on his new stealth against the backdrop of snow.

He got stronger and stronger, to the point where she was amazed anew each day by his abilities. He was like no tiger she'd ever known. He was like something out of legend.

Inwardly, she rejoiced. Her uncle's skills were not to be underestimated. Mitch would need every advantage he could find against someone of Gisli's cunning. He hadn't ruled over a stolen kingdom for this long without having superior skills and a deceitful nature.

At least, that's what Gina secretly thought. She didn't remember much about her uncle, but she'd tried to keep up with the intelligence reports her father received on a regular basis since she was old enough to understand them. She'd followed her uncle's activities from afar for many years. She knew he was a force to be reckoned with.

Mitch would need every bit of skill he could muster to win this challenge. Worry about the future was her constant companion now. That and the incredible joy being with Mitch brought her.

Every morning, they would go out for a run in their fur, prowling up snow banks and down hillocks, tussling sometimes in the loose powder, sliding fancifully on ice sheets and sharpening their claws on rocks and trees. This was their territory—okay, well, it was really her father's territory—but they were welcomed in his domain.

They ranged farther afield each day, bounding along the perimeter, through the woods, well hidden from prying eyes. Their snowy coats and ingrained camouflage made them very difficult to see against the backdrop of the snowy forest. At least, that's how it had always been for Gina. She'd roamed these woods all her life and never had a problem.

Until an arrow shot out of the misty morning to land not an inch from where her head had been and embedded deeply in the bark of a pine tree.

Mitch growled and jumped in front of her, ushering her to

relative safety behind a large boulder while he covered her body with his own. If more projectiles were coming, he had put himself in position to be hit first, protecting her as best he could.

When nothing happened for several minutes, he got up and peeked around the boulder, raising a paw, then an ear, then his head. No more arrows flew at them. Finally, he darted out from behind the boulder and swatted the arrow loose, dragging it back to cover with him.

He shifted quickly to his human form and unrolled a slip of paper that had been wrapped around the shaft of the arrow. Crouching behind the boulder, he read it and cursed.

"We need to get back to the cabin. This place isn't safe anymore and your uncle is well aware of my existence. He's issued the challenge."

Gina rubbed her head against his shoulder in distress. She'd stayed in cat form, knowing she was faster on ice and snow in her fur than her human form. The news made her want to gasp, while at the same time the tigress in her was ready to fight. She wanted this ordeal over with. And she wanted to taste the blood of her enemies.

With a growl, she moved back, watching Mitch shift into his stunning black and white fur. Together, they ran to the cabin, keeping to cover as much as possible. Fear followed her tracks and determination to end this once and for all spurred her on. Their idle time was over.

Whether they were ready or not, the challenge had to be met. This morning's demonstration only emphasized the point that they weren't as safe here as she'd always thought they were. Uncle Gisli had let them fall into a false sense of security. It was clear now that they'd been under surveillance all this time. How else could he know about Mitch?

Gina put on a burst of speed to get to the cabin. She had to check on her parents and the other families on the mountain. They needed to send up the alarm. Her sense of peace had been well and truly shattered.

Mitch checked out the cabin before he would allow her to

go inside. Things were okay this far inside the perimeter, but it was clear Gisli had his agents in the area and they couldn't take anything for granted anymore.

Gina shifted to her human form and reached for the phone even before she reached for her clothes. Hitting speed dial, she threw on her clothing as the phone rang at her parents' house, farther up the mountain.

"Mom. Thank the Lady. Is everything okay?" Gina knew she should probably be a little calmer and explain things, but panic had her in its grip. Her mother seemed to pick up on her urgency, reporting that everything was green up at the house. Gina was able to take a breath and regroup. She knew what she had to do. They'd rehearsed this many times. "Lockdown," she said in a no-nonsense voice. "Someone launched an arrow at my head near the southeastern perimeter. No damage, but there was a note attached. Gisli has issued the challenge."

Her mother, much better in a crisis than Gina herself, went immediately into battle mode. She let Gina know as she started the chain that would automatically notify every family on the mountain that the alert status had changed. Reports would start filtering in any minute, so Gina hung up with a promise that she and Mitch were going to head up to the house. It was the most fortified location on the mountain and everyone would be gathering there before long.

The storm had gathered and was almost upon them all.

Mitch's first view of the king's home in exile impressed him. They'd built a good, old fashioned stone keep up on top of the mountain. How they'd managed to do so in the middle of the native forest without changing anything too drastically, he'd never know. The structure was only two or three stories high, but it still managed to have an air of antiquity about it. The stone was all native grey rock. Granite, Mitch thought. Very thick.

Windows were small and raised well off the ground with no perch points that a shifter could take advantage of in either human or shifted form. The only real danger would be from the sky—if any raptor shifters decided to come after the tiger king in exile for some reason. That was unlikely, so the place was darn near impregnable by conventional means.

And if that granite was as thick as it looked, Mitch doubted anything short of a bunker-buster bomb would make a dent in it. He ushered Gina inside as others began to arrive. The queen met them all at the door, her lips tight as she directed everyone to the war room.

They'd named it aptly. Two floors down into the bedrock of the mountain, the war room could hold them all—and there was quite a crowd gathering. Representatives from every Guard family on the mountain filtered into the space. Mitch had met a few of the other families as he'd prowled the perimeter of the mountain over the past week, but he knew the Millers best.

Paul Miller was sitting with his brother Tad and his wife, Mandy. Her mother, Hilda, was seated on her other side. Mitch recognized a few other people from the dojo, where various neighbors had come to meet Mitch and train over the past few afternoons.

Gina gave Mitch a quick tour of the facility while they waited for everyone to gather. There were state-of-the-art monitoring systems that showed all points on the mountain. There were also maps and banks of computers that held who knew what kinds of information.

Mitch was impressed. This was a real control center. He could see the house above and the perimeter already guarded by groups of tigers in human and shifted form. They weren't easy to spot, but Mitch knew what he was looking for. Despite that, he was impressed by the skill of the Old Guard—as he'd heard those who had gone with the king into exile call themselves.

When Frederick and Candis entered, the energy in the room crackled. They came right up to Mitch and Gina and the king held out his hand. Mitch knew what he wanted. Mitch had already examined the small piece of paper with all the tools available to him and didn't think it was dangerous in itself. It was the message it held that was the real danger. Mitch handed it over with grim stoicism.

The king unrolled it and read it, his lips turning down in to a troubled frown. He paused a moment before turning to the assembly.

"You know the bare bones of what has happened. An arrow was shot at Mitch and Gina while they prowled near the southeastern perimeter. We logged the intrusion at oh-seven-twenty-six and have video surveillance of a rented car speeding away down Dawson Road shortly thereafter. Heat signatures indicate two humans inside. Enhancement shows what is likely a compound bow lying across the back seat."

Mitch was impressed all over again by the technology the king had at his command. They were even better equipped than he'd thought.

"The message wrapped around the arrow," the king went on, "reads as follows. *By right of Rule, I, Gisli of House Scangarten, invoke challenge upon the tiger known as Mitch, for I know my brother is too cowardly to face me in single combat himself.*"

Candis placed her hand over her husband's, which had started to tremble with anger.

"It is not cowardice that keeps me from shedding his blood," the king growled. "And he knows it!"

"We all know it, majesty." Paul Miller stood, his voice filled with the conviction of his beliefs. "We, born of the Old Guard, know the truth of the matter and we support you to our dying breath."

Around the room, everyone added their agreement with Paul's bold words. Mitch realized these Guards—both the ones who had gone with the king into exile and their children—understood better than any others why Frederick had chosen the path they were all on together.

The king bowed his head for a short moment, visibly calming. "Thank you, my friends. You all know this has not been an easy existence for me, my family and all of you and your families. Yet we were not given much choice. The

Mother of All sets our path and we must follow it as best we can."

Paul sat down again at the king's gesture and the mood changed in the room once more. King Frederick seemed to firm his resolve as he brought up displays on one wall.

"Those of you born here or who left our chosen homeland when you were too small to really know it will need to look at these maps. The rest of us will have to study up on them as well. Things have changed since last we walked the ice fields of home."

"We're going back?" Mandy's mother asked, her tone hopeful.

"If the Mother of All wills it. But first, a small group will go. With Mitch."

All eyes turned to Mitch. He felt the weight of their regard and realized this was what every moment since he'd awakened from the poison had been leading toward.

"I'm going too," Gina piped up beside him.

He wanted to argue, but he knew they should not—could not—be parted. Not now. Their tigers demanded they stay close by each other. They were mates and they needed to face adversity together.

"Kitten—" her father began, shaking his head, but Gina took Mitch's arm and snuggled close to his side.

"Father, Mitch is my mate. I will not be parted from him."

Silence reigned for a long moment until finally her father relented. He moved forward and held out his hand to Mitch for a firm shake.

"I wish it could be easier for you both, but I can't say I didn't know this day was coming. I had hoped you could wait until after the challenge was settled, but I know you must follow your hearts and your natures. Congratulations and welcome to the family, Mitch."

Frederick gave Mitch a back-pounding half-hug and then kissed his daughter on her cheek and stepped back. If this had been a normal mating among normal tigers, the rest of the room would have jumped up to congratulate them. But this was not normal. Nothing about the circumstances, timing or situation was normal.

"Mitch Thorburn ne Gustavson." The king was once more in formal mode, calling Mitch by a combination of the surnames he was entitled to use. "Do you accept the challenge?"

Mitch understood the king's formality. He stepped forward and answered with due consideration.

"I accept the challenge," he said in a clear, firm voice. At that moment, he felt something lock into place. Some kind of magical knowing settled in place that would not be removed until the challenge was answered one way...or another.

Things moved fast from there. The moment Mitch accepted the challenge, wheels were put in motion. Simply uttering the words invoked the ancient magic of the challenge and the clock started ticking. They spent time debating details of the trip, but it was a foregone conclusion that Mitch and Gina were on their way to Iceland to face the music.

The whirlwind caught them in its heart and the exiled king's support staff went into action, arranging flights, ground transport, supplies, clothing and everything else they'd need for the journey.

Mitch and Gina did not return to the snug cabin in the woods. They'd packed their few belongings and brought them along, but one of the Millers would see to closing up the cabin for them. They had bigger fish to fry. Travel plans were being made and Mitch knew he was ready. Physically ready. He'd spent a week getting his body back up to speed. He was at peak performance now and ready to face the fight.

Mentally, he didn't think he'd ever be prepared to risk so much. He knew if he lost, Gina would be in terrible peril. Not only would she be in danger from her uncle's court, but Mitch knew—without false humility—that she'd be heartbroken. Just as he would be if anything happened to her.

They were mates now. A pair. Two hearts made whole. One. Together. If one of them fell, the other would be diminished in strength and cast into despair.

He'd talked to her about it. He knew there was every chance that the challenge could go against him. He was prepared to meet his fate, but not if it meant Gina would be in danger. It put added pressure on him to win, though he didn't really need any additional incentive. Everything was riding on his shoulders, and he knew it. Gina, her parents, all those Old Guard families...even the entirety of the *tigre d'or*.

The Clan had suffered under Gisli's rule. Mitch knew it from firsthand experience, though nobody dared speak against the acting ruler of all tigers. Even so, Mitch felt the weight of responsibility on his shoulders for not only his friends and their families, but for all tiger shifters everywhere.

Nobody commented when, after a full day of planning and checking security, Gina brought Mitch to her room. She'd be damned if she'd sleep apart from him now that she'd declared him as her mate in front of her parents and everybody.

It wasn't a traditional mating ceremony, but these weren't ordinary times. Things were haywire. If they ever settled down, Gina promised herself they'd throw the biggest party the tiger Clan had ever seen to celebrate their mating.

If. Her entire future was riding on that tiny word. If Mitch won the challenge. If her uncle was defeated and his supporters could be ousted. If her father reclaimed his rightful place. If they all lived through the coming trouble in one piece. If. If. If.

She didn't want to think about it. She wanted only to lie in Mitch's arms and not think about tomorrow.

She led him by the hand over to the small bed that had been hers throughout her teen years. It would be a tight fit, but she didn't care. She didn't need much room and she was more than happy to use him as a pillow all night. She didn't think he'd mind either. Not after she got through with what she planned to do to him.

No words were spoken as they stopped at the side of the bed. She tugged the hem of his shirt up over his washboard abs and urged him to slip it off over his head. When it was gone, she stroked her fingers downward from his shoulders, over his muscular torso and then sank to her knees in front of him. She searched for and found the string to his sweatpants with her teeth, earning a groan of appreciation from him that made her smile.

They'd played this game before and she already knew he was a big fan of her oral skills. Almost as big a fan as she was of his oral skills. And oddly enough, she enjoyed pleasing him this way. It gave her a little thrill to think she had so much power over his pleasure.

He was such an Alpha. All in charge—all the time. Only with her did he let go.

And she loved the way he purred for her. She knew how special that was. Only she could evoke that response in him—as he did in her. Purring in human form was something special, reserved only for mates. It was just one of the ways a cat shifter could recognize the one truly meant for him or her.

She tugged his pants down by the elastic waistband. He'd been wearing sweats most of the time since he'd been spending every free moment when he wasn't helping plan their trip working out with the guys down at the dojo. He'd been in amazing physical shape already, but now he was like a chiseled marble statue of a Greek god. His muscles were hard and supple, his body honed to a fine knife's edge.

He would need every advantage in the challenge to come, but she still appreciated the sheer animal beauty of him at this peak of physical perfection. Everything about him was constantly amazing to her and she thought she'd never get tired of him. Never get tired of talking to him—for she'd discovered he had a quick and agile mind and interests that marched with hers. Never get tired of laughing with him—for their senses of humor complimented and augmented each other's. Never get tired of being with him, or simply sitting with him watching the fire. Never get tired of loving him.

He was her perfect mate. And she intended to show him just how much she appreciated him as often as possible before…before the trouble that hounded them caught up.

Gina kissed her way down his abs, pausing to lick each hollow and nibble on the six pack that begged for her touch. She liked the way he grunted when she bit a little harder than he'd expected and then purred when she bathed the area with long sweeps of her tongue. His breathing hitched as she angled downward, pushing his pants away and freeing him to her further exploration.

She took him in her hands, fondling him in the way she knew he liked, teasing him with tiny forays of her tongue over the domed head of his hard cock. She looked up into his golden eyes, entranced by the way his pupils dilated as she touched him. The gold of his irises was a thin ring around the fathomless black pupils as she took him into her mouth. And then she had to look away, angling her head so she could take him deep.

Her fingers squeezed as her mouth enveloped what she could take of him. He was a big man and it took some maneuvering for her to make sure every inch of him was attended. She wanted to do the job right. To give him all she could—as he gave her. Pleasing him was her pleasure and she knew he felt the same way when it was his turn to see to her. They were compatible like that. Each tuned to the other's needs and desires.

She was just getting into a rhythm when Mitch pushed gently away from her, taking himself out of her reach. She was disappointed for only a moment before he lifted her to a standing position and proceeded to undress her with swift, urgent movements. Yeah, this is how she liked him, commanding and ready to take control. It was her turn to purr.

He drove her to distraction, kissing every inch of her skin he uncovered. She had to bite her tongue when he placed her on the bed, spread her legs wide and proceeded to kiss his way up one thigh and down the other, pausing for a long, blissful moment right in the middle. Mitch had a talented tongue and he certainly knew how to use it.

He blew her mind at least twice before finally joining their bodies and rocking her to the rhythm unique to them alone. He knew just how to touch her, just how to soothe her, just how to drive her wild with delight and passion. She tried her best to give as good as she got, but she was nearly incoherent with need by the time he finally drove them both to the point of no return.

She stifled her cries of delight as she came, not wanting to wake the household. More than just her parents were sleeping in the big house now that they'd moved into the active phase of preparing for the challenge. Every one of the Old Guard families had members taking turns on watch and using the guest rooms on this floor. If she screamed, some of them might just come running to see what was up—and probably tease her and Mitch to death because they'd damn well know what was going on in this room.

She wouldn't give them any reason to burst in on them, even if any teasing would all be meant in good-natured fun. She just wasn't ready to share the special thing that was their relationship with anyone yet. Not *that* graphically, at any rate. She especially didn't want any of those horny female tigers ogling her man's amazing body. He was for her alone—just as she was for him.

She tried not to think about how little time they might have together. Each day that passed brought them closer to the trip to Iceland that would decide their fate once and for all. She clung to him in the dark of the night, fearing the future but knowing it must come.

CHAPTER TEN

Only a few days later, they touched down in Iceland and had to pick up their pre-arranged transport to the secret tiger enclave. The stronghold was located near the famous Grímsvötn volcano in the highlands on the northwestern side of the Vatnajökull ice cap. There was a human geological research and monitoring station not too far away, but over the years, the *tigre blanche* had employed mages of various kinds to help hide their presence from the humans who closely watched the volcano.

Grímsvötn—which many tigers just called the Grim for short—was the most active of the nation's volcanoes, and because most of it lay below the ice cap, the subglacial eruptions could be both explosive and very, very dangerous. If the hot magma managed to melt too much water beneath the ice cap, it could release suddenly in an outburst called a *jökulhlaup*. The Icelandic word had even made its way into the English language to describe any large, abrupt release of water from a subglacial reservoir.

Mitch had studied up on the area as part of his reading over the past week. He found the combination of fire and ice in this harsh environment a thing of beauty, and now that he was here, he thought he understood why some long-ago tiger king had moved his seat of power to this stark landscape.

When the *tigre blanche* had first claimed part of this land for themselves, there hadn't been many humans here and their technology had been primitive. Now though, humans had the ability and need to monitor the volcano and glacier that had become the tigers' refuge with all kinds of scientific devices.

The tigers had countered technology with magic, paying human mages to make their hidden enclave as protected as possible from electronic observation. In fact, there was even some kind of repulsion charm on the area right around the tiger stronghold that made most humans want to avoid it altogether. Only a few had been foolish enough to ignore their inner fears over the years, and they had been dealt with by the ever-present Guard that either redirected them in subtle ways or confronted them and ran them off.

Mitch drove one of the rented vehicles as they left Reykjavík and took the Ring Road, known in Iceland as the Hringvegur, which made a complete circuit around the edge of the island nation. It took them within hiking distance of the stronghold. They'd leave their vehicles in the village where most of the the tiger Clan living in Iceland had gathered. The village paid the government handsomely for certain priveleges of autonomy and silence. Most of the Guard families lived there and helped keep the route to the stronghold both secret and safe even while off-duty.

As their small party parked their rented vehicles, Mitch could feel the tingling sensation of eyes on them. They were being observed. He was surrounded by the group that had set out from the United States with him. Each member of the team had been chosen for their skill and dedication. Paul Miller led the group, organizing the rest.

They had no sooner stepped out of their vehicles than they were surrounded by a contingent of Icelandic tigers. Mitch knew their scent, if not their loyalties.

"This is private property," one of them called out as he stood forward.

He was young—maybe in his early twenties—and seemed to be the eldest of the group that surrounded them. Mitch was surprised. Was the whole town guarded only by children and youths? If so, what had happened here?

Mitch moved to meet the young tiger despite Paul's hiss of warning. Now was not the time to show any weakness or fear.

"We have safe passage," Mitch declared as he faced the younger man, only ten paces or so between them now. "I'm Mitch Gustavson and I come to answer the challenge offered by Gisli."

"King Gisli," the young man repeated, but with no heat, merely in a corrective tone.

"He is no king." Gina burst forward to stand beside Mitch. He knew she was angry but he wasn't sure if this was the best time for it. What could a bunch of kids do anyway? "He is merely the steward," she added.

"And who are you to question our leader?" the younger man asked in a curious tone.

"I am Gleda, daughter of Fridrik and Snaedis of the *tigre blanche*." Mitch had never been prouder of her regal bearing. Then she smiled and softened her tone, and there was the woman he loved. "But my friends call me Gina."

The reaction of the youths was immediate. They all sank to one knee in respect while Mitch eyed each one for any sign of subterfuge. But this looked genuine. They all seemed humbled by the presence of the tiger princess.

And then an old woman stepped forward from the outer edges of the ring of youths. He hadn't seen her approach and she had the tingle of magic around her. Her face was lined and her eyes were somewhat clouded with age. Her scent was that of a tiger shifter and she was the oldest-looking tiger Mitch had ever seen.

"Praise the Mother of All for your return, Princess Gleda. I am Hilda Berenson, priestess of this village and your great grandmother, Mitchell Gustavson." Her aged eyes twinkled at him and he realized there were tears sparkling on her pale lashes. He'd made the old lady cry, and that didn't sit well with him. Mitch shifted on his feet in discomfort. "I wish we had time to talk, but haste is your friend at this crucial juncture," she went on, surprising him with her knowledge. "Gisli prepares even now. His spies at the airport in Reykjavík have no doubt alerted him to your arrival. You must prepare yourself and meet him at the challenge grounds just outside the stronghold. Gunnar will show you the way." She touched the young man's shoulder, though he remained down on one knee.

"Where are all the older folk, madam," Gina asked in a respectful tone, asking the question that had been bothering Mitch since the beginning of this confrontation.

"Serving up at the stronghold, taken prisoner, dead or run off," Hilda replied with acidic candor. "Times have not been good here since your father's departure, princess. And after the financial crash of 2008, it's been worse. Gisli is a fool in many ways, but especially with money."

"Amma," the young man named Gunnar reproved his elder gently. "Be careful what you say." Mitch knew the Icelandic word for grandmother was amma. Whether Gunnar was related or not remained to be seen. It could be the old woman was called amma by the entire village due to her advanced age.

She laughed in reply. "The time has come, lad. Do you not see your salvation when it is standing before you? The real royals have returned. The Goddess blesses their path. They have only to prove themselves worthy and nimble, and our people may yet recover from this terrible time."

"It's not over yet, Amma. Be more cautious in your speech, please." Gunnar looked pained by the old woman's candor and Mitch saw the value in playing it safe. What if he didn't win the challenge? What if Gisli exacted revenge for her words here today? How many would suffer or die if Mitch didn't win?

He stepped forward and touched the old lady's shoulder with one hand. "If you really are my great grandmother—and I believe you are—then please heed Gunnar's caution. I don't want anything to happen to you if I fail."

She covered his hand with hers, lined with age but still strong. Her watery eyes met his and he could actually feel the strength radiating from her toward him.

"You must prevail, Mitchell. The Clan needs its rightful leadership. We've been too long without it and have paid the Lady's price for our hubris. We have suffered for a generation. The Clan is nearly bankrupt and cannot sustain its people. These youngsters here have never known the rule of a true king. You must return honor to our people. It is your sacred duty."

"I know, Amma, I know." Mitch bowed his head, receiving her words like a benediction. He felt the Goddess's power in the old woman's touch. "I'll do my best."

The wrinkled hand moved to his cheek and she smiled at him. "Your best is all we ask, grandson. I see my Maria and her mother, Marli, in you. You have Maria's smile."

Mitch was touched by her words. This old woman had known his birth mother and his grandmother. She was related to him by blood. Mitch had never had a blood relation before. He wanted to talk more with his great grandmother, but there was no time. Not now. Maybe not ever if he didn't win the day.

He couldn't answer her. He was too choked up. But he squeezed her hand gently and returned her smile. He hoped she understood how precious this moment was to him. If he had anything to say about it, he would return and talk with her at length once this was all over.

She stepped back and touched the young man's shoulder again. "Gunnar, this is your cousin Mitchell. You must take him to the challenge field near the stronghold. Be careful and watch for magical attacks." She turned toward Mitch to offer one last word of warning. "Gisli has a mage. A perverse and powerful creature. Gunnar has enough of my gift to detect magical attacks before they happen. Heed him and take cover if Gisli's pet mage comes into play. Gunnar can help you there—and perhaps you inherited some of my abilities as well—but you cannot count on it, I fear. Your best bet is to take Gisli out as quickly as possible, and don't give his mage any opportunity to snare you. Many men have died by that mage's hand. I would not see you join their number."

With that, she turned and left abruptly, and the rest of the youths went with her. Only Gunnar remained and he tilted his head, looking at Mitch with a twinkle in his eye that was much like the old woman's.

"So you're my cousin, eh?" Gunnar said.

Mitch didn't know what to make of him. He was younger by a few years, but he was definitely no child. He was Mitch's height, though he wasn't quite as broad in the shoulder. He still looked like he could handle himself and knew how to use those big fists of his. Mitch liked the look of him—and he did have enough of a resemblance that Mitch could believe he was related by blood. Now he had two blood relatives where only this morning he'd been an orphan with no family to claim him. This day was full of surprises.

"I guess so," Mitch replied, offering a hand to shake. "Call me Mitch."

Gunnar shook his hand and yep, there was the show of strength Mitch expected as the younger man tried to crush his hand. But Mitch was made of stronger stuff than that, and returned the grip—with interest. Gunnar grinned as they let go and shook out his fingers.

"Nice one, Mitch." He grinned and Mitch realized with a start that the kid had been testing him.

Guards often used little shows of strength to test each other. It was mostly harmless, and it helped establish hierarchy among so many Alphas. They couldn't all be top cat. And they couldn't waste time constantly fighting each other in dominance challenges. So they used little things to determine the pecking order among them. Gunnar had just proven that Mitch was stronger and therefore slightly more dominant. Gunnar would follow Mitch's lead. Excellent.

"I'm Gina." She stepped forward and took Gunnar's hand. Mitch watched closely. He didn't want the guy squeezing Gina's fragile fingers that way, but Gunnar surprised them both by raising her hand to his lips and offering a kiss instead. Gunnar's golden eyes danced with mischief and Mitch wanted to laugh at his antics. The kid was a jokester. Mitch liked him already.

Gunnar released her hand and bowed to her. "My princess," he intoned. "It is good to see you here in Iceland, where you belong."

Gina smiled back at Gunnar and then introduced him to the rest of the group. Paul seemed to come out on top from their handshake, but Gunnar surprised Mitch by proving slightly more dominant than the rest of his team. He was younger than all of them but already stronger. He'd make a damn fine Alpha one day…soon. If Mitch judged right, Gunnar wasn't far from reaching his full potential.

"Shall we set off?" Gunnar asked Mitch and Gina when he'd made the rounds. "Gisli is aware of your presence in the country. My father still serves as a Royal Guard, as do many others, who act as our eyes and ears in the court. Gisli hasn't let anyone come home for any length of time lately, wanting all his protectors around him, but the few who've come down from the stronghold for quick visits have kept the village informed."

"The sooner we get there, the sooner this ends," Mitch said in a grim tone. He wasn't looking forward to the battle, but he didn't want to live with this uncertainty any longer. He wanted it decided—one way or another.

Gina took his hand as they set off together, following where Gunnar led. Mitch had made a study of the terrain and knew the younger man was leading them in the right direction. Gunnar hadn't yet earned his trust—not the way the Millers and the other Old Guard families had—but Mitch would follow where the younger man led. For now.

One thing he wouldn't do was trust blindly. Treachery came in many forms, he well knew. Even when everything looked on the up-and-up on the surface, sometimes things weren't so clear cut. He'd follow Gunnar's lead, but only up to a point. Mitch had enough intel on the area from Gina's dad to know if the younger man was leading them astray.

They spoke in soft tones as they hiked. Their pace was fast but not tiring. They'd reach the challenge field before dark, Gunnar promised. Mitch walked beside Gina with Gunnar on his other side.

"You can sense magic?" Gina asked, clearly curious about Hilda's claims.

Gunnar shrugged. "A bit. Enough to know when it's building, and usually in enough time to take cover."

"I understand the need to hide the stronghold, but I can't say I'm comfortable with the casual use Gisli seems to have made of human mages in his court. In America, shifters and mages don't usually mix so freely," Mitch observed.

"Amma Hilda was born of a union of human mage and tiger sifter," Gunnar explained, surprising Mitch. "She inherited most of both her parents' skills. She also passed on a lot of her magic to subsequent generations. Your mother, for example, had weather sense and could always tell when a storm or volcanic eruption was coming. She was in tune with the earth in ways few of us are."

"How are you related to me exactly?" Mitch asked, curious.

"My mother and your mother were sisters. As it happened, they married brothers, so we have the same last name, but we're actually first cousins."

"Do your parents still live?" Mitch asked, feeling a pang for his own lost parents.

"They do. They are both up at the stronghold at the moment. Neither has been granted leave by Gisli to come down to the village in weeks."

"Who trains the younger generation, if all the Guards are constantly kept up at the stronghold?" Gina wanted to know.

Gunnar shrugged. "There are a few old timers who try, but it's not easy. Those of us who haven't been given spots in the Guard yet have had to take what we know and do our best to teach the cubs. I'm afraid our skills probably aren't up to the standard of the previous generation."

Was Gunnar lying? Trying to fool Mitch into a false sense of security? He thought not. Gunnar seemed to be on the level, but Mitch would remain cautious.

"That's irresponsible and short-sighted at best," Gina exclaimed. "My father would not have let this happen."

"Your father wasn't here." The tone was not accusatory, but Mitch felt Gina's instinctive recoil. He wished he could reprimand Gunnar, but he'd spoken only the truth. And sometimes, the truth was painful.

"You're right, Gunnar," Gina said after a long moment. "And I won't make any excuses. Father had his reasons."

"We know, princess. I didn't mean to condemn with my words. Amma Hilda has explained it to us many times, but it is still hard to live with. My apologies."

"Never apologize for speaking the truth," Gina countered, surprising Mitch—and Gunnar, if his expression was anything to go by.

"What did Hilda say about the king's exile?" Mitch was curious.

"That it was the will of the Lady and that we were not permitted to know Her reasons for every action. That we had to trust in the Mother of All to forgive us and return order to our kingdom."

"Forgive you for what?" Gina asked.

Gunnar frowned. "It is not for me to speak of, even if I did know all the details. I can only say that a misuse of magic brought all this about. At least, that's what Amma Hilda says."

Mitch would have probed more, but they'd arrived. In the distance, he could see a sheer ice wall that he knew from the king's descriptions was no ordinary ice wall. A hidden fissure lead to the tiger stronghold encased within the glacier. The ice palace. Hereditary seat of *tigre blanche* power.

As they drew closer, Mitch saw figures emerge from the fissure. Not stealthy. A mistake in Mitch's opinion. What if they'd been a party of human climbers? It was stupid to be so cavalier about what was supposed to be the *secret* entrance to a hidden stronghold. Mitch shook his head and kept walking.

The welcoming party was waiting.

"Gunnar Gustavson," a mountain of a man who had to be Gisli intoned. "Who have you brought to my doorstep?"

"Only those granted passage by the right of challenge, sire," Gunnar replied with seeming obedience. Mitch didn't blame him. It was best to play along with Gisli for now. If Mitch lost, Gunnar would have no chance against a tiger his size.

Gisli was a giant. Built on the scale of Gina's father but a lot younger, he was a tiger warrior in his prime. It was clear he kept in shape. He hadn't let soft living here at the stronghold weaken him. He looked like the kind of tiger that still got his claws bloody on a regular basis.

Mitch would have his work cut out for him. But he'd known that already. This had never been advertised as an easy task.

"I see no challenge here. Only cubs out for a walk." Gisli spat into the snow at his feet. "Run back home to your mothers, children, and leave the work of governing to the adults."

Mitch knew the usurper was trying to rile him. He did his best not to let idle words ruffle his fur. Instead, he very deliberately stripped off his pack and reached inside for the arrow they'd brought with them all the way from the States. It was the same arrow that had been shot at them, holding the challenge message.

Mitch lifted it in his hands and then threw it with dead-on accuracy to embed it in the snow an inch from Gisli's foot. To his credit, the usurper didn't even flinch. He didn't waiver. Didn't move back or give even a millimeter of ground. He simply stared at the arrow for a long moment and then looked back up at Mitch, a sneer on his face.

"So you're the puppy that comes to fight me in my brother's stead? I could have hoped you'd be a little bigger. As it is, I predict this fight will be a quick one."

Gisli threw off his fur robe, showing he wore only heavy cotton white gi pants beneath with some kind of light-colored footwear that appeared to grip the ice well. Had he come straight from training? He didn't look tired. In fact, he looked fresh as a daisy. Maybe he'd just been waiting around in his fighting gear, ready for the challenge. He'd definitely known they were coming.

Mitch didn't waste any time. He shrugged out of his coat and removed his shirt. He was wearing light-gray sweat pants and boots. He wasn't cold. In fact, the extreme atmosphere invigorated him. And his boots and pants wouldn't inhibit him if they shifted later in the fight. The boots would simply slip off his paws, and the pants would either tear or slide away when he shifted. Either way, he'd be unencumbered in his tiger form.

If this fight lasted any length of time at all, they'd end up in their fur, fighting beast to beast. May the best cat win.

Paul Miller was at Gina's side. Gunnar was next to her, slightly in front as if in a protective stance. She wasn't certain where Gunnar's loyalties lay just yet, but it certainly looked like he was trying to shield her.

Mitch had discarded most of his clothing and his knapsack on the ground. She scrambled to pick it up and hugged it to her chest. She wouldn't distract him now, no matter how much she wanted a final kiss. They'd said everything they needed to say already. She wouldn't dare break his concentration now that it was time to face the devil in his lair.

She sent a silent prayer upward to the Lady for Mitch's safety.

"We should withdraw to a safe distance," Paul said in a low voice near her ear.

"If he doesn't win, no place will be safe," she countered so that only Paul could hear. He met her gaze and nodded once, acknowledging her words, but continued to insist they move back, away from the fighting.

Gina complied, not wanting to get in the way. She would

give Gisli a wide berth and not be foolish enough to let him use her presence to his advantage. The last thing she needed was to be grabbed by him or one of his henchmen—or a group of them—and threatened to make Mitch concede.

She kept her group of loyal Old Guards around her. Truth be told, she wouldn't have been able to get away from them if she tried. They were stuck to her like glue for the duration and she was glad of it. She knew for certain that she wasn't going to be in any shape to watch out for herself until Mitch was in the clear. Worry for him distracted her too greatly.

She watched as Gisli and Mitch circled, sizing each other up. The challenge started slowly, cautiously. Each man testing the other, feinting to test reach and reflexes. She knew for a fact that Mitch was holding back. He wasn't showing all his cards in these opening rounds, and if her uncle had any sense, neither was he. Which made this confounded situation all the more dangerous and tense.

"I didn't know you were a Gustovson," Gisli said loud enough for Gina to hear from many yards away. Was he going to taunt Mitch now? She hoped Mitch wouldn't rise to the bait.

She was glad when Mitch didn't answer Gisli's question, but her uncle wasn't dissuaded. He kept talking and she heard every word of it.

"If I'd known you were going to grow up to cause me bother, I would've killed you along with your parents. They were always troublemakers. I've killed a lot of Gustavsons in my time, starting with your sire. Did you know he squealed like a stuck pig when I tore him open with my claws? I can still hear it," Gisli taunted, laughing.

But his words were taking on the mindlessness of a rant, in Gina's opinion. Was he not sane? Her mouth went dry at the thought that Mitch was facing a crazy man. Who knew what he would do when pushed? He'd been unpredictable before, but adding a little insanity into the mix made it all that much worse.

Mitch seemed to keep his cool even through the taunting,

but a moment later, Gisli launched himself at Mitch for real. Maybe he thought he'd weakened Mitch in some way with his words, but the furious attack was rebuffed at every turn. Gina clutched Mitch's jacket to her chest, digging her fingers into the fabric with each block, each parry, each tumbling leap out of the way.

It was clear to her now that Mitch was the more nimble of the two men, even though they were closely matched in size. Mitch was big, but he was light on his feet in a way Gisli wasn't anymore—if he'd ever been. Would it be enough to tip the scales in Mitch's favor? She prayed as hard as she could that it would.

And then Gisli landed a crushing blow to Mitch's right side, right near his kidney. It was very possible he'd broken ribs.

And the mountain in the distance shook.

CHAPTER ELEVEN

Mitch felt the pain in his side, even as the volcano stirred to life. A split second later, he felt the lava flowing—in his veins and under his feet. Somehow...he was connected to the mountain. He felt its anger and its pain reflected the pain in his own body. And somehow...it gave him power.

Broken ribs knit as lava flowed around them, setting them as hard as the Grim's basaltic magma when it hit the tempering air. He was invigorated by the fiery mountain. Enthralled by its pulsating magic that beat within his own heart. He was aware of it as he had never been aware of anything before. Almost as if it spoke to him in its deep, rumbling voice of fire.

Mitch shook his head and got back into the fight. Gisli had been thrown off for the moment but he was regrouping, ready for the next round. Mitch was ready too. His injuries had been healed in the mountain's fire, strengthened by the Grim's rocky heart and the magma powered his body as it flowed like fire through his veins. In that moment, he *was* the mountain.

And the mountain didn't like Gisli one bit.

"Bright Lady." Gina heard Gunnar whisper from in front of her. "I have never seen anything like this."

"What do you see?" she demanded.

Gunnar turned his shocked face to her. "He is one with Grímsvötn. The heart of the volcano works through him." And then Gunnar seemed to realize something. A smile spread over his handsome face. "Gisli doesn't stand a chance."

Gina watched Mitch with careful attention, wondering at Gunnar's words. If Amma Hilda was to be believed, Gunnar could sense magic. And if what he said was true...

Gina gasped as Mitch seemed to gain speed. His motions blurred as he and Gisli struggled against one another, acrobatic moves occurring at lightning speed as true lightning lit the dark sky behind them—the volcanic ash of the mountain's eruption attracting the charged electricity in the air.

Full night had fallen, and the flash and bang of the lightning and thunder was almost blinding as it hit so nearby. The two men joined in mortal combat didn't seem to notice that the fury of the storm and the anger of the mountain reflected their own conflict.

But Gina saw. And she started to realize the truth behind what Gunnar had said. The mountain responded to Mitch's actions. It growled and spat molten rock when he got hit. It brought lightning bolts to earth, almost in triumph, when Mitch scored a hit on Gisli.

She realized then that the mountain was truly on Mitch's side.

Sweet Mother of All. The implications were staggering.

Mitch began to dominate the fight. In his human form, he was unstoppable, clearly more than a match for Gisli. When her uncle realized it, he shifted to his tiger form.

Mitch shifted a moment behind him, and where Gisli's magic had shown dull and sickly against the snow and dark night sky, Mitch's magical transformation shone like sparkling ice crystals, glistening in the air. His fur was sparkling as well, where Gisli's was a dull off-white. Seeing the two white tigers side-by side, it was strikingly clear who was more powerful.

Gisli was huge and had artificially sharpened claws. Mitch was the natural. The way things ought to be. His claws were sharpened by nature and his dark-black stripes stood out in vibrant contrast against the glistening white of his fur. He was truly magnificent.

The two giant cats began to circle, lashing out with claws as they came together, tails tangling in an effort to trip each other up. In this form, they were more evenly matched—at least at first.

Gisli seemed to tire faster than Mitch. In fact, Mitch seemed to lose nothing despite the length of the battle. It was as if he was being powered from somewhere outside his own being. Before long, the black and white mixed with the red of blood as each scored hits—some deeper than others—on one another. The black of the volcanic mountain behind them. The white of the ice cap beneath them and the red of the magma that lay just below the surface. All were represented as the fight dragged on and on.

"I've never seen him this strong," she whispered to Paul at her side, but apparently Gunnar heard her comment as well.

He turned briefly to look back at her. "Grímsvötn is feeding him energy. The mountain favors him. It heals him as he fights. He is unstoppable as long as the Grim gives him its power."

The mountain rumbled in the distance and an eerie ice fog began to steam down the slope, heading toward them. Gina watched the battle carefully, keeping one eye on the creeping fog. It seemed almost...alive?

"The mage gathers himself," Gunnar warned in a tense voice. "Be ready."

Ready to do what, she wondered? Gina didn't know what good her martial arts training would be against a magical attack, but maybe her gymnastics might come in handy. If the mage started sending something she could see toward her, she might be quick enough to spring out of the way.

Lowering Mitch's jacket and backpack to the snow in front of her, she quickly shrugged out of her coat. She wanted to be ready and able to move without the somewhat binding coat encumbering her. Out of the corner of her eye, she saw her friends do the same. They knew what to do without being told. Every one of them had trained for all contingencies, though none of this group had ever come up against a mage before.

But they weren't the first choice of target. Gina actually saw the fireball streaking for Mitch's back as Gisli stepped away. The bastard had positioned Mitch just so, but something made Mitch turn a moment before the fireball was set to envelop him. Gina held her breath as the fireball streaked closer. Mitch put out one hand as if to ward it off and then something amazing happened.

The magical fire seemed to hesitate and then stop as if blocked. It went around Mitch as it dissipated against what looked like a shield of some sort that rerouted the magical energy into the earth, away from him.

Gina was shocked and thankful that Mitch had somehow developed magical shields. That wasn't anything he'd ever talked about before. She didn't think he'd ever *had* them before.

"Was that Mitch or the mountain?" she whispered.

Gunnar smiled at her. "There is no difference at this point. They are one and the same right now."

"So I'm not imagining things. You see it too?" She had to get confirmation of her incredible suppositions.

"Oh, yes, milady. My cousin is everything the Goddess promised us and more." Gunnar's expression changed from joy to concern in a flash. "Prepare yourself. The mage gathers energy once more. He may aim for us now that his way to your mate is blocked. He will seek to distract so Gisli can get an opening."

"He won't get it from me," Gina vowed, nodding to Paul and the others. They were all braced, ready to move at a moment's notice.

And then the fireballs were raining down on them and they were springing away in all directions. Gina checked on her people and everybody was safe—for now. But the mage was using a slightly different tactic. Where he'd shot one giant fireball at Mitch, he was sending multiple little ones at their group. And they kept coming. As soon as one volley ended, another began and everyone was kept moving in order to avoid them.

Inevitably, someone got hit. A cry of pain came from the edge of her little scattered group. Adele Miller was being supported by her brother Harold for the moment. He was helping her avoid the small fireballs for now, but they were much less mobile with her injury and the two of them together made a bigger target. Something had to change soon.

She looked across the battlefield and saw Mitch looking at her. She nodded to him, telling him without words that he should concentrate on his opponent and not fall for this distraction. They would deal with this. Somehow.

And then Mitch looked up at the mountain and it rumbled as if in response. Hot rocks spewed from the crater with such energy they made it all the way down the slope to where the small group of shifters stood. But the molten chunks didn't fall anywhere near Gina. No, they rained down on the watchers on the other side of the challenge field. They all dove for cover as the mage's concentration was broken.

And then the ice fog that had been making its way down the slope arrived. It was thicker than any mist Gina had seen before and it moved as if it was…alive. It enveloped the field of battle, shrouding the two tigers in mist as they battled. The magic of the ice fog sparked off Mitch's fur as it rolled over the combatants locked in flashes of teeth and claws and blood.

The fog continued spreading, moving toward the onlookers. It enveloped Gina and her entourage in a gentle wave of fog that gave them some cover. But when it hit the other side of the field, a scream went up from the mage, drawing Gina's gaze as he was physically imprisoned by tendrils of dense fog. It dragged him downward as she watched, swallowing him whole.

And then he simply disappeared. The fog had taken him and Gina didn't even *want* to speculate on where or how. What mattered most was that he was gone. Out of the action. Unable to lob any more fireballs at her and her people.

To them, the fog was a benevolent shield of sorts. To the human mage who'd dared interfere with a sacred challenge, it had been a deadly form of justice.

There were ancient rules about challenges. No outside interference was allowed. Targeting others to distract the two champions was not allowed. Gisli's pet mage hadn't played by the rules, and somehow the ice fog had come to set that right.

"There's powerful magic in the fog," Gunnar said as he returned to his position in front of her. Now that the fireballs had stopped, her people were regrouping around her.

"It healed me," Adele whispered loud enough for Gina to hear. "When the fog touched my wound, I could feel fire and ice, and then the pain was gone and the wound with it."

Gunnar merely nodded as if he'd expected no less and returned his attention to the combat that was ongoing in the center of the field of challenge. The two tigers were upright on their hind legs, locked in an epic struggle.

And then Gisli roared in pain as Mitch scored a solid hit. Blood gushed from deep gouges on Gisli's flank. The two tigers broke apart and went down on all fours, hidden mostly from view in the fog. It parted as Mitch made his next move. He crashed down on Gisli with all his power and Gina heard the snap of bones as Gisli cried out.

The fog dissipated and the two tigers remained. Gisli was on the ground broken beyond repair, while Mitch stood above him, prowling back and forth, his tail twitching with agitation. The most confusing part of all was that Gisli…had turned orange.

His dull fur was no longer the sickly off-white. He was no longer *blanche*. And as he breathed his last, it was clear that any magic he'd had once upon a time had left him for good.

Mitch shifted back to his human form and walked toward Gina. He scooped up his sweatpants and boots along the way, stepping into his pants as he went. He climbed the little rise in the ice on which Gina and her small group of Guards had watched the battle.

When he reached her, he simply opened his arms and she stepped into his embrace. They were both shaking with emotion, clinging to each other while the rest of the onlookers remained speechless.

Before long, Gisli's supporters began to wake up and try to make a run for it, but the mountain wasn't done with them yet. Without warning, a huge flood of water swept down the slope at an incredible pace. The source of the water was a new fissure that had opened up just below the peak of the mountain, lined up perfectly with the battlefield.

It all happened so fast, there was no time for anyone to get out of the way. Gisli's body was swept away first, followed by the tight knot of his supporters. Within moments, they were gone from sight, lost to the torrent.

Oddly—or perhaps magically—the water just missed the small hill on which Gina and Mitch clung to each other, surrounded by their friends. Only a thin line of Royal Guards who had stood behind Gisli at the perimeter of the cliff had escaped the flood on that side of the field.

"What the hell was that?" Gina asked after the main force of the water died down.

"Jökulhlaup," Gunnar answered from a few feet away. "When the volcano erupts, the heat melts a huge amount of snow and ice under the ice cap. It builds up in the caldera and can release all at once, sweeping away everything in its path. It wiped out a big section of the Ring Road last time it let loose." Gunnar looked into the darkness, his gaze following the path of the water. "It is doubtful their bodies will ever be found."

"I hope no innocents were caught up in that," Gina whispered.

"Have no fear, princess," Gunnar went on. "Only Gisli's staunchest supporters were in that group. He kept his sycophants close to him at all times. The Clan is better off without them. They were as poisonous as he was."

As they talked, the row of Royal Guards came closer. The waters were finished gushing and had gone as quickly as they had come.

"What happens now?" Gina asked Mitch, still held close in his arms. He was bloody, but she didn't care. He was alive and that's all that mattered.

"I'm not sure. I hadn't really thought beyond the challenge," he admitted, moving slightly away to smile down at her.

"You did it. Praise the Lady. You did it!"

He looked around, moving a little farther back from her. "Yeah, I guess so. Hot damn."

The Guards neared, and one by one, they slid to one knee as they formed a semi-circle around Gina and Mitch. Gunnar joined them. Only the Old Guard friends they'd brought with them from the States kept their feet, watching intently, ever vigilant.

"Gunnar..." Gina stepped away from Mitch so that they stood side-by-side. "What's going on?"

The younger man rose and bowed toward both her and Mitch. Then he winked and turned to address the people who were kneeling all around.

"Royal Guard!" he called out in a ringing tone that carried to all present. "The winner of the challenge is Mitchell Gustavson. He is one of us. A Royal Guard born and bred." Those kneeling cheered. Mitch stood his ground though Gina knew he was uncomfortable with all the attention focused on him. Then Gunnar held up a hand, signaling for silence. "By right of combat, he is our new king."

Gina felt Mitch tense at her side. The others seemed skeptical as well, even though Gunnar's tone had held no doubt whatsoever. One of the Guard stood and faced Mitch.

"Gustavsons are always *d'or*. Were you born *blanche*?"

It was an older woman who asked the question. She had battle scars and looked as if she had served many years as a Royal Guard. Her tone was curious, not accusing, so Gina took her question as a good sign. These people wanted to know more about Mitch before they made any decisions. After living under Gisli's rule for so long, she didn't blame them one bit.

"I've always been golden," Mitch admitted, clearly uncomfortable. "Until a couple of weeks ago. I was poisoned in battle and nearly died protecting another monarch, as was my duty. Princess Gina saved me and the first time I shifted fully, I…changed."

"Goddess touched," the same woman breathed and then sank back to one knee. "I will accept you as my king," she went on in a firmer voice.

"Now wait a minute." Mitch held up one hand, palm outward, already backpedaling.

Gina had a feeling he meant to renounce the throne, but she didn't want him to be hasty. Her father wasn't here, and if given a chance, she doubted her dad would want to come back and rule. He'd given up on being king of the Clan a long time ago, and she thought she knew him well enough to be able to say that he'd made peace with his decision. He wasn't power hungry. He didn't really want the throne. He just wanted peace and prosperity for the Clan and safety for his family.

Mitch had accomplished the latter by defeating Gisli in battle. The terror her uncle had imposed on her family for so many years was finally at an end. But what would happen next was unclear.

She put one hand on Mitch's arm to halt his words. "Emotions are high," she said in a strong voice that she knew would carry to the assembled Guards. "Let's take stock of where we all stand before any more decisions are made. We first must deal with Gisli's defeat and the impact on the Clan. Everything else can be decided later." She looked at the kneeling Guards. "For one thing, I understand that none of you have been given leave to be with your families in the village for weeks." Many of the Guards couldn't hide their hopeful expressions as they met her gaze. "Any of you who want to go home, should. Come back when you can. We will be sorting out the mess my uncle left behind. Anyone who can assist in that task is welcome. The Clan comes first."

Gunnar rose, smiling brightly. "Spoken like a true queen," he complimented her as the other Royal Guards stood as well.

About half of them didn't wait another minute before shifting shape and running for the village. Their families were waiting, she was sure. And word would spread from them as to Gisli's fate.

"Should we go see what's become of the stronghold since your father's time?"

CHAPTER TWELVE

Surrounded by the core group of friends who had come with them from America and the rest of Gisli's Guard, they entered the stronghold. Gina held her breath. She had been born here, but she wasn't sure how the memories of her childhood would measure up to the reality.

She shouldn't have worried. It was even more majestic than she remembered. The fissure in the ice wall created a narrow passage that went up for hundreds of feet until it met in the solid block of glacial ice far over their heads. They moved down the small corridor, heading toward the series of chambers that led eventually to the heart of the stronghold, deep inside the mountain.

Ice and sleek black volcanic rock blended to create something utterly unique in the world. As they moved deeper inside, the floors under their feet went from ice to basaltic rock that had flowed as if directed by the hand of the Goddess into perfectly flat, level sheets. The deeper they went, the more rock formed the walls of the chambers in fluted spires that joined seamlessly with the ice that soared high above their heads. Circuitous, winding shafts here and there allowed for air exchange, while the purity of the water let light to filter through the translucent ice and reflective snow to illuminate the halls deep beneath the surface.

In the great audience chamber—the largest room of the stronghold—the soaring arched walls were made of deceptively strong, delicate-looking columns of stone that had flowed into precise geometric shapes to mesh with the thick glacier in an arrangement that was nothing less than magical. Black and white, the room was a study in extremes and contrasts, yet somehow it formed a thing of intense beauty.

"This place is amazing," Mitch whispered as he stopped short just below the dais where two thrones of obsidian and ice rose from the floor created of the same shiny black, volcanic glass.

The steps up to the thrones weren't carved. They looked as if they had been created when some giant builder had poured sparkling obsidian in oval waves from above, each puddling an exact step higher than the last layer, decreasing in diameter as they rose to the final platform that was crowned by the two thrones made from spindly stalagmites of obsidian topped with even thinner spires of ice. Black and white. Like a Goddess-blessed white tiger's fur.

"It's just like I remember it," Gina agreed, looking around in wonder. "I wasn't sure. I was very small when we left. I thought maybe I'd over-romanticized the place, but this is even more than I remember."

Mitch reached out and took her hand. She could almost feel the power of the Grim running through him. His golden eyes had glowed with the magic of the mountain and though he was still bloodstained, he wasn't hurt. The Lady and Her sacred mountain had healed him even as it gave him strength. He was the most amazing man. If she didn't already know him and love him, she thought she might be really intimidated.

Mitch turned around and stopped short. Gina followed, realizing quickly that they had gathered quite an entourage during their journey in from the cliff face. Their friends created a buffer of sorts between them and what looked like the entire population of the stronghold. Everybody, it seemed, had turned out to see what Mitch would do next.

"I think you'd better say something to them," Gina whispered for Mitch's ears alone. "Some of them looked worried."

He tightened his hand on hers fractionally. "Some of them probably should be," he mused low enough so that only she could hear. "But you're right, my love." He lifted their joined hands to his lips and kissed her knuckles before lowering their hands again. He didn't let her go and she was glad. She needed the reassurance of his touch after everything that had just happened.

"For those of you who haven't heard yet, my name is Mitch." He raised his voice and it carried beautifully in the cavernous room. This near the dais, it was pretty clear that the acoustics of the room had been finely tuned by nature—or rather, by *Mother* Nature. "Much has happened here today and much will take place over the next few days as we take stock of the mess left behind by the former steward. Right now, I want everyone to cease all business operations until each section has been reviewed. We'll start with the most mission-critical areas tomorrow morning at five a.m. local time. In the meantime, I want each section head to lock their offices and allow no entry until someone from my staff comes to check things over tomorrow. Any non-compliance will earn detention and questioning, in that order. Understood?"

"You're really sexy when you get all businessy," Gina whispered, bringing a small grin to Mitch's mouth as he turned his head to look at her.

"Are you trying to make me crazy?" he answered back in the same low tone that kept the byplay between the two of them.

"Is it working?"

"They're wondering who you are. Shall we inform them officially?" he asked, changing the subject without answering. She gave him a small nod, taking a deep breath for courage.

She hadn't lived as a public figure since her early childhood, and back then she hadn't even realized it. This was a whole different ball game. Her entire life to this point had been about staying hidden. Putting herself and her true identity on display for all to see went against the grain. But she knew she had to step up and stand by Mitch. He'd done it. He'd put himself out there. Now she had to do the same.

"The honor guard we brought with us from the States is made up of children of those loyal Royal Guards who went into exile with my lady's father, King Frederick. They have my trust and you can regard them as acting for me. I don't know you yet and you certainly don't know me, but you should remember the rightful king and his family. This is Princess Gleda, my mate. You will treat her with respect due her as a born and bred *tigre blanche*. If you don't, you'll answer to me." The little growl that came through in his voice on that last bit made her feel all tingly inside.

He was staking his claim in front of their people and her inner tigress absolutely loved it. When he'd named her as his mate, she'd wanted to purr.

Quite a few of the faces in the crowd showed surprise and dare she hope—happiness? Some of the people looked very familiar, but she'd been so young when she left here, she couldn't be sure of her memories from when she was just a cub. Still, a little part of her hoped that some of the tigers here would remember her and her family with fondness and maybe feel a little more inclined to welcome her back.

She knew they had questions—probably more than she and Mitch could handle right now. He was still covered in blood and the sweat of the battle and she'd never seen anything sexier. Still, he needed to get cleaned up, and even with the power of the volcano running through him, it had been a long day.

"We should find one of the guest rooms and clean up a bit," she whispered to him and he looked over and nodded slightly in agreement.

He might be the all-powerful volcano whisperer, but she was starting to drag. The intense anxiety of the past hours had definitely taken a toll on her. All she wanted was a warm bath and then to lie in Mitch's arms for a few hours. To reassure herself that he was all right and with her. To be held in the security of her mate's embrace.

"Forgive me, love," Mitch rumbled near her ear as he bent to place a small kiss on her cheek.

She smiled up at him as he retreated. "There's nothing to forgive. Let's leave them to mull over the changes and face this fresh in a few hours. Five a.m. is going to come quickly, and before it does I want to ravish you at least a few times."

"You've just made me an offer I cannot refuse," he quipped with a grin. He turned without explaining anything further to the crowed and, still holding her hand, left the massive chamber and its tigers behind. "Where are these guest rooms you're so proud of?" he demanded in a teasing tone once they were out of the main chamber and back in the series of smaller hallways and antechambers that had characterized the majority of the stronghold.

"If I remember correctly, they're down the next corridor."

The Old Guard had followed them, she saw, stationing one of Gisli's Guards at the door to the audience chamber to keep curious cats from following them. The guest quarters were just where she remembered and they picked a suite at random.

Mitch tried not to become impatient when Paul insisted on searching the guest suite for any dangers before he'd allow them inside. Mitch understood the sense of it and silently approved of Paul's caution, but it felt distinctly odd to be on the other end of such precautions. Usually, it was Mitch clearing the way for the Nyx.

Finally, they were alone. Paul and some of his brethren would be guarding outside the chamber, but inside, it was just the two of them. As it should be.

As the door closed behind them, Gina turned into his arms and just held him for a long, long moment. He could feel her trembling and he hugged her tighter.

"It's okay. It's all over and we both made it through," he

whispered, trying to reassure her.

"Praise the Mother of All for that," she whispered against his chest, her head tucked tightly below his chin.

He was still grimy and bloodstained from battle, but she didn't seem to care. Now that they were finally alone, they were both free to cling to each other and be grateful that they had both lived to fight another day. Mitch just hoped that the rest of his battles for the foreseeable future would be in the boardroom and not on the challenge field. Even with the volcano backing him up, it had still taken a lot out of him to fight Gisli.

"Whatever power that mage had—" he thought aloud, "—it kept Gisli white—or off-white at least. Did you notice, after the mage was swallowed by the fog Gisli turned gold again?"

"He looked awful," Gina agreed in a small voice. "I thought that mage was going to kill you and then you pulled that shield out of nowhere."

"Strictly the Lady's doing. Whatever Her divine intentions are by linking me to the Grim, She gave me incredible amounts of power and abilities I don't even fully understand. Perhaps I never will. But when I saw the fireball coming, I somehow knew what to do."

"Thank the Goddess," she whispered.

"Indeed," Mitch agreed. So much had happened to them both in such a short time. It was all a little hard to take in. "And then the mage turned on you and my heart nearly stopped in my chest, Gina." His hands shook as he remembered the terror of those moments when he realized the attack had turned on her and the small group of supporters standing on his side of the challenge field.

"It turned out okay. I'm pretty good at evasion." She stretched her neck upward and moved back just far enough that she could look into his eyes. "I'm so glad that's over and that you lived to tell the tale."

"Me too." He couldn't resist. He lowered his lips to hers and gave her the sweet kiss he'd been dreaming of for the past hour.

He hadn't enjoyed being the center of attention since the challenge, but he knew his duty and he knew the Clan needed him to be strong and serve them in whatever capacity made the most sense. For now, it was as figurehead and leader. He'd start tomorrow, sorting out the business problems that had nearly bankrupted the Clan and thrown an entire country into economic turmoil. That couldn't wait.

But first, he would see to his mate. Mitch ended the kiss but kept her in his arms. He had to clean up before he took her to bed. He lifted her into his arms and strode through the sitting room, into the bedroom and straight into the attached bath. The tub was a work of art made by the Lady Herself, poured of molten basaltic lava and solidified centuries ago. The stone and ice walls of the stronghold rose upward around it.

The giant tub was the central focus of the room, but there was a smaller basin at about waist height with a polished mirror hanging over it a few feet away and a discrete toilet seat hidden in a little alcove beyond that. All the luxuries of modern living, fed by water melted from the glacier and heated in the earth by the magma running far beneath their feet. A perfect blend of magic and practicality.

Mitch put Gina on her feet and flipped open the taps on the bathtub and let it fill, carefully monitoring the temperature. He didn't want it too hot for Gina. He needed to bathe, but he didn't want to let her go too far. His tiger needed her presence and he got the idea she felt the same.

She stripped off her clothes as he did, joining him to stand by the rim of the giant tub. Together, they stepped into the warm water, the taps still running, filling the huge basin around them. They remained standing while he scooped warm water over her shoulders, loving the feel of her wet skin under his fingers. Then Gina took control.

She insisted on checking every inch of his body for scars under the blood. When he realized there was still a great deal of blood on him, he opened the drain and let the dirty water slide away, to be replaced with fresh. Gina used the soft sponge that had been tucked into a crevice in the rim of the tub to remove the last of the blood and grime from his body.

When the water ran clear, he replaced the stopper in the drain and let the tub fill around them again. This time, they sank into the pooling water, sitting on the wide floor of the natural basin. The hot water felt good on his muscles, and having Gina here with him made the experience perfect. The only thing better would be if he was inside her.

Realizing that, he lifted her into his arms and arranged her legs on either side of his as she faced him. Essentially, she was sitting in his lap, her arms wrapped loosely around his neck as she smiled at him.

"You are so beautiful," he whispered, tracing his fingers over her delicate skin, flushed now with the heat of the water and the light layer of steam near its surface. "You're too good for me."

"Never," she contradicted him. "You were always meant to be my mate, Mitch. You are my perfect match and I couldn't love or admire you more. You *are* perfect. In every way. I'm the one who has to stay on my toes if I want to keep up with you." She smiled, leaning in and kissing him, forestalling any further comment he might've made on the subject.

He let his hands roam down her body, pausing to play with the hard tips of her breasts, loving the way she responded so eagerly to his lightest touch. She squirmed against him in the buoyant water, little sounds of need issuing from her throat. He moved his hands around to her back, tracing her spine and the curves of her waist, then down over her shapely butt, squeezing lightly.

She growled low in her throat with passion, and he had to smile. His mate was everything he'd always dreamed of and never thought to find. He was a truly blessed man.

Then he moved one hand around to the front, keeping the other on her ass, delving between her cheeks, teasing lightly. He played with her, touching and moving back, then allowing the water to slide between them as he touched the apex of her splayed legs, zeroing in on the little nub at the top that made her squirm on his lap.

Mitch kissed her, pushing his tongue deep into her mouth as he speared two of his fingers into her liquid warmth, priming her, testing her readiness. She moaned and it was music to his ears. His mate was with him and as eager for him as he was for her. He could wait no longer.

He removed his hand from within her and, rearranging her only slightly on his lap, he positioned him cock at her entrance. He pushed forward, sliding through the water and the even slicker fluids of her desire, entering the gates of paradise. He broke their tempestuous kiss as she cried out, her head thrown back as he slid into her fully. They were one.

He stilled, waiting for her to signal when she was ready to proceed. He was happy. He was one with his mate and his tiger purred. Gina's head rolled as her body shivered, but eventually she lifted her gaze to meet his. He saw the fire, the passion in her eyes, and it made him want to move.

Mitch waited for her to initiate though. He didn't want to rush this. He wanted everything to be perfect for her. Just being here with her, inside her, already made it perfect for him.

Then she began to move. Slowly at first, she put her hands on his shoulders, using him for leverage as she pumped up and down on his hard shaft. He let her set the pace, gradually assisting her movements, his hands on her hips, guiding, lending her his strength. He could feel the volcano under them. He knew its pulse. And he felt its power and its approval of their activities. The mountain was happy when they were happy.

The mountain had claimed Mitch for its own and now it claimed Gina as well. They were the sacred servants of the Grim and its power flowed into them and back again. The very earth was pleased with them.

Mitch increased the pace, unable to hold out for too much longer, though they'd already stayed in the water so long their skin was beginning to wrinkle. He'd wanted this to last—and it had—but even amazingly good things had to come to an end. The thing was he knew he could have this again and again. Gina was his now, and as long as he kept her safe, he could be with her whenever he wanted. She was his mate. She wouldn't leave him. Not ever.

Only death could part them, and he didn't plan on dying anytime soon. Now that he'd lived through the challenge, Mitch felt free to make plans for the next sixty years or so. Each and every one of them included Gina. And eventually, if they were so blessed, maybe a family of their own.

Mitch strained against her, pumping hard and fast now as Gina strained above him. Her breath came in ragged pants as he growled low in his throat, the animal inside him showing as his climax neared.

And then it was upon him. Gina roared as her climax hit and he was only a second behind, reaching for the stars with her, in her. Together, they transcended the earth, the mountain and the ice cap. They soared into the stars and back, shared pleasure taking them to magical places few mortals dared to go. He almost glimpsed eternity before falling back to earth…to his mate.

"I love you, Gina mine," he whispered, rocking her in his arms, their bodies still joined in the most intimate of ways.

"I love you too, Mitch, and I always will."

CHAPTER THIRTEEN

A little before five a.m., Mitch woke and took stock of their situation. Much as he would've loved to spend the early morning hours making love to his mate again and again, he knew today was meant for work. Hard work. They had many things to do to get the Clan up and running again.

As he'd expected, when he poked his head out the door, a stack of messages waited for him. Adele Miller handed them over, along with the small bags Mitch and Gina had brought with them from New York. Clothes and some essential toiletries would help them both face the day fresh and prepared.

Mitch cleaned up, dressed and was going through the messages by the time a tap sounded on the outer door. He'd set up shop in the sitting room, leaving Gina asleep in the bedroom. She needed the rest and he didn't have the heart to wake her up so early after the day they'd had yesterday.

He answered the door to find breakfast had been delivered on a tray. Adele verified the food had been tested, which was something Mitch had done for the Nyx once upon a time. He thanked the Guards with a nod and took the tray back into the room. He had just enough time to share a little bedroom picnic with his beloved before he had to get to work.

He turned toward the bedroom, but Gina was already up,

dressed and standing in the doorway to the bedroom looking at him. She had a smile on her face.

"I was going to serve you breakfast in bed." Mitch lifted the tray in his hands.

"Too late." Gina shrugged and walked into the sitting room. She took a seat on the couch in front of the glass coffee table he'd been working on, sorting messages. "Can I help with any of this?"

Mitch put the tray down on the coffee table and sat next to her, pulling her into his arms for a quick kiss. Well, maybe it wasn't as quick as he'd planned, but he wasn't complaining and more importantly, neither was she. He let her up for air only because he didn't want their breakfast to get too cold.

"To answer your question, yes, you can be of great help. I need a doctor—maybe a few in different specialties actually—to help sort out the Clan's biggest holding. Have you ever heard of Phelix Corporation?"

He had already served her a cup of coffee and uncovered the plates that had been stacked on the tray. Healthy portions of eggs, bacon, sausage and potatoes were on each plate. He looked up when she didn't answer and realized she had stilled completely.

"Phelix Pharmaceuticals?" Her eyes had narrowed in thought and she seemed wary.

"The pharmaceutical operation is just one subsidiary. They're a hi-tech company with multiple arms and the tiger Clan is by far the biggest shareholder. I also think, based on what I saw last night and some of the information I've managed to glean from this stack of messages, it's also our biggest problem."

"Maybe more than you think. I've been working with a shifter doctor who runs a special project for Phelix." That was news to him. "Actually, the project goes back quite a ways to when my family first went to America. I became involved in it later, but it was always designed and meant for shifter use. We call it royal nectar. It's a distillation of what we think is the active component in my blood." She sighed and shook her head. "When I was called down to Ellie's apartment to treat you, I gave you my blood. It stopped the poison, but then you were unconscious again when Cade brought you up to my apartment. He needed you awake again, so I gave you a dose of the nectar. It roused you for a little while but then you took a turn for the worse. Much worse, actually. Mitch, the combination of the poison you were given and the nectar almost killed you."

"What do you think that means?"

"I think if Phelix is corrupt, it means that something we were creating to help shifters has been targeted. The poison seemed to react violently with the nectar. Maybe whoever created the poison knew about the nectar and deliberately cultivated an agent that it wouldn't work on." The implications were terrible.

"Let's hope not. Let's hope we're getting ahead of ourselves. All I have right now is a suspicion of financial wrongdoing. Let's take this one step at a time for now. And be very cautious. It still might be nothing. I could be way off base. I'm going to look at the books in depth today and see what's what."

"I'm happy to help in whatever way I can." Her steadfast support meant the world to him.

"I'm counting on it."

After they'd finished breakfast, they went out to face the day together. Adele was the ranking Old Guard on duty but Gunnar was with her. He was a font of information.

As it turned out, the majority of Gisli's followers had been swept up in the flood. The crooked bookkeeper, the complicit accountant, the shark of a lawyer who had systematically bankrupted the Clan. According to Gunnar, they were all gone.

Mitch and Gina were taken on a tour of the stronghold. There were the expected audience chambers and living quarters, but there was also the hi-tech area Mitch had ordered closed the night before. This was the area reserved for the running of the Clan's many business interests. This was the area Mitch wanted to study first.

It was time he put his MBA to use.

What he discovered was troubling, to say the least. First of all, the supposedly hi-tech equipment was woefully out of date. From the look of the account books, it was clear they hadn't spent any time or money on upgrades in the past decade at least.

Mitch spent part of an hour going quickly over the personnel records and realized right away that someone would have to personally visit some of the corporate offices of the companies owned or heavily invested in by the Clan—especially their greatest investment, Phelix Corporation. The executives needed to know that things were going to be done differently now, and if Gisli's handpicked lackeys didn't want to comply, they would be summarily replaced.

He started to make notes for whoever ended up in charge. He still couldn't wrap his head around the idea that they wanted him to be the king. He was more of the opinion that Frederick should come back and retake the throne, though Mitch would be glad to help him. Fixing the Clan's finances was an urgent matter and Mitch was already strategizing the best way to go about implementing changes. The Clan couldn't wait. They needed help now.

"Mitch." Gina's voice came to him from a few feet away. He'd been so intent on the ledger he'd been reading, he hadn't noticed her approach.

When he looked up at her, the older female guard who had questioned him on the challenge field was beside her. A quick glance told him that a few of their Old Guard friends were near enough to assist should there be any attempt at treachery. Just because Mitch had won the challenge didn't mean these Guards who had served Gisli had earned Mitch's trust yet.

"This is Helga," Gina said, indicating the woman at her side. "We've been talking about the state of the Royal Guard."

"Thor was washed away in the flood and good riddance,"

Helga said in a flinty tone. "He was Gisli's chosen to lead our ranks. Now we have no leader and are in chaos. This is not good for the Royal Guard or the Clan, but I didn't want to act without your permission." She tilted her head to the side in a slight bow of respect and Mitch realized this seasoned warrior was deferring to him. He'd known on some level that winning the challenge would change things, but he hadn't quite realized how much. Frankly, he'd never really thought much about what came after the challenge.

He tried to think fast now about how to proceed. He scanned the room, his gaze alighting on Harold Miller. Harry was a warrior's warrior. He might be young, but he would easily earn the respect of any Royal Guard for his skill and courage. He could be of great help here. He also had a mind for strategy that was unmatched among the Old Guard he'd met and worked with.

"Harry," Mitch spoke the younger man's name in a firm voice. Harry came over promptly. "Helga, this is Harold Miller. He is a Royal Guard descended from the Old Guard that followed King Frederick into exile. He was taught in the old ways and I have found him to be a warrior of great prowess with a knack for tactics and teamwork. I'd like you to consult together to see what can be done with the Guard."

Helga nodded. "It will be done."

They trotted off, already talking about how they would go about reorganizing the Guard corps. They were an odd set—the older female and the young male—but Mitch was pleased to see they seemed to be getting along. He had little doubt about Harry's skills, but he didn't know this other group of Guards at all. He'd have to tread carefully with them and trust to Harry's judgment for now.

Gina put her arm around him and leaned down to rest her chin on his shoulder as he sat at a tempered-glass desk. All the manmade furniture he'd seen in this ice fortress was sleek metal and glass. Ultra-modern in design but not very welcoming. Mitch didn't like it. It seemed overly pompous to him. And cold. And though the colors were complimentary to the black rock and ice out of which the place was formed, the style was angular and awful. Very jarring and unnatural.

"You've had your nose buried in these ledgers for a couple of hours. Is it as bad as it seems?" She kissed his cheek before moving back to sit in the empty rolling chair at his side.

"Worse," he answered in a voice that only she could hear. He didn't want to alert everyone to the trouble he'd found from his initial examination of the records. He wanted to have all his ducks in a row before he broke the news to the other members of the Clan. "I'll have to recheck these figures a few times, but it doesn't look good."

"Well, frankly, neither does the rest of the place. Gisli put all my parents' furniture—what he didn't sell—in storage. He's the one who bought all this tacky glass and chrome stuff." She ran one hand along the glass tabletop. "The good news is I can get most of the old furnishings back, but it'll take a little while. I talked to all of the household staff and put Maribeth in charge of reorganizing things there. Some of them didn't want to serve anymore, with good reason. Gisli had abused them and forced at least two of the women into living up here at the stronghold to see to his every whim. The pig."

Mitch caught her hand and squeezed. "I'm glad he's dead."

She moved closer and rested her head on his shoulder. "I'm glad you won," she whispered. "I was so afraid...until I realized the mountain was helping you." She drew back to look into his eyes. "How in the world did you manage that? The volcano stopped erupting when the fight ended."

"I'm not really sure, but I can feel the mountain in the back of my mind now. Its energy is waiting. And I think..." He considered his words carefully before forging ahead. "I think it'll come at my call. I think I finally understand that part in the Rule about the power of the fire and ice reserved for the king. I bet your dad had this kind of communion with the Grim. Actually, I can't wait to talk to him about it."

"Well, he's on his way. I called them as soon as I saw I

had a signal." The phones had been down last night because of the volcanic eruption. The ash plume had wrought havoc with the cell towers. "I wanted to let them know how it turned out, but Dad said he already knew. He'd seen your victory in a vision. They spent the night in a vigil at the stone circle praying for you."

Mitch was touched by the idea that the king and queen had kept vigil for him.

"They're coming here?" Mitch was glad. He wanted the title settled once and for all. The sooner the better. Some of the Guards had been calling him *sire*, and it wasn't a comfortable fit at all.

"They chartered a plane and are already on their way. They should be here late tonight and they're bringing most of the Old Guard with them."

Mitch didn't even blink at what had to be a huge expense. He knew the exiled king had done well in business over the years.

"Unlike the Clan's finances, your father has run a tight ship with his personal money. He left here with nothing and built a small empire of his own. He's the perfect man to help the Clan recover financially." Gears were turning in Mitch's mind and things were falling into place.

"So are you, Mr. MBA." She leaned in to kiss his cheek.

He realized by that simple touch that he needed her presence. He needed the touch of his mate. She'd stood by him through everything, and he couldn't love her more. They left the office area and ate lunch with some of the Millers and a few of the more highly placed staff members. Everyone wanted to get to know him and Gina, it seemed, which he understood, but it made it hard to find any time alone with his mate. The tiger bristled at the constant scrutiny, but Mitch knew it was only natural.

After lunch, he and Gina took a quick walk outside to view the path of the flood from the day before. The day outside the stronghold was bright and sparkling. The mountain was silent and the mood was somber as they took in the scene of last night's battle. Mitch listened to Harold and Hilda's reports on the damage assessment from the flood. The stronghold had escaped with very little damage, which Mitch put up to the Lady. Her divine hand had been clear to him in the mountain's actions during the battle.

They went back into the ice palace reassured that its location had not been compromised by the challenge. By late afternoon, the mood in the stronghold had grown expectant. Frederick and Candis arrived just after dark with a large contingent of the Old Guard, and Mitch was really glad to see them.

He watched while Gina greeted her parents with big hugs. He noticed there were also a few tears shed on the part of many of those who had not seen Iceland—their original homeland—in years.

They all moved to one of the smaller audience chambers. The largest of the chambers would hold the entire village plus all the newcomers, so the room that was considered *small* was still huge by Mitch's reckoning. There was a big central table and plenty of chairs. It almost looked like the round table of Arthurian legend, but Mitch didn't dare say so out loud.

Frederick and Candis sat first, followed by Gina and Mitch. Then everyone else took seats around the table. Mitch hadn't planned it that way. It just sort of happened, but it was clear that everyone else was watching very closely to be certain they didn't seat themselves before any of the white tigers.

Mitch wasn't sure how that made him feel. Being *blanche* was still very new to him and he felt like he was still the same person he'd always been. But people around here sure were treating him differently. He tried not to notice the way they quieted and moved aside when he and Gina passed.

As an Alpha, Mitch was somewhat used to commanding the respect of other shifters, but this was much more. This was almost…reverence. And it didn't sit comfortably.

Some of the other things though, they came naturally. Fixing problems was part of his nature. Applying creative recovery strategies to the multiple messes left by the previous administration was right in his bailiwick. He'd already mapped out a tentative business plan to move the various companies the Clan owned or had an interest in, forward.

Mitch wanted to run his ideas past Frederick and see what he thought. In fact, Mitch was almost nervous about it—in a good way. He might have an MBA, but he'd never used it much, and here was an opportunity to really get his hands dirty, resurrecting a group of companies that had been nearly run into the ground. He was eager to start—if Frederick agreed.

But they had even bigger fish to fry at the moment. They had to settle the leadership of the Clan publicly, so it would be clear and as stable as they could make it for the good of their people. Mitch fully intended to make it plain he'd acted as Frederick's champion and nothing more. He would happily take a background role and do what he'd always done—protect the monarchy and support the royal family in whatever way he could.

It would be a little different now because he would technically be part of the royal family. That was new and more than a little uncomfortable, but there was no way he would ever give up Gina. She was his mate in all ways and *for* always. He would walk through fire to be with her. It would be an adjustment—one he was willing and eager to make if it meant spending the rest of his life with her.

So Mitch sat back and let Frederick handle the gathering. Many key members of the Old Guard were present, as well as the highest ranking among Gisli's Guard. The most important of the support staff were also present, waiting to hear what would happen next.

"I want to start this meeting by stating unequivocally that I will not be reclaiming the throne," Frederick began, shocking Mitch with his words. "Mitchell Gustavson won the seat of power by right of challenge and I have seen with my own eyes that he carries the Goddess's favor. I followed Her direction when I went into exile all those years ago. I follow

Her still." Frederick looked directly at Mitch and his blue eyes were sparkling with emotion. "You have served Her well, Mitch, and you are the rightful king of our people now. Candis and I have discussed this at length. It's time for you and Gina to rule. We will support you in any way we can, but our time on the obsidian thrones is over. Let this be a new start for our people. And may the Mother of All continue to bless your path."

Silence reigned and Mitch felt at sea for a moment. He hadn't expected this. He'd been fully prepared to turn over what little authority he'd gained since the battle to Frederick...and now this. Mitch was stunned.

"Sire, I..." Mitch had to clear his throat before continuing. He wasn't sure what to say. "I've never imagined I would rule. I am a simple soldier. A Royal Guard. I serve. It's what I've trained my entire life to do. I don't know the first thing about ruling."

"And yet you are a leader of men. An Alpha all other Alphas look up to. You have served the monarchs among the big-cat shifter Clans. It is time you came home to your rightful place. Time you served the tiger Clan in our time of need. You alone have the mandate of the Goddess, Mitch. And you have proven able to call on the sacred mountain as it was of old. I've heard about your battle in detail. All our people know that you are one with the Grim. You are the leader they will follow. You are the leader I place my faith in, now and for the rest of my days. Whether you like it or not—whether you are prepared or not—this is your time."

The weight of Frederick's words hung heavily in the air and on Mitch's shoulders. He was at a loss. But some of the things Frederick had said rang true in his heart. Mitch had read accounts of the kings of old in the histories of their people. It was often said they could command both fire and ice. Mitch had done that by being one with the mountain. He still didn't quite know how, but he'd done it easily during the battle with Gisli. It had felt natural.

In the history books Frederick had asked him to read, that

was one of the main signs of kingship among the tigers of old. And it had happened to Mitch. For the first time in centuries, a Tig'Ra could tap into the full power and magic of the Grim. He couldn't deny it. If he thought about it, the mountain was there now…in the back of his mind…an ever-present well of ancient energy just waiting for him. It welcomed him. It was eager to serve.

As Mitch had served all his life. His had been a life of service. He'd honed his Alpha tendencies in a specific direction. As an orphan with no family of his own, he'd chosen to serve the monarchs of their kind. It had been his life's work.

Maybe… Mitch paused, allowing a few moments for his thoughts to process before he responded to Frederick's words. Maybe his old life *had* ended that day. Maybe, with Gina's help, he had been reborn into this new existence where his chosen role of protector and servant had expanded to include the entire tiger Clan rather than just a few monarchs of other big-cat shifter Clans. It made a lovely sort of sense if he was willing to accept it.

He realized belatedly that he really had no other choice. He could not argue with the vision the Mother of All had granted him at the stone circle any more than he could argue with Her allowing him to feel her presence in the Grim, in her guise as Gaia, Mother Earth. He could not argue that She had taken a very personal interest in him for some unfathomable reason, and he had no choice but to accept and serve Her, as he had always tried to do. It was his nature, and his personal honor demanded he do no less.

"Although I never thought to rule, I will accept the role." Mitch reached for Gina's hand. "But I want it made clear from the start that I serve the Clan, not the other way around. I will not repeat Gisli's mistakes. The good of the Clan comes before my own. I promise to do all in my power to restore the peace and prosperity we once knew, and heal the schism that has kept us scattered and apart for all these years." Mitch looked around at everyone, judging their responses by the expressions on their eager faces. There was a sense of joy in the room that could not be faked, and he could read approval in almost every gaze. He'd said the right thing. Thank the Lady. "And I don't intend to spend all my time up here in Iceland. I'm sorry, but the world has changed and our business interests are all over the place. I think we're going to have to form a secondary headquarters closer to where the action is. Maybe London, New York or Los Angeles. Maybe elsewhere. Maybe it'll be a more mobile presence, but if we're going to rebuild our finances, we need to be more agile."

Mitch outlined some of his ideas for reestablishing the Clan's business interests, much to the surprise of many of those gathered in the small audience chamber. He could see that the Guards hadn't had a clue about his business background, but they seemed to approve of his forward-thinking plans. The support staff was beaming. They'd been more involved in the day-to-day running of the Clan and they were in a better position to understand what Mitch had in mind.

He invited comments and suggestions and with Frederick, Candis and Gina's help—along with those support staff most impacted—they ironed out a preliminary plan to get the expenses under control. That was the first step. Gisli had spent the Clan into near bankruptcy with his extravagant and foolish ways. Mitch would put a stop to that right away and then begin a regimen that would hopefully bring the finances back into the black over time.

He left the specifics of that part of the plan for later. This meeting was all about putting people to work right away to stop the bleeding Gisli had caused. After they got through with the business side of things, Mitch invited Harold and Helga to outline their plans for the Royal Guard. They'd spent time coming up with a well-thought-out plan that Mitch approved of whole-heartedly. The Old Guard was going to start training those that had been in residence at the stronghold. Any of those who wanted to retire to village life would be allowed to do so and the interested youngsters who had Guard tendencies would be put into a more rigorous training regimen.

Harold was proving his worth and Mitch thought in time he'd be an excellent choice for Captain of the Guard. The Captain oversaw all the Guards of the Clan—a position of great power and authority. Helga, on the other hand, showed herself to be thoughtful and fully capable of taking charge of any given situation. Mitch could use someone like her—if she continued to prove her loyalty—to oversee Gina's safety when Mitch couldn't be by her side.

Gina needed her own contingent of Guards dedicated to her alone. Most of them would be female, naturally, so they could easily go everywhere Gina might go. Mitch would probably have to have his own group too, but he saw them as more of a formality. He didn't necessarily want a group of guys following him around wherever he went, but he understood the necessity. He'd go along with it, if only to make sure Gina did the same. Mitch thought Paul Miller would be a good choice to lead his own personal Guard, if he was agreeable, but he'd take that up with Paul in private.

The meeting lasted more than two hours. At that point, Mitch broke it up with a promise to meet again the next day. He took a much smaller group that included Gina and her parents as well as a few of their friends from America to another chamber where snacks had been set up for them. Paul checked over all the food without even being asked, already falling into the role of Royal Guard without being formally appointed. Mitch silently approved.

Everyone *seemed* happy with the change in leadership, but Mitch knew they couldn't be too careful. He'd already been poisoned once. He didn't want to repeat the experience.

They shared a more relaxed atmosphere, talking about the events of the past week. Mitch felt more at ease with this group of friends and was almost able to forget all the crazy shit that had happened to him in the past day or two.

"I still don't understand why or how Gisli turned golden during the battle," Paul said as he reached for another serving of mutton stew.

"I think I have an answer for that one," Harry said from the other end of the table. "I was talking to Amma Hilda—your great-grandmother, they said—" Harry nodded toward Mitch. "She told us she'd had her suspicions about Gisli's color for a long time. She thinks his pet mage was keeping him white magically and that's why the color was kind of sickly. When the mage disappeared, the color went with him." Harry bit into a drumstick as if he hadn't just dropped a bombshell into the conversation.

"Well, that would explain a lot," Frederick said finally after a moment of silence in which everyone seemed to think about the old woman's theory. "I could never figure why he remained *blanche* when it was so clear he'd strayed well off the path of the Lady. Being *blanche* isn't just an hereditary thing. It's a magical, sacred thing—as you well know, Mitch." Frederick nodded toward him and then returned his attention to his glass. "I mourned Gisli's loss back when he turned from the path of Light. I am sad at his death, but I know it was the only way to save our people—to save our Clan. I'm only sorry he didn't redeem himself in some way before the end."

Everyone fell silent, the mood turning solemn.

"I'm sorry," Mitch said finally. "I know he was your brother. Even though he was in the wrong, I will never celebrate his death. Just as I have never celebrated any of the lives I've had to take in the course of my duties. I will pray to the Lady for his spirit."

Frederick met his gaze. "You are wise beyond your years, Mitch Gustavson. I have lost a brother, but I'm proud to have gained you as my son-in-law." He raised his glass and everyone followed suit in a silent toast to family both lost and found.

"Which reminds me…" Candis said after the toast had been completed. "Have you given any thought to a formal mating ceremony? It's traditional among the royal families to have some kind of ceremony and reception to acknowledge the union publicly."

Mitch wasn't sure what to think. The expense of a big party wasn't something he wanted to contemplate after looking at the Clan's books. He might be able to pay for it out of his own pocket, but he wasn't a rich man. He'd put aside part of his salary over the years and invested wisely, but his bank account wasn't that of a king's just yet.

"It doesn't have to be anything lavish," Candis went on as if reading his mind. Or maybe she was just reading his expression. "In fact, anything too fancy or expensive would be foolhardy in the current situation. But a formal mating ceremony, witnessed by as many of the Clan and shifter dignitaries who wish to come, plus an informal get-together after would be a nice thing to do. With help from the ladies in the village, I bet we could put something together that would satisfy the dignity of the occasion and the need for our people to celebrate life once again. It would be a good gesture to begin your reign."

Mitch knew the former queen had several valid points. He couldn't argue with anything she'd said and an idea was beginning to form for the ceremony that wouldn't cost the Clan anything but might go a long way toward demonstrating his true power to those he would invite to attend. Now that he'd accepted he was going to be Tig'Ra, he had to cement his position. He wouldn't let any perceived weakness on his part reflect poorly on the Clan.

The other shifters had to understand he was much more than a jumped-up Guard. He was Tig'Ra by right of challenge and forbearance of the Lady. He'd proven the first part by defeating Gisli. Proving the Goddess's blessing was harder, but he had an idea of how to demonstrate it beyond the shadow of a doubt.

"Gina?" Mitch turned to his mate. He loved her so much, it was a special moment each time he looked at her and realized she truly was his mate. "I'm up for it if you are. What do you think?"

She smiled at him and stole his breath. "I think it's a good idea. Mom and I can plan the party. Do you want to handle the ceremony?"

How did she know what he had in mind? He tilted his head and smiled at her. His woman never stopped surprising him. She gave him an answering grin and held his hand through the chorus of approvals coming from around the table. It seemed everybody liked the idea of a party.

CHAPTER FOURTEEN

They set a date a little over a month away so they would have time to invite dignitaries from the other big-cat shifter Clans. Matings among royals were few and far between. It was customary to at least invite the other big-cat shifter royalty to bear witness to a royal match. In this particular case, it would also give Mitch and Gina a chance to get to know the other monarchs. They were new to their roles as Tig'Ra and Tig'Ren. The other monarchs didn't know them and needed to understand that things in the tiger Clan were going to change radically from here on out.

The phrase about two birds, one stone fit, Gina thought. She'd get to meet the other monarchs—if they came to the wedding—and take their measure. At the same time, the guests would get to see Mitch and Gina in action. They'd soon learn that Gisli's corrupt management style was over.

Mitch spent his mornings over the next week working out with the Guard—Old and new—making sure they were integrating and learning from each other while he kept himself in shape. Gina joined them, since keeping fit was important to her. She had to be sure she could help defend herself if it became necessary. Monarchs were natural targets for enemies who wanted to destabilize the Clans.

And the tiger Clan was already in chaos from Gisli's poor

handling of everything. After lunch, Mitch and Gina would spend hours going over the books with her parents' help. The long-standing investments in the biotech conglomerate called Phelix Corporation was of particular concern. Phelix had multiple smaller companies under its corporate umbrella such as Phelix Genomix, Phelix Scientifix, Phelix Pharmex and a slew of similarly named hi-tech companies.

Most of the specialty areas of these smaller companies were deeply grounded in medical, scientific and pharmaceutical research. That was where Gina's background really came into play. She helped by going over the scientific reports of the company's divisions while Mitch sorted out the financial statements. Between the two of them, they were able to discover some serious mismanagement and possible embezzlement of huge amounts of the Clan's money.

The problem was so bad and the executives so unresponsive via phone and videoconference that they decided to visit the corporate offices in person. A surprise inspection from the main shareholder ought to shake them up a bit.

So only a week after arriving in Iceland, Mitch and Gina were on their way back to the States—to the very city Gina had lived in and Mitch had been poisoned in—to corner a few very skittish executives in their high-rise ivory towers. They brought along a contingent of Royal Guard with them. Gina supposed her days of traveling alone and incognito were at an end.

But having Mitch in her life was a more than fair trade-off. She didn't really care about being queen. The only thing that was truly important to her was Mitch. It hadn't really hit her that she was the Tig'Ren yet. Her mother had tried to tell her a few things about the position, but Gina didn't really feel it. Not yet. Maybe not ever.

She'd just have to adjust as she went along. She'd do her best to make the position into something she could live with—a compromise between the formality of the past and the more or less regular life she'd tried to make for herself before meeting Mitch.

Gina had used up all her leave from the hospital and now that she was back in the city, she'd set aside some time to go down there and end her employment for good. It was a big step but one that she felt okay about taking. She'd enjoyed her job and her freedom to live and work in the human world, but she loved Mitch. He'd given up his relative anonymity and his job as Royal Guard to be with her. She had to show the same willingness to bend.

They'd discussed it at length and had come to the conclusion that they were both starting fresh. Neither of them really knew what to expect, but they would face whatever came together.

She went to the hospital without Mitch. He'd wanted to come with her, but having him in tow would've made the trip a lot longer. She would have had to introduce him to nosy coworkers at every turn. Better she make her exit as quietly as possible. Paul Miller went with her. The hospital staff was used to seeing him—another doctor—from time to time. His brother Tad and his mate, Mandy, were pre-arranged to meet them there. They would all help to keep Gina safe for the hour or so it took to clear out her things and tender her formal resignation.

Everything went off without a hitch, and while Gina was sorry to see that part of her life end, she was looking forward to the next step. Mitch had arranged an emergency board meeting at the Phelix headquarters building downtown. Paul stayed by her side and Mandy and Tad came along with them. The more doctors she had to consult with on some of the more questionable of the experiments she'd uncovered, the better. And she wanted to get to the bottom of the nectar's reaction with the poison Mitch had been given, if she possibly could.

Mitch met her in the lobby of the office building Phelix Corporation owned. It was a marble and glass monstrosity that dominated the downtown skyline and Gina had to shake her head at the enormous expense of both the design and the décor. It had been built in the last decade and the Clan had paid for all of it. She was disgusted. The gaudy building looked more like a monument to somebody's overblown ego than a serious place of business.

Their little entourage took an express elevator to the penthouse where the board was scheduled to meet. Security couldn't stop them, but she knew there were some fast and furious phone calls being made the moment they stated who they were and where they were going.

When the elevator door opened at the top level of the building, the first thing she smelled were shifters. Lots of them. Not just tigers, though there were a few distinct tiger scents. She also smelled the wet-dog scent she associated with werewolves, the subtle differences of other big cats and one or two that she couldn't quite place.

"Magic," Gunnar hissed, moving to take point. "There's at least one mage here. Possibly more." Mitch had decided to bring Gunnar. He'd proven himself to be both loyal and brave.

Mitch growled and the rest of their group bristled. In addition to Gunnar and two more of their new friends from Iceland, Paul, Tad and Mandy were still with them.

Their small group of eight advanced steadily toward the board room. Everyone was on guard and the few workers who saw them pass took visible steps back. So far, so good. Nobody was fool enough to challenge their right to be there.

Gunnar led the way to the board room that was situated on the east side of the building. It was a large room with a bank of windows that displayed the city skyline and streets far below. It was quite a view, but what interested Gina most as they barged in were the reactions of the various board members sitting around the giant, oblong table.

"Who are you?" a tiger shifter nearest the door asked in a snotty tone. Gina didn't like the look of the man, but she'd give him the benefit of the doubt before making up her mind about him.

"My name is Mitch and I've just recently become your

biggest shareholder." His tone was just casual enough to convey the true meaning of his words. He left them in no doubt of his position as he continued. "Gisli is dead. I'm in charge now."

"You're the new Tig'Ra?" the same tiger asked in a disbelieving voice. He wasn't showing the least bit of respect for either Mitch or his new position, and Gina watched to see how her mate would handle the situation. The Guards with them bristled but wouldn't move until Mitch gave the word.

Their group moved farther into the room and Mandy and Tad closed and locked the doors, standing in front of them.

"Now then," Mitch took control of the room. "I'd like you all to identify yourselves and what your role is here. I've had a hell of a time getting any of you to videoconference with me the past week, so I've had to come all the way here. I'm not happy about it."

Silence reigned for a long moment before one of the two humans in the room stepped forward.

"I'm Norbert Grange, corporate secretary."

Even Gina felt the wave of magic that leapt from the man. Gunnar growled even as Mitch casually repulsed the subtle magical attack. They'd learned by trial and error that even a thousand miles away from the Grim, Mitch could still use the magic of the earth to protect himself and others. He truly was the Tig'Ra and had powers like the tiger kings of old, seen only in history books until now.

"Your sorcerer's tricks have no effect on us, so you might as well back off, Norbert," Mitch informed the man. "The very fact that you've tried to attack rather than talk, puts you under arrest."

Mitch wiggled one finger and the heavy braided silk that bound the drapes to one side untied itself from the curtains and wound itself around Norbert's resisting hands. It continued snaking around the struggling mage until he was completely immobilized—bound and gagged. Mitch crooked his finger one last time and the man fell back into the chair behind him, well and truly quelled for the time being.

"Now, who else here wants to test me?" Mitch turned on the remaining people in the room. Heads shook and one woman burst into tears. Mitch sighed even as Gina's gaze traveled from person to person, sizing up their reactions.

"Are you a mage or a tiger?" one brave werewolf asked.

"Yes," Mitch answered with a grim twist of his lips.

"You're a fraud. I recognize you. You were part of the Nyx's household. You're nothing but a jumped-up Royal Guard." The man who spoke was smaller than Mitch but not by much. His scent said he was one of the other big-cat species. Gina figured *pantera noir* by the fact that he'd mentioned the Nyx.

"Horace van Cleef," Mitch intoned flatly. "Imagine finding you here. Looks like you've been up to your old tricks since the Nyx threw you out."

Outside the bank of windows, the sky darkened with storm clouds. Gina knew enough by now to realize that Mitch's anger was affecting the weather. He had that ability now—though it seemed to manifest only in moments of intense anger.

"It was a misunderstanding," Horace tried to defend himself, but it wasn't very convincing.

"Oh, so she misunderstood that you'd drained the accounts you'd been in charge of to buy yourself a mansion on a hundred acres of prime real estate? Interesting. Seems to me she thought you were setting up your own little kingdom, even though you have absolutely no right to a throne of any kind."

"The old system is corrupt!" he shouted back, clearly agitated by the way his whole body shook. "Look at you—the Tig'Ra simply because you defeated a wimp like Gisli."

"My uncle was a lying, cheating bastard," Gina stepped in, unable to hear her mate insulted. "He never should have ruled anything. And he was *never* the Tig'Ra." She looked around the room to press her point, meeting each set of eyes. "Mitch is Goddess-touched. You've seen his magic. He is one with the Grim."

Shocked silence greeted her words and at least a few of the board members sat back, defeat written on their faces. Chief among those was the man who'd sat in the chairman's seat at the head of the table.

"I'm Walter Sorenson, the CEO," he said with great dignity as he stood and adjusted his suit jacket. "I was appointed chairman of this board by Gisli and I've never been comfortable in the role he made me play. I recognize the new Tig'Ra and resign my position with the company."

Mitch seemed to weigh the man's words and then finally nodded. "I accept. Do any of you feel the same?" A few hands went up around the room, including the woman who was still crying. "Good. You may all be excused to the next room, where you will remain until we have talked with each one of you. Do not leave the building on penalty of death. I know who you are and the Grim can reach you wherever you try to hide."

The woman started crying even harder and the others looked either hostile or whipped. Slowly, they exited the room, Mandy showing them the way to the chamber next door. Not a single one of them tried to make a run for it. Wise choice, Gina thought.

That just left the trussed-up mage, the mutinous *pantera* named Horace and one other person...a werewolf if Gina sniffed correctly. And he was growling at Mitch as they faced off across the table.

"You're the slimy bastard that poisoned me," Mitch said in a lethal tone.

Gina was shocked. Mitch had come face-to-face with the man—wolf—who had almost killed him. He was utterly calm on the surface, but Gina knew there had to be a firestorm brewing beneath his placid exterior.

"You should be dead." The werewolf sealed his own fate with those words of acknowledgment.

"Why? Why did you target him like that? He was only a Royal Guard back then," Gina wanted to know.

"Because of what he's become, of course. Foresight is

rare, but my friends knew what could happen. They knew Mitch Thorburn would be a threat. They wanted him out of the way and sent me to do it." The werewolf's eyes weren't quite sane.

"Your friends in the *Venifucus?*" Mitch asked quietly. "It's no use denying it. I see the evil glyphs on your face, Victor."

Gina did a mental review of the list of board members she'd studied on the plane ride here. Victor French was listed as the Chief Financial Officer of the company. He had ready access to the billions of dollars at Phelix's command. The implications were horrific. A *Venifucus* agent with that kind of entrée could do—and had probably already done—a lot of damage.

The big-cat Clans had been organized into their current political structure during the Renaissance in Europe. The *Venifucus* went back even further than that. They had once been led by a fey mage named Elspeth, who had come to be known as the Destroyer of Worlds. She and her followers had almost won the last war, but the forces of Light had defeated them and sent Elspeth into the farthest realms, never to return.

Or so everyone hoped. Recently though, the *Venifucus*— thought gone for centuries—had been making a comeback. The few agents who had been caught all professed one alarming goal. They wanted to rescue Elspeth from the farthest realms and bring her back to the mortal world to wage her evil war once more.

The fact that the *Venifucus* had someone in its ranks that could see the future was very, very disturbing. The fact that they'd felt so sure of the foreseer's information as to send someone after Mitch on the theory that he might be important later, was even more alarming. They were acting on the foreseer's visions. Who knew how many innocents who might've done good things were now dead or derailed because of that evilly placed gift of foresight.

The werewolf growled and leapt onto the table in a single bound, baring his fangs and brandishing his claws at Mitch.

Everyone reacted in a split second, even as Mitch sprang over Gunnar's head to meet Victor on the surface of the heavy table. Mitch's hands were partially shifted, just like the werewolf's.

The werewolf tried, but he was no match for Mitch without what he now realized had been the magical support of the mage. A group had ambushed Mitch that night when the dojo had burned. He'd only seen the one he'd fought up close and personal—this werewolf—but he'd known there had been at least one or two more behind him. One of them had wielded the needle filled with poison that had almost killed him.

Mitch needed to know more. He leapt at the werewolf, grabbing him around the throat as he slammed the bastard clear off the table against the heavy glass of the large windows. The werewolf whimpered as his head connected hard with the thick glass. Mitch squeezed his airway and though he tried to fight free, he was immobilized. The moment Victor understood that little fact, he stopped fighting.

That was the moment Mitch had been waiting for.

He took a quick glance around. The mage was still immobilized, but Horace had risen and tried to head toward the door. He'd been intercepted and Gunnar and Paul had one arm each. Horace wouldn't be able to get away from both of them.

"So is this the evil triumvirate?" Mitch asked in a disgusted tone. "The three that jumped me near the dojo. If you knew who I was, why didn't you skip town the moment I took over as Tig'Ra? You've known for a week that I was in charge."

"We thought you were dead," Horace spat from across the room. "We killed Mitch Thorburn. We didn't know Mitchell Gustavson was the same guy. We figured he was just some lucky Icelandic bastard who had managed to kill Gisli."

"You should've taken my calls." Mitch smiled, knowing their own hubris had been their downfall. They'd thought they were too good to talk with the new Tig'Ra. They'd been too sure of themselves and their superiority. How the mighty had fallen.

"Yeah. I see that now." Horace grimaced as Gunnar tightened his grip on the panther's arm.

Victor passed out due to lack of air and Mitch threw him aside. Guards moved quickly to tie him up so he couldn't attack anybody when he woke.

Mitch checked the mage, noting the glyphs on his face. Mitch had never had any real magic before, but and suddenly he could see the magical tattoos that were only visible to those with a specific kind of magical sight. He'd read reports about such things, which is why it had finally registered what he was seeing, but only after the mage had already attacked. These three were going to be prisoners and they were going to be questioned very carefully before being sentenced and punished for their crimes against the Clan.

Finally, Mitch turned to Horace. He'd known of the man from his days with the Nyx, and everything he knew about him told him the panther wasn't trustworthy. He'd been a con man and had swindled members of the *pantera noir* to support his lavish lifestyle. His actions had gotten him thrown out of his Clan, which was one of the worst punishments imaginable to shifters.

"Are you working for the *Venifucus* too? I don't see any glyphs on you. Or are they hidden?" Mitch asked Horace point blank.

The panther shook his head. "I'm in this for the money. Vic and Norbert pay me for services rendered—including the intel on where you would be the night of the dojo fire."

"So you're the inside man that's been leaking the Nyx's itinerary. I bet she'll be happy to find that out so she can finally stop running. Horace, you've made that girl's life a living hell."

"She's the almighty panther queen. She should be able to deal with it," Horace countered with a sneer. It was clear he had no respect for the Goddess-granted authority given to the monarchs.

"What you fail to realize here is that I *like* Ria. It was my honor and duty to protect her for a lot of years. I didn't like seeing her hurt each time she had to run and someone else tasked with helping or protecting her got hurt because of the leaks in her security. Because of *you*, Horace."

Finally, Horace backed off, paling under Mitch's scrutiny.

"I'm not disposed to cut you any deals, but if you tell me everything you know, things will go easier for you."

Yeah, good old Horace was thinking about it, weighing his options—which weren't very many at the moment. Unlike the two fanatics with the *Venifucus* tattoos, Horace was motivated by greed and his desire for personal comfort. That was something Mitch could work with.

"I'll cooperate," he said finally. "As long as you protect me from those two. They'll kill me without hesitation."

"Done," Mitch agreed.

CHAPTER FIFTEEN

Mitch arranged for discrete transport of the three out of the country on a private jet. The tiger stronghold was the safest place for them. He could imprison them there indefinitely while they were questioned and the intense power of the volcano would nullify anything the mage tried to throw out.

Mitch and Gina stayed in the city a little longer so they could get in touch with their friends Cade and Ellie. Mitch was shocked, but Gina was not surprised to find out the two had mated. Most of Mitch's surprise was regarding the fact that Cade had taken a human, but Gina set him straight, championing her friend. Mitch conceded after a while that such a paragon of human stubbornness as Gina described was the perfect mate for his best friend, Cade.

Ellie had also informed Gina that her apartment was no more. There had been a fire in the building while Ellie and Cade had been dealing with the threat to the Nyx. The bad guys had targeted Ellie's apartment and Gina's had been directly above. There was essentially nothing left worth salvaging. It was tough to hear, but Gina could deal. Most of her truly cherished possessions had been left at her parents' house anyway. She'd lost all her furniture and clothing though.

Cade and Ellie were on the road, but they promised to stay

in touch by phone and they all exchanged numbers and their new contact information. They were also invited to the mating ceremony in Iceland and promised to be there with bells on to party with their friends. Mitch couldn't wait to meet the human who had managed to ensnare his best friend.

He also had to thank her for helping him that night after the attack on the dojo. Ellie had taken Cade and an unconscious Mitch back to her place and the rest, as they say, was history. Without Ellie's kindness to a stranger, Mitch would have never met Gina and would most likely be dead. He owed a lot to the human woman.

Mitch spent most of the next week working at Phelix Corporation's headquarters, weeding out the bad apples and replacing them with new people. Gina had been of incalculable help, overseeing the scientific and medical aspects of the various divisions. She and her team of Old Guard sons and daughters who had all gone to medical school together—not to mention some of Gina's human medical colleagues that she called to consult—had gone through the majority of the ongoing experiments.

One sinister find had been the very poison Mitch had been given. There was a lab dedicated to certain black projects that all seemed aimed at killing shifters. The two scientists who had run the lab with rather telling autonomy had mysteriously disappeared almost immediately after Mitch had stormed the conference room that first day.

And worst of all, vials of the nectar had been found among the materials in that lab. It was as Gina had feared—they'd been trying to counteract the very substance that could have saved so many lives. The nectar wasn't finished yet. They hadn't been able to synthesize much of it and it hadn't been tested fully, but it had been a promising experiment. She wanted it to continue. If the component in her blood that healed could be made available to all—even in a diluted state—it would mean a great deal to shifters and humans alike. She hated that they'd taken what had been a good project and actively worked against it.

Mitch seethed to think that a corporation mostly owned by the Clan had secretly funded research into ways to kill shifters. He'd bet anything that the two scientists were dyed-in-the-wool *Venifucus* foot soldiers.

Another thing he'd discovered was that Phelix had once been wholly owned by the Clan. Gisli had sold off shares to raise money over the years. Mitch vowed he would repurchase those shares and return the company to the Clan in time. He was already laying the groundwork for the plan and would—if all went well—be able to start on it in the next fiscal year. Sooner, if Ria was willing to help. He thought she would, but he wanted to see her face-to-face to put forward his plan.

Ria might be young, but she'd been Nyx for a while. She was a smart young woman with a head for business. In fact, her Clan of panthers had thrived financially under her leadership these past years. He'd been so proud of her for making the tough decisions that had ultimately turned out so well for her people. He'd even given her advice now and again when she'd asked his opinion on business matters. He liked to think that she'd help him now, when his people needed a little boost.

He wouldn't mind the other investors in the company being fellow big-cat shifters. He'd even reach out to the *were* Tribes of North America if he had to, but one way or another, he was going to take back the company for shifters alone. It was a goal that might take a few years—maybe decades—but he'd do it.

On the personal front, Mitch was able to get his things out of storage. He spent an hour or two sorting through his stuff and selecting the items he wanted sent to the stronghold. He sent the rest to the highly defensible apartment he'd rented through the corporation. It would do for a U.S. base of operations.

The apartment was in a more expensive part of town than Gina's old place and it boasted its own swimming pool. It was the penthouse in a relatively shorter building near the river. Nothing in the area overlooked their top-floor space and it wasn't so high up in the air that the escape routes were limited. It was a nice compromise between safety and privacy.

Mitch carried Gina over the threshold on the first night they spent there together. She'd helped him pick it out and had already bought some new furniture. Mitch had his complete wardrobe—with items suitable for everything from state dinners to working out—and a few keepsakes he'd picked up over the years. Gina had gone shopping, picking up enough clothes and shoes to keep her presentable.

"You have more clothes than I do," Gina complained when he showed her the dual walk-in closets. His was already full. Hers was woefully empty. "That's not right. Women are supposed to have more clothes than men."

He kissed her cheek. "We'll fix it at the earliest opportunity, my love. But in my defense, I had to be prepared for anything Ria threw at us. As her Royal Guard, I had to be neat and inconspicuous at every kind of event she might be invited to attend. You were a doctor. I think you pretty much lived in scrubs, right?"

She sighed heavily, clearly not placated but willing to admit defeat. "I'm not a clotheshorse. It's going to be hard to find the right stuff I'll need to be queen. Maybe Ellie can help. Or my mom."

She seemed so depressed about the idea of clothes shopping that Mitch had to laugh. He scooped her up in his arms and left the closet behind, heading for the bedroom.

A night of thorough loving had her back in a good mood come morning. Mitch had a way of doing that to her. It seemed anything could be solved by spending a few hours alone together, preferably in each other's arms.

They headed back to Iceland, having accomplished a great deal in a short amount of time. Mitch had uncovered even more treachery by going over the account books held in the States than he had by looking at the duplicate—but altered—set kept in the tiger stronghold. He knew where the rats were now and it was about time to spring his traps.

One rat in particular was going to be caught before the day was through. It seemed Walter Sorenson, the ex-CEO of Phelix Corporation, had family back in Iceland. Gisli's handpicked stooge was only a puppet. The real puppet master was his older brother, Sven, who did the accounting for the Clan.

Sven had been oh so helpful when Mitch had taken over after the challenge. He'd been almost eager to show Mitch the doctored books. But now that Mitch had seen the other side of the coin back in the States, he knew without a doubt that Sven was in this up to his eyeballs.

Mitch wasted little time confronting the accountant the moment he reached the stronghold. He gave Sven credit for still being there. He had probably thought nobody would understand what they were looking at in the cleverly doctored books, but Mitch had seen the numbers for what they were. A great big fat pack of lies. Smoke and mirrors. Deception.

One thing was certain. Sven had been systematically working against the interests of the Clan for years. He'd secreted vast sums of money in Swiss bank accounts. Mitch needed that money, which rightfully belonged to the Clan. He needed it to retake control of the Clan's business interests. He needed it to rebuild the framework in which his people might thrive.

Mitch caught up with Sven in his office, just inside the business area of the stronghold. It was another chamber of chrome and glass, hung with expensive medieval tapestries that had set the Clan back a bundle. Waste. That was Sven's specialty. Decadent waste on personal fripperies.

Mitch had already seized the homes and condominiums bought in Sven's name all over the world. His agents were moving on them even as Mitch moved on the small man behind the overlarge desk.

"Sire, you're back." Sven seemed to smile as he rose, but the smile didn't quite reach his eyes.

"Yes, I am, and you're under arrest." Mitch nodded to the

205

Guards who flanked him and they moved forward.

"What is this?" Sven shouted, evading the Guards as best he could. He fumbled for something in his desk drawer and a split second later, a dart whizzed past Mitch's ear to embed itself in the wall. A sickly green fluid came out of the tip.

One of the Guards—Helga—smashed her hand down on top of Sven's wrist, making him let go of the pistol. Mitch heard the distinct sound of bones crushing as the accountant cried out, but it seemed he wasn't done. He crouched as if to spring, but Mitch held out one hand, stopping him with the magic that was his to command.

He was strong now wherever he was, but never more so than when he was near the mountain that lent him its power. Mitch held the man in place without even touching him. A quick glance told the Guards to let go and stand by.

"You can't do this!" Sven shouted in a squeaky, annoying voice.

"By the Goddess, I certainly can," Mitch begged to differ.

"You…you're just an upstart. A flash in the pan. You won't last a week before they kill you, and I'll still be here long after you're gone." The man was raving now and it wasn't pretty.

Mitch lost his temper.

"By the grace of the Goddess I serve, the power of the Grim runs through me. If you want to feel my displeasure, keep pushing. If you want to know my mood, monitor the volcano," Mitch warned, fed up with the man's posturing. He was going down. One way or another.

No longer would incompetence be tolerated or rewarded.

"That's not p-p-possible," the man stuttered.

"Look into my eyes and tell me what you see." Mitch allowed the heat of the mountain's fiery depths to show in his eyes for a moment.

"Lava," he whispered. "It burns!"

He got a little hysterical after that, falling back to land hard on the edge of the desk, his hands covering his eyes.

"Now you know the truth of it." Mitch pulled back his

power and adopted a bored stance. "You're going to stand trial for crimes against the Clan."

Mitch nodded to the Guards once more and watched with satisfaction as Sven was taken into custody. The ice palace had plenty of hidden, secure chambers where prisoners could be kept for years. Already, Mitch was adding to the number of prisoners kept there.

He'd freed anyone wrongfully imprisoned by Gisli and given them whatever assistance they needed to recuperate and rejoin their families if possible. Now he was filling the place with legitimate wrongdoers who would face judgment fair and square. As soon as the true extent of their crimes had been established and they had been questioned to Mitch's satisfaction, the work of justice would proceed. Once he had all the information he could get out of them, he'd figure out what to do with them next.

Some would face the volcano's wrath. Anyone who had sold his soul to the *Venifucus* would have to be cleansed in the Lady's Light. What better way than to use the fire of Mother Earth ever-present in the Grim. There was a reason, after all, that the tigers of old had chosen this place to build their stronghold.

The rest of the villains would have to be dealt with according to the severity of their crimes. Already, Mitch was thinking of ways some of the lesser offenders could make it up to the Clan. Walter Sorenson, for one, could be useful—if he had truly repented.

Everything was coming together, and little by little, Mitch and Gina were weeding out the evil in their midst. It would take more time, but eventually they'd be free to get to the real work of rebuilding the Clan. They had plans to put in motion, including planning the mating ceremony and reception.

Gunnar had been helpful in clearing out the rooms used by Gisli's pet mage. He could sense magic, but it took Mitch to go in and disarm the traps the mage had left behind. With the power of the mountain behind him, nothing the now-dead mage had set up could withstand his presence. Mitch didn't fully understand magic, but at times like this, he gave himself up to the Goddess and let Her work through him.

In a locked box in a hidden compartment of the wardrobe, Mitch discovered something that made his stomach turn. He immediately sent for Gina and her parents, knowing that no matter how much this hurt, they needed to see it. They needed closure.

When they arrived, Mitch met them outside in the hallway—away from the residual taint of the mage who had lived in the rooms behind him. He held the box out before him and silently opened the lid.

Candis gasped and grabbed Gina's arm for support. Frederick moved forward a step, tears in his eyes at the dazzling light coming from within the box.

"It's the missing part of young Fridrik's pelt. I recognize his scent and his magic. He was a truly dazzling white." The old king's voice cracked as he took the box into his hands and cradled it to his chest.

"I believe this is what was keeping Gisli white. The true white tiger pelt was used to mask Gisli's blotchy brown. That is why the mage took it from your son in the first place," Mitch said with regret. "I'm sorry, but at least now your son can be at peace in the next realm."

Frederick bowed his head, tears rolling unheeded down his face as he turned to his wife and daughter. They huddled around him, arms linked around his shoulders, supporting each other in their moment of renewed grief.

At length, the old king and queen moved off down the hall and Gina came to Mitch's side and walked with him. They wouldn't wait. It was time to free the remaining part of Fridrick. They walked, people joining the silent procession as they went through the twisting halls and chambers of the stronghold. Whispers spread the word of what was occurring and the mood was somber and respectful.

Everyone who was able turned out to support the white tigers as they walked toward the sacred mountain. They went as far as they dared. The darkness of the night was lit by the light of a trillion stars and the welcoming red glow of the fissure in the earth that was their destination.

Of them all, only Mitch and Fredrick could withstand the heat of the earth at the mouth of the fissure. They left Gina and Candis some yards behind them, clinging to each other. The two men were protected from the searing heat by the Lady's magic, Her chosen warriors.

Frederick opened the box and handed it to Mitch. He held it, acting as servant to the father who had lost his son much too soon. Without words, Frederick lifted the small patch of sparkling-white fur out of the box and held it aloft.

"I return him to you, Mother Goddess. Please be kind to my son. He was a brave and heroic warrior who gave his life for his sister and Clan." The old king's voice rang through the night, touching all who heard it.

Mitch remained silent, his heart breaking for the old king and the women who sobbed behind him. He felt the need to offer comfort.

"He is surely with the Goddess," Mitch said in a quiet voice, meant for the king alone.

The old king nodded tightly, bowing his head as he watched the last little sparkling bit of his son. He held the patch of fur over the fissure in the earth and Mitch could clearly see the pool of magma below. They were standing over a crack in the earth on the side of the Grim. The Lady's sacred mountain. And Mitch could feel Her presence.

"Lady bless him," the old king whispered, releasing the small patch of fur to the fire below.

Mitch tried to watch the pelt as it combusted on the magma, but it caught fire with a blinding white light that erupted out of the fissure to take form on the other side of the crack in the earth, lighting the night sky with its radiance. When he could see again, he realized the light had taken the form of a young man. A young white tiger. Somehow, he could see both images superimposed on the manifestation. Was it a ghost? A spirit? Mitch didn't know, but it smiled at them.

"Do not grieve for me, father. I will come again." Young Fridrik's face was calm and full of the eagerness of youth and the knowledge of the ancients. "I will come again. Sooner than you think. My work here is not yet done."

The sound of his voice was touched with the Lady's blessed chimes. He was a spirit—or maybe an avatar. Mitch didn't know, but the young tiger's words concerned him. It almost worried him that the Goddess was not yet done with them. But then again, who was he to question the will of the Lady?

Young Fridrik sent a smile toward his mother and sister. "Tell them both that I love them. I will always love them, and though I died to this existence, I will be back. The Lady I serve wills it."

"Are you all right, my son? Are you safe? Are you happy?" the old king asked.

Fridrik looked at his father and smiled again. It was a beatific smile that Mitch would remember for the rest of his days.

"I am blessed. All those things and more, Father. I am a Knight of the Light. I serve the Lady and Her Light in every realm."

The old king fell to his knees, his gaze on his son who glowed from within. Tears ran down his face.

"I'm so proud of you, my boy. So very proud and full of love. I am only sorry I will never get to know the man you would have become."

"Not in this realm, perhaps—" glowing Fridrik tilted his head, "—but never say never. There are many realms beyond this one and I have been promised that if we all work very hard, we may yet be reunited in another time and place. For now, I leave you knowing that I am well and missing you, though my existence is not without purpose. My purpose in the mortal realm was to save my sister. Now I serve the Lady and She guides my purpose."

Mitch could see the spirit was beginning to fade. Unless he

was mistaken, Fridrik would be gone soon. The old king seemed to realize it as well.

"Then you are truly blessed. Be well, my son. I love you." Tears ran unchecked down the old king's face.

"I love you too, Father. Tell Mom and Gina...and the little one." He looked at Mitch when he said the last and then he was gone. Only the light of the stars shone where he had been.

"Little one?" Mitch repeated, but the old king was too stunned to hear. Mitch helped Frederick to his feet and rejoined the women. They and all their people had witnessed a miracle on the mountain that night. It would take some time to process.

Some weeks later, the day of the ceremony dawned bright and clear. The mountain was quiet, but Mitch was pretty sure it would have a few rumbles to add to the celebration planned for that night. The ceremony would take place on the side of the volcano, but the party was being held in the village. The exact location of the stronghold would remain a secret known only to the most trusted friends and members of the tiger Clan.

The village had a big hall that had been decorated by the local people and accommodations had been set aside for a larger roster of guests than Mitch had expected. Apparently, all the big-cat shifter Clans had sent either their monarchs or representatives. It was turning out to be quite a little conclave, though they hadn't planned it that way.

In fact, it was bigger than a conclave. It actually had the makings of a shifter summit. The Lords of the North American *were* Tribes had come with their mate, Allie, who was also a priestess of the Lady. The Eurozone Lords had also come—a set of Alpha twins who were as yet unmated. The Russian Federation *were* had sent a highly ranked representative and other Tribes, Packs and Clans from around the world had either sent a representative or a gift, or both.

They were already comparing notes on recent unrest and *Venifucus* attacks. Mitch was even considering letting some of their new allies have a crack at the prisoners still being held in the stronghold, but that would come later. For now, they had a mating to celebrate.

Mitch knew Gina was a little overwhelmed by all the attention. Truth be told, he was a little intimidated himself. But having Cade and Ellie here in the stronghold helped considerably. They, along with Ria and a few of her Royal Guards Mitch had served with, were considered trustworthy enough to be allowed to stay at the stronghold. He actually enjoyed showing them around *his* domain, though it would take a lot of getting used to, being the landlord of a hidden, icy lair.

Ellie was a great help to Gina, Mitch knew. And when he finally saw Ellie with Cade, he thought he understood how the little human had completely stolen his best friend's heart. Ellie had a kind soul, and with his new instincts for magic, he could see the goodness shining in her eyes. She may be human, but she was definitely mate material in every sense of the word. She would protect her mate and her friends to her last breath and she was very protective of Gina, of which Mitch heartily approved.

Mitch's first meeting with Ria monarch-to-monarch felt odd, to say the least. Luckily, Ria put him at ease almost immediately, launching herself into his arms with a huge grin. She was like a little sister to him and he was touched by the happy smile on her pretty face. She kissed him on the cheek and gave him a big hug. Right there, the ice was broken and they were able to move on, comparing notes on the states of their respective Clans. Already they had a tentative agreement on working together to retake complete ownership of Phelix Corporation.

The two couples, plus Gina's folks, Ria and some of her Guard spent the day together, working out details of an even closer relationship between the two Clans. Mitch took the opportunity to have the *pantera* Guard work out with his tigers. They sparred in human form and in their fur, taking over the largest chamber in the stronghold for their fighting practice.

Cade threw Mitch one of the towels as they finished up their workout. Cade was the only one who didn't seem to be treating Mitch differently now that he was white instead of gold, and he valued his friend's easy acceptance of the change.

"You have such pretty fur now, I'm almost afraid to damage that field of sparkly white," Cade groused as they headed toward the hallway together.

"You suck at stealth in this part of the world, buddy," Mitch teased back. "All that black sticks out like a sore thumb against the snow and ice."

"But I bet I'd still be better than you at night crawling, even up here in Frozen Ass, Iceland, whitey."

"I guess we'll have to see about that."

"Maybe we will," Cade countered with a calculating grin.

"Yeah, but not tonight. Tonight's my mating night."

Mitch looked forward to spending part of the night partying with his friends and getting to know the dignitaries who had come to witness their mating. The rest of the night he intended to spend balls deep in his mate, showing her again and again just how much he loved her.

"Yeah, we have to party with the other shifters and make nice for the dignitaries. I'm actually kind of impressed by how many different Clans showed up to pay their respects. You done good, buddy. I think you may have the start of one hell of an alliance if you can get even half the groups these guys represent on board."

"You think?"

"Hell, yeah," Cade answered seriously. "Ria's age works against her. That and the fact that she's not mated. They'd pay more attention to her if she at least had a mate." Cade's gaze grew troubled.

Cade truly cared for the Nyx. She was more than just a queen to him. She was part of his family. Few people realized that if something happened to her, Cade would be in line for the *pantera* throne.

Mitch had never been in a position before to help Ria politically, but now that he was…

"You know she's got my full support. I'll make that clear to anybody who'll listen if you think it'll help."

Cade grinned. "I wasn't going to ask, but since you volunteered…" Cade laughed outright as they walked through the halls of the stronghold.

"You're the only guy I'd let get away with that manipulative shit, but hell, I love Ria like a kid sister. Now that I can actually help her cause—which I still find hard to believe—I'll do what I can. You panthers are sneaky sons of bitches. Why couldn't you just come out and ask?"

"Now where would be the fun in that?" Cade quipped.

It was a mark of the strength of their friendship that Cade could still tweak him like this. Mitch knew Cade and his powers of persuasion well enough to know that if he'd really wanted to manipulate Mitch—or anybody, for that matter—he could have easily done so without ever letting him realize it. Mitch had seen the sly *pantera* in action many times before and respected his skill.

Having settled the matter, the men split up, each heading for their own suite of rooms. Showers were in order and then they had to get ready for the party that night.

The bedchamber he and Gina had been sharing was empty when he got there. The women of the Clan had taken her off earlier that morning and kept them separate all day. He'd see her again at the ceremony. For now, he was on his own. Well, he and his Guards were on their own. Harry and Paul were silent shadows that followed him pretty much everywhere he went—even inside the stronghold.

Eventually, he hoped such precautions could be dropped. At least here, on tiger ground among the Clan. But for now, they had to play it safe. Mitch was too new to power to take anything for granted. Especially when there had been so many selfish bastards hiding in plain sight within the Clan itself.

Gisli's poisonous ways had filtered through the ranks until the weaker members of the group had become as dishonest as he was. Mitch was changing all that, but it was a slow process. He'd rounded up the worst of the thieves, but there were probably lesser offenders still out there. Only time would tell if they planned to reform or move into the spots left open by their predecessors' downfall.

Mitch spent time on his appearance, though he usually didn't care much about it. He dressed well, of course, befitting his old position as a Royal Guard, but that didn't mean he really cared what he wore. As long as he was comfortable, he was happy. But now it seemed he had a team of experts from the village debating every little aspect of his attire for this very special ceremony.

He put on what they'd prepared for him and felt only a little silly in the ermine-trimmed cloak. It was soft and warm. Since the ceremony would be held on top of the glacier that covered the volcano, he might need the warmth of the fur before the ceremony came to an end. They didn't call this country Iceland for nothing. It was cold out there. Especially at night.

Even if he wasn't looking forward to the freezing temperatures, Mitch strode eagerly up the slope of the glacier, his spiked boots crunching on the snow-covered ice. His Guards were with him and more waited above with his lady. Mitch couldn't wait to see her. They'd been apart all day and it had been hard to bear.

Mitch knew he was probably grinning like a fool when he walked up to Gina, but she smiled back at him and everything was okay. Amma Hilda was officiating as priestess, but Mitch noted with interest that the much younger mate of the North American Lords was at her side, helping the older priestess.

The ceremony wasn't very complicated and Mitch spent most of the time staring into Gina's eyes, wondering how he'd been so blessed. He felt the strength of the mountain flowing through his veins and knew he would do everything in his power to keep Gina safe and be the partner she deserved.

He only had one thing he really wanted to say to her on this most special of nights. When it came time for him to speak his vows, he knew exactly what to say.

"Gleda, Princess of the *tigre blanche*, daughter of Fridrik and Snaedis...my beautiful Gina..." He had to clear his throat before he could continue. Nothing had prepared him for the intense emotion of this moment. "My mother saved your life as a child, Gina. I like to think she saved you for me." Gina sniffed as her eyes filled with tears, but he had to say the rest of what was in his heart. "I will love you for the rest of my days, my love, my heart, my mate. I will protect you and cherish you for the rest of our lives and beyond. My heart to your heart. My soul to your soul. My life to yours, now and forever."

The mountain rumbled its approval, witnessing their vows from above. Mitch felt its presence in the back of his mind, a brooding energy that would come at his command.

Gina spoke her vows, but all Mitch really heard was her declaration of unending love. The mountain roared its approval in his mind and in reality. It spewed molten rock in a show of light, heat and smoke, calling lightning from the sky in a spectacular demonstration of its power and its joy.

Mitch knew just how far the mountain would go. This was only a small show of its power, but it seemed to impress the guests.

"Mother Earth approves the match," Amma Hilda shouted above the distant noise of the mountain, a broad smile on her face. Then she turned to Mitch and gave him quick, quiet instructions. "Show them your power, Mitchell. Call the lightning and silence the volcano. Then they will all know you are the true Tig'Ra."

He saw the merit in the old woman's suggestion, but did he dare? He looked at Gina for her input and she gave him a confident nod.

Mitch reached out to the mountain, raising one hand

skyward. The mountain immediately quieted while a lightning show played about the crest of the peak, sparking from particle to particle within the rising ash cloud.

"The Grim answers the Tig'Ra," Amma Hilda intoned, just in case there was any doubt. "The Mother Goddess has spoken."

Gina watched the people gathered just below them on the slope of the glacier. Mostly they seemed either astounded or troubled by the proof of Mitch's connection to the sacred mountain. Two identical men narrowed their gaze on Mitch and then looked past him—not to the mountain, but to the young priestess who stood just above her and Mitch on the glacier. Allie had been introduced to Gina earlier as a priestess, but she was also mate to the twin werewolf Alphas from America.

Gina looked at her and found wide-eyed approval in her gaze as she looked from Mitch to the mountain's fiery peak and back again. Then she turned her attention to Gina and winked.

"The Mother Goddess speaks in a booming voice of fire and ice to your mate, Lady Gina," Allie spoke in quiet tones only Gina could hear as the crowd continued to watch the spectacle of lightning and almost deafening thunder. "I see the truth of the Lady's presence here and I want you to know, the North American Lords will be your allies in whatever trials are coming. My mates stand firmly on the side of the Lady and the Light. As I now know beyond the shadow of a doubt you and your mate do too. I look forward to getting to know you both better."

Gina bowed her head slightly in acknowledgment. She knew an important part of holding this ceremony and the party after was to build alliances with other shifters. It looked like they might've just taken the first step on that political journey. Hopefully it would be the first of many. She couldn't wait to tell Mitch.

When the light show finally died down, Mitch took her

hand and together they walked down the slope of the glacier toward the waiting sleighs that would take them all into the village. It was time to party with her new husband.

Husband. She liked that word. Mate. She liked that one even better. And in about nine months' time, he'd also be a father. She hadn't told Mitch yet, but she knew he'd figure it out any hour now as her scent deepened and twined with that of the baby.

And her brother had known. She'd heard what his spirit had said about *telling the little one*. Gina had known what he meant right away, but apparently Mitch hadn't quite figured it out yet. He would though. She cut him some slack considering how much had been going on lately. He'd had a lot of changes thrust upon him in a very short time and he was handling it magnificently, in her opinion. He was just amazing. The most amazing man in the world.

She was truly blessed to have found the man who made her life perfect. They'd had a hard road to get to this place, but with a little luck and a whole lot of blessings, they would forge a future for themselves, their Clan and their new family.

She couldn't wait to get started on her very own happily ever after.

EPILOGUE

Ria was enjoying the party. Most of the other monarchs were looking at her a little differently now that Mitch treated her as an equal. How things had changed in such a short time. A few weeks ago, Mitch had been just another part of her Guard corps. Now he was a king. Her equal. *More* than her equal, if truth be told. The man was able to command a volcano, for cripes sake.

She'd had no idea he had that kind of power lying dormant within him. For that matter, she didn't think he had realized it either. My, how times had changed.

Now Mitch was mated and happy in his new life with a ready-made stronghold that was absolutely incredible. The ice palace was like something out of a comic book, only cooler. Why hadn't the previous *pantera noir* rulers built themselves a stronghold somewhere? She would've enjoyed not having to move all the time, on the run from her enemies.

Although Mitch had done her a great service in finding the mole that had been feeding her location to their enemies. Horace had done so much damage, even after she'd booted him out of the Clan. He'd still had friends and family among her loyal followers and they hadn't thought talking to him would put Ria's life in danger.

They knew better now. Cade had done a good job of

impressing the need for discretion upon all the members of the Clan after Horace had been exposed. She could breathe a little easier—maybe. For a little while, at least.

"May I have this dance?" a male voice asked at her elbow.

Ria hadn't sensed anyone approach. She jumped a little and turned to face the man who'd managed to get the drop on her. She was ready to give him a polite refusal, but her words caught in her throat when she looked up into the bluest eyes she had ever seen.

The man stood taller than her. He was taller than most of her Guards. Probably a half inch taller than Cade, which was saying something. And he was all lean muscle and hard sinew. She could see that just from the way his tailored suit fit his lithe body. He moved like a man who knew how to use that body—as a weapon, or a tool. She'd bet he was as lethal as he was handsome.

He had a finely chiseled face that reminded her of...someone. She wasn't quite sure who, but he looked vaguely familiar. And those eyes...they were almost spooky in their clarity, as if they could see through to her very soul.

She realized belatedly that he held out one hand to her and her sluggish mind knew she had to take it. She wanted to feel his skin against hers, even in such an innocent way.

She put her hand in his and time stood still. For just a moment, they were the only two people in the room. In the world. In the universe. She saw infinity in his eyes and her life in a flash of sacred time.

And then the world started up again. The earth commenced spinning and time flowed once more.

"What was that?" she muttered, unable to censor her thoughts, so jumbled they were.

"Destiny," he answered in a very serious tone.

She looked up into his eyes and was caught once more. And then she remembered to breathe as he ushered her gently onto the dance floor.

They were playing a slow waltz that suited her just fine. She wanted to be held close in this stranger's arms. She wanted to talk to him and dance with him face to face, body to body.

"I'm Ria," she offered, hoping he didn't realize her position. She wanted this marvelous man to want to dance with her just for her—not for her title.

"I know," he replied, crushing her hopes that he had sought her out just for herself alone. "I'm Ellie's brother, Jacob. I've been seeing you in my dreams for months now, lovely Ria. Now that the time is right, I came here specifically to meet you."

"Why?" she wanted to know.

He smiled, and she was enchanted, falling even more deeply under his spell.

"It's simple, really. I'm here to help you save the world."

ABOUT THE AUTHOR

Bianca D'Arc has run a laboratory, climbed the corporate ladder in the shark-infested streets of lower Manhattan, studied and taught martial arts, and earned the right to put a whole bunch of letters after her name, but she's always enjoyed writing more than any of her other pursuits. She grew up and still lives on Long Island, where she keeps busy with an extensive garden, several aquariums full of very demanding fish, and writing her favorite genres of paranormal, fantasy and sci-fi romance.

Bianca loves to hear from readers and can be reached through Twitter (@BiancaDArc), Facebook (BiancaDArcAuthor) or through the various links on her website.

WELCOME TO THE D'ARC SIDE…
WWW.BIANCADARC.COM

OTHER BOOKS BY BIANCA D'ARC

Now Available

Brotherhood of Blood
One & Only
Rare Vintage
Phantom Desires
Sweeter Than Wine
Forever Valentine
Wolf Hills
Wolf Quest

Tales of the Were
Lords of the Were
Inferno

Tales of the Were – The Others
Rocky
Slade

Tales of the Were – Redstone Clan
Grif
Red
Magnus

String of Fate
Cat's Cradle
King's Throne

Guardians of the Dark
Half Past Dead
Once Bitten, Twice Dead
A Darker Shade of Dead
The Beast Within
Dead Alert

Gifts of the Ancients
Warrior's Heart

Dragon Knights
Maiden Flight
The Dragon Healer
Border Lair
Master at Arms
The Ice Dragon
Prince of Spies
Wings of Change
FireDrake
Dragon Storm
Keeper of the Flame

Resonance Mates
Hara's Legacy
Davin's Quest
Jaci's Experiment
Grady's Awakening
Harry's Sacrifice

Jit'Suku Chronicles
Arcana: King of Swords
Arcana: King of Cups
Arcana: King of Clubs
End of the Line
Sons of Amber: Ezekiel
Sons of Amber: Michael

StarLords: Hidden Talent

Print Anthologies
Ladies of the Lair
I Dream of Dragons Vol. 1
Brotherhood of Blood
Caught by Cupid

OTHER BOOKS BY BIANCA D'ARC
(continued)

Coming Soon

Tales of the Were - Redstone Clan #4
Bobcat
June 2014

Jit'Suku Chronicles ~ Arcana #4
King of Stars
Summer 2014

String of Fate #3
Jacob's Ladder
Fall 2014

Tales of the Were - Redstone Clan #5
Matt
Fall 2014

TALES OF THE WERE – THE OTHERS
ROCKY
BY BIANCA D'ARC

On the run from her husband's killers, there is only one man who can help her now... her Rock.

Maggie is on the run from those who killed her husband nine months ago. She knows the only one who can help her is Rocco, a grizzly shifter she knew in her youth. She arrives on his doorstep in labor with twins. Magical, shapeshifting, bear cub twins destined to lead the next generation of werecreatures in North America.

Rocky is devastated by the news of his Clan brother's death, but he cannot deny the attraction that has never waned for the small human woman who stole his heart a long time ago. Rocky absented himself from her life when she chose to marry his childhood friend, but the years haven't changed the way he feels for her.

And now there are two young lives to protect. Rocky will do everything in his power to end the threat to the small family and claim them for himself. He knows he is the perfect Alpha to teach the cubs as they grow into their power... if their mother will let him love her as he has always longed to do.

TALES OF THE WERE – THE OTHERS
SLADE
BY BIANCA D'ARC

The fate of all shifters rests on his broad shoulders, but all he can think of is her.

Slade is a warrior and spy sent to Nevada to track a brutal murderer before the existence of all shifters is revealed to a world not ready to know.

Kate is a priestess serving the large community of shifters that have gathered around the Redstone cougars. When their matriarch is murdered and the scene polluted by dark magic, she knows she must help the enigmatic man sent to track the killer.

Together, Slade and Kate find not one but two evil mages that they alone can neutralize. Slade finds it hard to keep his hands off his sexy new partner, the cougars are out for blood, and the killers have an even more sinister plan in mind.

Can Kate somehow keep her hands to herself when the most attractive man she's ever met makes her want to throw caution to the wind? And can Slade do his job and save the situation when he's finally found a woman who can make him purr?

Warning: Contains a tiny bit of sexy ménage action with two smokin' hot men..

TALES OF THE WERE – REDSTONE CLAN
GRIF
BY BIANCA D'ARC

Griffon Redstone is the eldest of five brothers and the leader of one of the most influential shifter Clans in North America. He seeks solace in the mountains, away from the horrific events of the past months, for both himself and his young sister. The deaths of their older sister and mother have hit them both very hard.

Lindsey Tate is human, but very aware of the werewolf Pack that lives near her grandfather's old cabin. She's come to right a wrong her grandfather committed against the Pack and salvage what's left of her family's honor—if the wolves will let her. Mostly, they seem intent on running her out of town on a rail.

But the golden haired stranger, Grif, comes to her rescue more than once. He stands up for her against the wolf Pack and then helps her fix the old generator at the cabin. When she performs a ceremony she expects will end in her death, the shifter deity has other ideas. Thrown together by fate, neither of them can deny their deep attraction, but will an old enemy tear them apart?

Warning: Frisky cats get up to all sorts of naughtiness, including a frenzy-induced multi-partner situation that might be a little intense for some readers.

TALES OF THE WERE – REDSTONE CLAN
RED
BY BIANCA D'ARC

A water nymph and a werecougar meet in a bar fight… No joke.

Steve Redstone agrees to keep an eye on his friend's little sister while she's partying in Las Vegas. He's happy to do the favor for an old Army buddy. What he doesn't expect is the wild woman who heats his blood and attracts too much attention from Others in the area.

Steve ends up defending her honor, breaking his cover and seducing the woman all within hours of meeting her, but he's helpless to resist her. She is his mate and that startling fact is going to open up a whole can of worms with her, her brother and the rest of the Redstone Clan.

KING OF SWORDS
BY BIANCA D'ARC
Arcana, Book 1

David is a newly retired special ops soldier, looking to find his way in an unfamiliar civilian world. His first step is to visit an old friend, the owner of a bar called *The Rabbit Hole* on a distant space station. While there, he meets an intriguing woman who holds the keys to his future.

Adele has a special ability, handed down through her family. Adele can sometimes see the future. She doesn't know exactly why she's been drawn to the space station where her aunt deals cards in a bar that caters to station workers and ex-military. She only knows that she needs to be there. When she meets David, sparks of desire fly between them and she begins to suspect that he is part of the reason she traveled halfway across the galaxy.

Pirates gas the inhabitants of the station while Adele and David are safe inside a transport tube and it's up to them to repel the invaders. Passion flares while they wait for the right moment to overcome the alien threat and retake the station. But what good can one retired soldier and a civilian do against a ship full of alien pirates?

BIANCA D'ARC

WWW.BIANCADARC.COM

Printed in Great Britain
by Amazon.co.uk, Ltd.,
Marston Gate.